A COUNTRY RIVALRY

Also by Sasha Morgan

A Country Scandal

A COUNTRY RIVALRY

Sasha Morgan

First published in the United Kingdom in 2019 by Aria,
an imprint of Head of Zeus Ltd

Copyright © Sasha Morgan, 2019

The moral right of Sasha Morgan to be identified as the author of this work has been asserted in accordance with the Copyright, Designs and Patents Act of 1988.

All rights reserved. No part of this publication may be reproduced, stored in a retrieval system, or transmitted, in any form or by any means, electronic, mechanical, photocopying, recording, or otherwise, without the prior permission of both the copyright owner and the above publisher of this book.

This is a work of fiction. All characters, organizations, and events portrayed in this novel are either products of the author's imagination or are used fictitiously.

9 7 5 3 1 2 4 6 8

A CIP catalogue record for this book is available from the British Library.

ISBN 9781786699039

Aria
an imprint of Head of Zeus
First Floor East
5–8 Hardwick Street
London EC1R 4RG

www.ariafiction.com
www.headofzeus.com

For my mum, a tough old bird who tells it like it is.

I

Tobias raised his glass. 'To the last night of our honeymoon.'

Megan raised hers to his. 'And the beginning of our lives together. Cheers.'

It had been a magical holiday, spent in tranquil, rural Normandy in an enormous farmhouse oozing with character. The ancient beams, stone walls and huge open fireplaces had been a welcome sight for the newlyweds, as had the south-facing terrace, which caught the sun all day. But what made the farmhouse so special was the garden and its wild Parma violets growing in abundance. Their sweet aroma had hit Megan immediately, transporting her back in time and bringing to mind memories of her gran, who always wore the fragrance of violets.

None of this was coincidence, of course. Tobias had known exactly what he was doing when booking the accommodation. It had been Ted, Megan's grandfather, who had told him about the farmhouse and the part it played in his life years ago during the war. It was here that the kind French family had helped him recuperate from his injuries. He had lived with them for almost a year, as his lost memory slowly eased its way back to life, and the smell of Parma violets had given him the jolt he needed to recover the faded memories of his first love, Grace, Megan's grandmother. Now the farmhouse was a luxurious B & B, which retained its rustic charm. Tobias had been thorough in his research and, with Ted's help, he had managed to track it down and make his wife's honeymoon all the more special for the sentimental link.

Together Tobias and Megan had lazed by the still, turquoise pool, walked through the wooded valley, meandered through the busy market square, eaten fine French cuisine and drunk rich, fruity wine in the dusk by candlelight, listening to the cicadas. They had all they needed: each other and the promise of a family on the way. As Lord Cavendish-Blake and the new custodian to the ancestral home, Treweham Hall, it fell on Tobias' head to produce an heir, an obligation he had fulfilled with Megan a month before marrying her. They had yet to announce the good news, choosing to keep it secret for the moment.

For Tobias, this was a cherished time. Having been dubbed a 'wild child' in his youth, along with his two close friends, Seamus Fox and Dylan Delany, his meeting Megan only seven months ago and falling head over heels in love was somewhat out of character, or so the tabloids would have their readers believe. According to them 'Lord Cavendish-Blake-the-rake' had been untameable, a hell-raiser, who, together with Seamus, had been nicknamed 'the Heir and the Fox'. Their antics had been reported in many a newspaper, but now it appeared they *had* been tamed and disciplined, just like the stallions they rode. Seamus was now the obedient husband to the fiery Tatum, who was more than capable of cracking the whip, and a doting father to their two little girls. Tobias was the love-struck new husband to Megan, who had moved into Treweham village last spring after inheriting her grandmother's cottage.

Megan had worked in the local pub, The Templar, becoming close friends to Finula, who was the landlord's daughter and who couldn't speak highly enough of Tobias and his family. Megan had been instantly attracted to the dark-haired, green-eyed, devilishly handsome lord, who made her laugh. She also fell for the caring, compassionate side to him that had never been described in the papers. It had been a whirlwind romance, leaving Megan a touch dizzy. Tobias had provided practical help whilst renovating her grandmother's cottage and offered emotional support when she had discovered the truth about who her granddad actually was. He'd made no secret of his attraction towards her either, and despite her wariness of his notorious past, his charm had won her. And when she had realised she was pregnant, her whole being had well and truly spun.

For Tobias, it was simply the icing on the cake; all he ever wanted. He'd craved a deep, loving relationship and yearned for children, especially when witnessing how happy his best friend, Seamus, was with his wife and two daughters. From the moment he first set eyes on Megan he knew she had to be his. He'd fallen under the spell of her brown, almond-shaped eyes, her freckled, button nose and silky, brown hair cut neatly into a bob. The feeling he had wasn't just lust, of that he was certain. He found her company refreshing; she often made him laugh and her quiet confidence gave her a pleasant self-assuredness, not like the brash, overbearing women who had thrown themselves at him. Her interest in his upbringing hadn't been crass, it was genuine, his background being a total contrast to her own. Despite his reputation and all the glamorous girlfriends that had been pictured on his arm, he had only felt like this once before. He had previously been engaged to another local girl, years ago. Tragically she had been hit and killed by a drunk driver, leaving Tobias heartbroken. The press still hadn't relented, choosing to home in on a young man's desperate grief. In the end Tobias had retaliated and given them something to write about, each exploit getting more daring and outrageous than the next. Now it was different: now he had settled down.

Even so, he was ever mindful of the media's presence. Not wanting to alarm his new wife, Tobias had secretly had the French B & B 'looked over' before arriving, and he had it on good authority that the only guests staying in the five-star hotel were genuine holidaymakers like themselves. The staff had been made well aware of the high profile of their visitors, although Tobias and his new wife were at pains not to give any clues to their status. Tobias had wanted the two of them to blend in anonymously, so that he and Megan could enjoy a much-needed peaceful honeymoon.

The last few months had been hectic with Treweham Hall opening for the first time to the public, and the renovation of the old stable block into a superb racehorse training yard, which his friend Dylan had taken over. Dylan Delany was the most famous jockey on the circuit. His dark, gypsy looks, black curls and piercing blue eyes made him the most attractive, too. His reputation matched that of his best friends, Tobias and Seamus, although there had been a shift in the sand of late. It appeared even Dylan was on the verge of calming down, if his relationship with his pretty, fresh-faced assistant trainer, Flora, was anything to go by. Together they were working every hour God sent to make the stable yard work. Dylan was seriously hoping to make Delany's Racing Yard a huge success and Tobias was more than happy to collect the rent his renovated stable block and land would bring. When he had first assessed the estate's accounts last spring, Tobias had been astounded at the state his late father, Lord Richard Cavendish-Blake, had left them in. With mounting debts threatening to close the Hall, Tobias had had to put urgent financial plans in place and thankfully he had started to turn things round.

'How are you feeling?' Tobias asked yet again, looking towards his wife's stomach.

'Fine. Really.' She could tell he wasn't convinced, hardly surprising when she had started with morning sickness two days into their honeymoon.

Once the first few hours of the morning had passed, and after keeping most of her breakfast down, Megan's face had started to regain colour and they were able to enjoy the rest of the day. Although they wanted to keep her pregnancy secret for a little while longer, Megan feared that when they returned to live in Treweham Hall, with Tobias' mother, brother and a team of staff, it would be hard to conceal, especially if she was throwing up most mornings. She imagined the look of disdain on Henry, the butler's, face and couldn't help but laugh to herself. It was going to take some adjustment, living in such a grand place, especially when comparing the greatness of the Hall to the humble cottage that her gran had bequeathed her.

Megan couldn't bear the thought of selling. Bluebell Cottage. It held such fond memories of her beloved grandmother and she had treated it as a second home since she was little. Tobias had promised that they would still have their privacy and they were going to have the rooms in the south wing of the Hall. Megan was looking forward to choosing the décor and really making it their own, although she wasn't confident she would have the final say, as Tobias ran his own property development business and it was second nature for him to get involved.

'Looking forward to going home?' he smiled, admiring her beautiful face in the moonlight. They were sitting on the small balcony of their room and a lantern flickered brightly on the table. It was mid-September, but luckily the summer was proving hard to shake off and the air was still pleasantly warm.

'Yes, but if I'm honest, a bit apprehensive.' Megan had always been made to feel welcome at Treweham Hall, but even so, the thought of having staff permanently on call was nerve-racking and she feared they would be intrusive. Little had she known when first arriving in the picturesque village of Treweham that she would end up being Lady Cavendish-Blake, living in Treweham Hall. It still felt surreal.

Then she turned to her husband, who had become her rock; the reassurance, kindness and care he had shown her meant she couldn't help but fall for him. That and the fact she'd found him utterly irresistible with those mesmerising green eyes that twinkled with mischief and blazed with passion. He still made her heart flutter and she couldn't imagine a time when he wouldn't.

Tobias understood Megan's apprehension and he was anxious for his wife to settle at Treweham Hall. He knew she was popular with the staff, having seen her interact with them. Megan had overseen the guided tours of the Hall when it had first opened, along with the tearoom and gift shop, into which he had converted part of the ground floor. She was a natural with the staff; even his butler was finally succumbing to her charm.

'Don't worry, my darling, everything will be fine. We have our own rooms waiting for you to furnish.' He took her hand in his and squeezed it.

'I think I'll start with the nursery,' she replied with a smile.

'Good idea.' He kissed her lingeringly on the lips. 'And now, let's go to bed,' he whispered in her ear.

2

The quaint country inn of Treweham village was still recovering. The Templar was well used to playing host to its local celebs and all the hullabaloo that entailed, but the village's latest event had taken its toll on the sixteenth-century coaching inn. Lord Cavendish-Blake's wedding had caused utter mayhem, attracting local and national press, not to mention the public, who had flocked to Treweham to capture anything they could of this momentous occasion. Dermot O'Grady, landlord of The Templar, wasn't complaining, though: business had boomed and profits had soared. He made sure his staff had reaped the rewards, giving them hefty bonuses as well as the tips they'd earned.

Finula, his daughter and chef at The Templar, was worn out. He could see she needed a break and was going to suggest she take a few days off. He knew she missed her best friend, Megan, who had worked alongside her in the pub. Now that Megan was the new Lady Cavendish-Blake and had a role in the revamp of Treweham Hall, he doubted

Finula would see her as much, which was a shame as he'd enjoyed the camaraderie between the two of them.

Dermot bent down to pick up the post that had been delivered that morning and noticed a cream envelope addressed to Finula. It was thick good-quality paper and had bold black writing in fountain pen. Dermot frowned; whose handwriting could that be? He walked through to the bar area, where the traditional wooden benches, oak panelling and stone floor gave it real character. Finula was behind the bar.

'Fancy a coffee, Dad?'

He nodded. 'Thanks, Fin. You've got a letter.' He held up the cream envelope before passing it to her.

Finula looked at it curiously. She didn't recognise the curvy handwriting. Choosing to open it later, alone, she passed Dermot his coffee and made herself one.

'Finula, I've been thinking.' He eyed his daughter thoughtfully.

'About what?' She sipped her cappuccino and winced as it burnt her lips.

'Maybe you should take a break. Have a few days away from this place.'

'But what would you do?' she answered, surprised at his suggestion.

'I can always get help in, no one's indispensable.'

She raised her eyebrows. 'Thanks.'

'Now you know what I mean,' he gently reproached. 'You know I think you're the best chef ever, but seriously, Fin, you need a rest.'

She couldn't argue with that. The last week had certainly been taxing, working long hours to accommodate the fully booked inn. Only now was normal life gradually returning, although being Megan's bridesmaid and having the media buzz on her own doorstep was an experience Finula would never forget. The day had been wildly thrilling. She'd worn a beautiful bronze dress and had been driven in a horse-drawn carriage to Treweham Hall. Reporters, journalists, and the public had lined the country footpaths, waving as Dylan had gently guided the two carriage horses through the cheering crowds. It had felt surreal, and once the carriage had made its way through the security of the cast-iron gates of Treweham Hall, Finula had sighed with relief.

Even now she couldn't help smiling when she thought of it. She smiled when she thought about a certain guest who had stayed at The Templar last week, too. Originally assuming he had been a reporter, she had been corrected by her dad, who had informed her that he was in fact a film producer called Marcus Devlin. From the short conversation she had had with him, Finula immediately realised he was from the same county as her dad, Roscommon, which was clear from his soft, Irish lilt. Dermot had soon struck up a rapport with their guest, exchanging tales from their home turf. Finula tried to deny her attraction to Marcus, knowing he'd be gone all too soon, but that hadn't stopped her looking him up on the internet. Marcus Devlin apparently was an up-and-coming documentary producer with vision, flair and plenty of grit. Finula had admired his profile picture, the way his green eyes with amber flecks had stared broodingly into the camera. They reminded her of someone, but she couldn't place who. His dark stubble and hair looked slightly unkempt, which gave him a rugged look. Finula read that he had been born in Roscommon thirty-two years ago, had attended the Institute of Art, Design and Technology in Dún Laoghaire, County Dublin, obtaining a BA Hons Degree in Film and Television Production, and thereafter had gone from strength to strength. He'd started out as a runner, quickly climbing up the career ladder to production assistant, director, then finally to the award-winning documentary producer he now was.

'When I'm making a documentary, I live with it twenty-four hours a day,' he'd stated in an interview. 'It takes over my life.'

He certainly looked intense, thought Finula, as her interest continued to grow. He'd lived in London, but had recently moved to Shropshire, taking a liking to it whilst filming on location there.

'Shropshire's the nearest thing to home,' the article had quoted him saying. 'It's green, with lots of space, a real charm of its own. Here I can completely relax and let the creative juices flow. London suffocated my energy with its pace of life.'

Once Finula had started researching Marcus Devlin, she found it hard to stop. Apparently, he had been married once, a long time ago, but didn't have any children. She'd even watched some of his documentaries and found them moving, invoking real emotion. From the horrific, cold truth of sex trafficking, to the heart-breaking, compassion of organ donation, Finula had been first hooked and then reduced to tears. Marcus had taken real risks, filming in dangerous territory, interviewing victims and exposing the ruthless, powerful gangs that terrorised and controlled the vulnerable. He had followed the plight of a child desperately needing a heart transplant, covering the emotional scenes before his operation and the joyful ones at its success.

Unable to resist, she'd tapped in his address on a satellite map site and homed in on the Tudor cottage nestled in the Shropshire hills. A white building with black timber frame, it was covered with ivy, and the surrounding colourful garden bursting with hydrangeas was utterly charming. It unnerved Finula a little that she had gone to such lengths to find out more about a person she had met so briefly. If Megan had known, after she'd teased her about looking him up, she would have encouraged her to try to contact him. Her best friend was eager to see Finula happy in a relationship, given how awful Finula's ex-boyfriend, Nick, the hunky local vet, had proved to be. Often Megan and Finula had laughed about 'a tall, dark stranger, walking into her gin joint'. Well, now it appeared he had…

3

Dylan was sitting at his desk. The window in front of him overlooked the training yard where three of his staff were busy preparing the stables for the racehorses that were due to be delivered that afternoon. Flora, his assistant trainer and girlfriend, had asked for fresh hay, water and clean swept floors. Not that the grooms really needed telling, all having previously worked at Sean Fox's training yard. Meanwhile, Flora was busy making phone calls, ensuring final preparations for the arrival of the horses were in place. Dylan had opened Delany's Racing Yard only a few weeks ago and already the stables were half full. He had room for thirty horses, and at this rate they'd soon be training at full capacity and would need more staff.

He couldn't expect Flora to continue working at her current pace, particularly as she was still recovering from a virus. As Flora's parents were travelling around Europe and her brother was at university, Dylan had insisted she come and stay with him for a few days until she had recovered, but that few days had turned into weeks. Together they had rubbed along nicely, living and working alongside each other in an easy, uncomplicated way.

Although Flora was only twenty, Dylan held her in high esteem. She had an innocent, honest sincerity about her, which he admired, especially when comparing her to the many crude, licentious women who threw themselves at him. Dylan had a reputation, which up until Flora came into his life he had been more than happy to uphold. He was the sexiest and most successful jockey, both on and off the racecourse. His dark curls, twinkling blue eyes and thoroughly toned body had sent many a lady's heart pounding, and Dylan had been chased, a lot, sometimes leading to rather unfortunate circumstances. One lover had handcuffed him to the bed and sold her kiss-and-tell story to a newspaper; another, the wife of a client, had been seducing him in the hot tub when her husband had arrived home early. All water under the bridge now, Dylan liked to think.

Flora, however, didn't. She might be ten years younger than he, but she was well aware of Dylan's lothario days. Still, she couldn't fault the care and attention he had shown her whilst she was ill. Like Dylan, Flora had grown to love their living together and, whilst nothing officially had been said, it had gradually become the norm for her to stay at his house. Flora had noticed how clinically clean and ordered Dylan's home was when she had first arrived but now it had turned into a proper home, which looked lived-in.

Working together, they had flourished, each intuitively understanding the other, and each had a way with horses so it was little wonder that already they had had quite a few runners thundering past the finishing line in first place. In fact, it was all going so well that Dylan was about to announce his retirement as a jockey, to dedicate all his time to the training yard, and keeping Flora happy. She had shown her fiery, stubborn side once and he didn't wish to see it again.

Now he looked sideways at her whilst she was talking on the phone. His gaze automatically homed in on her pale, flawless complexion. She was biting her bottom lip and frowning slightly, deep in concentration. Her blond hair hung in waves to her shoulders and he suddenly longed to feel its silky touch between his fingers.

Dylan got up from his desk and stood behind her on the sofa. He bent down and kissed her neck and she turned slightly and smiled, continuing to talk into the phone. His lips ran across her collarbone; then, deciding he wanted more of her, his hands started to unbutton her shirt. She giggled slightly, then quickly coughed and carried on her conversation. She playfully slapped his hand. He ignored it and continued to pop her buttons until he pulled the shirt apart, to reveal her splendid creamy breasts, spilling out of a red lace bra. How was he supposed to concentrate on work, knowing she was wearing this? His hands cupped her breasts, which felt soft and warm. His tongue found one of her nipples and slowly licked it and instantly it hardened. He heard her release a sigh. Flora quickly wrapped up the phone call and released another sigh as Dylan's hand moved further down to delve inside her jeans.

'Let's go home,' he whispered thickly into her ear.

It was so tempting, but how could they, with so much to do? 'We can't Dylan,' she replied faintly, as his thumb rubbed her intimately. She was fully aroused and he could feel she was ready for him. He couldn't stop now; his need was way too strong. He moved to stand in front of her, then picked her up with ease and placed her on the edge of his desk. His eyes blazed with passion as he pulled her jeans and red lace knickers down over her legs and onto the floor. 'Dylan, we can't,' she protested quietly, knowing full well they could and would.

Dylan didn't reply, but kissed away her unconvincing objections. As his tongue explored her mouth, she could feel his stubble against her face and smell his aftershave. Intoxicated by him, Flora closed her eyes in surrender as Dylan gently parted her thighs. He'd undone his jeans to fully expose his large, hard erection. He edged himself slowly into her silky heat and groaned with pleasure while she clasped his buttocks and let out a gasp. He pushed further into her, making her cry out again. Dylan wanted more and ground deeper and harder until finally he burst with absolute satisfaction. She clung to him panting, her legs wrapped tightly round him.

'What if someone had come in?' she asked, breathlessly.

Dylan was zipping himself up. He looked at her affectionately. 'Well, nobody did, did they?' He winked and kissed her hard on the lips until they were interrupted by the phone ringing. Picking it up he answered smoothly, 'Hello, Delany's Racing Yard,' whilst watching Flora quickly fumble with her clothes.

4

Marcus Devlin marched into the office with purpose, a look of determination on his handsome face. He was late and the rest of the production team were all sitting round the table waiting. They had worked with him before and knew exactly what to expect. His tardiness was the least of their problems. He threw down his clipboard with force, making Jamie, the young runner, jump. He then plonked himself down. There was no pre-amble, no cosy introduction with Marcus, just straight down to business.

'Right, I've managed to secure the funding for this documentary.' There was slight applause and a round of congratulations from the assembled team, which Marcus cut short. 'Now we have to decide locations, schedules and the budget.' Silence fell. He glared at the woman sitting on his right. 'Viola, what you got for me?' he asked directly, in his southern Irish lilt.

She answered with ease, refusing to be intimidated by him.

'As the documentary is exploring quaint, English traditions and customs, I suggest we call it *Green and Pleasant Land*.' This was greeted with nods and murmurs of agreement.

Marcus didn't give away any opinion. On the face of it, this documentary didn't appear his usual, gritty style. He did, however, have every intention of adding his own harsh, stark mix, blowing away any image of 'a chocolate-box village'.

'Go on,' he ordered.

Viola shuffled in her chair and cleared her throat. 'Regarding the location, for me, this would work best in the heart of some quintessential countryside, steeped in folklore in the olde worlde villages.' Again, mumblings of encouragement echoed from all the team except the producer.

'Where?' interrupted Marcus.

'I've done some research. The Cotswolds.' This finally seemed to evoke a reaction from Marcus. For the first time since stomping through the door, his face relaxed a little.

'And?' he asked.

'I've come up with two villages. Bellebrook and Treweham.'

Now he *was* interested. He stared straight into Viola's face intently. 'Continue.'

'Both have good stories to tell, with colourful characters. They have history, aristocracy and well-known faces. Both villages have hit the headlines for various reasons, from arson to flash, celebrity weddings. Heard of Christian Burgoyne?'

'He's a barrister, isn't he?' Marcus raised his eyebrow.

'That's him: a top-class barrister who defended a young, single mother accused of harming her child.'

'I remember that!' butted in Jamie. 'The baby had brittle-bone disease.'

Viola nodded and continued, 'What about Tobias Cavendish-Blake?'

Marcus' eyes narrowed and there was an awkward pause. 'That's the wild child, Lord Cavendish-Blake, recently married,' he replied flatly.

'His brother is Sebastian Cavendish-Blake, rising star at the Royal Shakespeare Theatre,' gushed Jamie, his eyes shining with admiration.

'Also,' Viola carried on, 'there are two country inns oozing with rustic charm. The Bluebell at Bellebrook and—'

'The Templar,' finished Marcus.

Viola's brow furrowed: how did he know that? Typical, always one step ahead.

For Marcus it was a no-brainer. After staying at The Templar a week ago and acquainting himself with the landlord's daughter, a redhead with porcelain skin, who could have been hand-picked from his home town of Roscommon, his mind was made up.

'Treweham. We'll go for Treweham,' he said decisively.

'Ri-ght...' Viola answered, a little perplexed. Normally she would have had to pitch things much harder to Marcus for him to decide and she had been prepared to do so. He'd quite taken the wind from her sails. She knew damn well that being his assistant producer would be taxing. She was originally a researcher, but had wanted to gain further experience and relished the opportunity when Marcus had offered her the position of his assistant on his last could only afford everyday supermarket specials. To him, the country set had double standards, wanting a greener, healthier environment, yet they all drove unnecessarily gas-guzzling four-by-fours to take their children to school. He wanted to kick their sorry, tweed-clad arses into the real world, where some poor families were living off food banks. Poverty was on the up. Homelessness was rising. Meanwhile the rich were flourishing in their country estates. Statistics proved this and Marcus wanted his documentary to be the catalyst that highlighted the glaring inequalities.

'I'll arrange an interview with Tobias Cavendish-Blake,' Viola said.

'You'll be lucky; he hates the media,' chipped in Jamie.

'Leave it with me,' Viola smiled sweetly.

'I'll shoot Treweham Hall, if he agrees,' added Len.

'Don't see why not. He just opened it up to the public,' replied Marcus.

Again, Viola noticed how he seemed already to know a bit about Treweham village.

'What about interviewing his brother?' Jamie asked, his face alight with excitement. 'He's currently staring as Richard III at Stratford.'

Viola's lips twitched: it was obvious Jamie's latest crush was Sebastian Cavendish-Blake. Why not give him a break and include him? 'Good idea, Jamie.' She gave a supportive smile.

'Hmm,' replied Marcus, quite liking the *Richard III* spin they could utilise. 'Why not? If it doesn't work, it'll just end up on Libby's cutting-room floor.'

'I'm sure it won't,' soothed Libby, who could see Jamie's face beginning to fall.

'What about the locals? The landlord of the...' Viola looked back at her notes.

'The Templar,' interrupted Marcus. 'Leave that with me.'

Viola frowned. She was desperate to ask why he was going to take this on himself, but knew better than to do so.

'When do we start filming?' Len asked.

'A week's time,' Marcus answered, as always enjoying making people drop everything for him at short notice.

'A week?' they all cried.

Marcus rolled his eyes. What was it with these people? Did they want to make a documentary or not?

5

Now is the winter of our discontent
Made glorious summer by this sun of York;
And all the clouds that lour'd upon our house
In the deep bosom of the ocean buried.

Sebastian Cavendish-Blake surveyed the audience as he spoke, his eyes roaming over the dark rows of seats with silhouettes of still heads, all turned to focus on him. It didn't unnerve him. In fact it thrilled him and he revelled in the attention. When all eyes were on him, adrenalin pumped through his veins, making his performance all the better. And what a performance he had to give when portraying evil King Richard III. The padded jacket he wore contained a small pillow in the back panel, giving him that infamous hump. It dug into him slightly, making him stoop further, but Sebastian didn't mind as it made him look even more like the character. His crooked posture made his lumbering walk appear more life-like, too, as he hobbled across the stage.

He was an absolutely natural performer, and had taken to this role like a duck to water, gaining rave reviews. 'A Shakespeare star in the making,' announced the *Guardian*. 'Cavendish-Blake's attention to detail is exquisite,' opined the *Stage*, 'his acting is so credible.' But the finest, making even Sebastian himself double-take when he first read it was *The Times*, which simply stated, 'The new Laurence Olivier.'

His mother, the Dowager Lady Cavendish-Blake, had wept with pride on his opening night. Even his aunt Celia, who was notoriously tough as old boots and hard to please, had had a tear in her eye. Sebastian had excelled himself. After years of acting with a small travelling theatre, he had finally made his mark. Already offers were pouring in, with future roles on the horizon. Sebastian, however, didn't want to commit to anything just yet, as he was still recovering from a rather bruised heart. Whilst being cast as Richard III had been the distraction he had badly needed, it still didn't fill his time whilst off stage. Alone in the apartment that he was renting in Stratford-upon-Avon, he could often feel himself slowly edging into a black hole. His last relationship had been turbulent, to say the least. Nick lived in Treweham. He was the local vet and a bit of a heart-throb. The trouble was, Nick hadn't played fair. Sebastian realised their relationship wasn't exactly exclusive when he had discovered Nick was also dating Finula from The Templar. In Nick's mind this shouldn't have been a problem – after all, what was he supposed to do when Sebastian was off travelling with the theatre? The lack of empathy Nick showed staggered Sebastian. Not only for himself, but poor Finula too, who had been devastated when learning the full facts of Nick's bi-sexuality. The inability to see things from any point of view other than his own made Nick an unpopular resident in Treweham where, as in many small villages, a kick to one resident meant they all fell.

Landing the role of Richard III had been a blessing, giving Sebastian purpose. He was popular amongst the cast and crew, reducing them to laughter whilst regaling them with tales from his past. He intrigued them. It wasn't often a member of the aristocracy had a starring role, yet he never lorded his social position over them. He had invited the cast back to Treweham Hall for a weekend before the play opened and it had proved a great success, with the Cavendish-Blake family welcoming this small motley crew, delighted that Sebastian was smiling again. He fitted in at the theatre well. With his sparkling personality and acting skills he had earned the respect of his fellow actors and the director of the play.

Now it looked like he was impressing the audience too, especially someone sitting on the front row, who appeared mesmerised. Sebastian had spotted him earlier on whilst secretly watching his audience take their seats, hidden in the wings. He often enjoyed people watching, seeing their reactions as they entered the theatre. Sebastian was close enough to note this boy's large, smoky-grey eyes drinking in every minute detail of the red seats, the curve of the two tiered balconies and the surrounding spotlights. The stage was up close to the seating and veered off into two pathways at the bottom, allowing the actors almost to walk amongst the audience. This guy had short, blond hair and wore a denim shirt. Sebastian had noticed some kind of business card sticking out from its front pocket and had wondered what this young man did for a living. Or could he be a student? He'd certainly looked young enough to be one. There were always groups of one drama club or another traipsing in and out of the theatre, but this boy looked to be sitting alone. For some reason he stood out to Sebastian as he'd watched everyone shuffle sideways into their rows.

Then he'd realised the young man reminded him of himself a few years ago, when he was at his most vulnerable: blond, pale, thin, unsure, a touch susceptible, not quite certain of his life path. It was different these days, though, he had reminded himself as he took a deep breath and walked backstage to prepare for his performance; now he was sure where he was going: all the way to the top.

6

'How does it feel to be back?' Megan asked, looking sideways at Tobias as he drove up the gravel driveway to the magnificent Treweham Hall.

Even now, she still couldn't quite believe this huge, stone building, with its buttresses and four turrets, giving it a castle like-appearance, was actually her home. Stained-glass windows glimmered in the sunshine. It was a magical place and opening it up to the public a couple of months ago had already proved profitable. The Hall's grandeur cost greatly. A small team of staff ran Treweham Hall like a well-oiled machine. Not only was the Hall open for tours, but the estate grew fruit and vegetables in its three thousand acres of land. Its orchards burst with apple, pear and cherry trees, plus plots containing herbs and vegetables, which were picked, packed and sold to local businesses. The new racehorse training yard was at the far end of the estate with a separate entrance, well out of the way from the paying public.

Visitors had flocked to Treweham Hall, not just to see the splendour of the building, but in the hope of seeing its family living there. With Tobias' wedding to the beautiful young Megan Taylor splashed across the papers, and Sebastian's rising fame, not to mention Dylan Delany, the very attractive jockey, in the nearby stable yard, it was hardly surprising that so many people wanted to visit.

Tobias smiled and turned to his wife. 'It feels good. How about you?' His hand squeezed hers in her lap.

'A little daunting, but I'll get used to it.'

Tobias appreciated how she must feel coming back to such a place, even if he had been at pains to make it feel like home to her. Given time, he was sure she'd feel more at ease, and God help any member of staff who didn't treat her well.

His thoughts turned to Henry, his butler, who hadn't given Megan the warmest of welcomes. Being entrusted with the duty of looking after her dog whilst they were away hadn't helped matters.

As if on cue, Henry appeared at the front entrance, ready to receive them. Tobias got out of the sports car and went round to help Megan to her feet, and hand in hand they climbed the stone steps into the Hall.

'Good day, sir.' Henry bowed slightly, then quickly added, 'Good day, madam.'

'Hello, Henry. Could you have the car unpacked, please?'

'Certainly, sir. Tea, madam?' He looked in Megan's direction. Megan smiled.

'Lovely, thank you, Henry. We'll have it in the drawing room.'

'Make that the south wing drawing room, please, in our apartment, Henry,' butted in Tobias.

documentary. He had done so again, expecting her to act as assistant producer and researcher, thus saving money on a very tight budget.

'Now, let's talk schedules. We'll want to interview the villagers. We need to home in on any eccentrics, recluses, country bumpkins, people that will entertain, or provoke. Viola, you mentioned folklore. I like that, but take it further, exploit it, think... think...' he narrowed his eyes again, '*The Wicker Man.*'

There was a stunned silence. Libby, the editor, a quiet, middle-aged lady, who had worked several times with Marcus, coughed slightly. 'Is that really the angle we're going for, Marcus?'

He looked surprised by her question. 'Yes. Why?'

'I thought it was more quaint English country tradition we were interested in?' added Len, the cameraman.

'We are,' replied Marcus, 'but that alone isn't going to make this a good documentary. We'll need that twist to give it dimension.'

After consideration, the team began to see his point. Marcus Devlin wasn't an award-winning documentary producer for no reason. He was going to examine a small, country village and, besides depicting its charm, was going to expose all its idiosyncrasies, even if that meant uncovering its darker side too. He'd seen too many programmes focusing on the idealism of country life. It was boring, repetitive and in his opinion, unrealistic. As if anybody lived the good life to the extent that had often been portrayed! And so smugly, too. It prickled him the way the green-welly brigade lorded over their organic way of life and looked down their snooty noses at those who

Henry looked a little surprised, but nodded all the same. Megan smiled again. Obviously Tobias was making a point; he was a married man now, with separate rooms from the rest of the household, and she felt a sense of relief that he had set the boundaries.

Tobias put his arm round her and pulled her in to him. She felt further reassured. He kissed her cheek. 'We'll dine with Mother tonight. She'll want to see us. Is that all right?'

'Of course. I'm sure she's dying to see you.' Megan threaded her arm round him.

'Aunt Celia may still be here,' he gently warned, making her giggle.

'Even better.' Well, she was going to have to get used to all this sooner or later, wasn't she? She only hoped she'd manage to keep dinner down and her pregnancy a secret.

Together they walked along the tiled floors of the corridor, past the oak-panelled Great Hall and up the sweeping staircase to the south wing. The rooms had been aired and cleaned, but it was to be Megan's project to redecorate them. At the moment the walls were bare, all pale yellow and white with polished wooden floors. Nice enough, but she wanted to inject warmth and character into her home, to personalise the rooms with photographs, cosy it up with throws, rugs and gentler lighting. Tobias had had his great four-poster bed moved into their bedroom, and a matching dressing table with the same heavy style of carving had been placed there too. Beatrice, no doubt, thought Megan, appreciating her thoughtfulness. The two large sash windows in the drawing room overlooked the gardens, manicured to perfection, giving them splendid views. It was a vast contrast to the small cottage garden at her old home.

There was a knock at the door and a young girl wearing a white apron carried in a tea tray. Placing it on the coffee table she quickly smiled before leaving the room.

'Thanks!' Megan called after her.

Tobias was on his mobile, staring out of the window. Far in the distance the white railings of the training track could be seen. Beyond that was the old stable block, which he had converted for Dylan's business, and it was Dylan he was talking to, with an intense expression on his face. Clearly they were talking business. Megan understood how much her husband worried about keeping Treweham Hall afloat and out of the red. The training yard promised to have a huge positive impact on their finances, and both Tobias and Dylan were determined to grow the business as quickly as possible. Seeing the tea had arrived and Megan was waiting on the sofa for him to join her, however, he finished the conversation quickly.

'Everything all right?' Megan asked, pouring the tea.

'Fine. The yard's filling up; more horses are arriving this week.'

'That's great, isn't it?' she replied, passing him a cup.

'Certainly is.' He took his cup, put it down, and then turned to her. She got more beautiful as the days passed. Pregnancy certainly suited her, making her skin shine healthily and her brown eyes sparkle. Her body was starting to change shape slightly, with her full breasts and stomach beginning to swell. Megan saw her husband looking at her and it felt good that he still reacted this way. He leant forward to kiss her and she met his lips while her hands ran through his long, dark hair. He pulled her towards him, his arms enclosing her as he deepened the kiss. Her hands crept under his shirt and felt his toned back. She heard him quietly groan as he ran his lips down her neck and began to reach for the zip at the back of her dress.

'Tobias! Tobias, are you there?' Suddenly they jumped apart. Beatrice bustled into the room, closely followed by Zac, Megan's black Labrador. 'There you are! How wonderful to see you both!' Her petite frame was outstretched for Tobias to hug, which he dutifully did.

'Mother, how lovely to see you,' he answered.

Megan chewed her bottom lip to stop the laughter that threatened to escape, whilst hugging an excited Zac.

Dinner that evening was a curious affair. Beatrice and Celia made rather humorous company, without any intention to be funny on their parts.

'So, how did the honeymoon go?' Celia asked directly whilst breaking into her bread roll.

'France was divine, thank you, Celia,' replied Tobias. Celia then turned to Megan.

'All settled in then?' Her eyebrow arched. Megan couldn't decide if that was a genuine question, or a bit of a dig at them having their own private quarters.

'Yes. How about you?' replied Megan, referencing the fact Celia was still there since coming to stay for the wedding, instead of returning to her luxury retirement complex. *Touché*, thought Tobias grinning to himself. Celia chose to ignore the question and carried on.

'You look a little pale, Megan. Are you feeling all right?'

Megan's soup spoon hovered before her mouth. 'Fine, thanks.' Had the old bat guessed? With her hawk eyes she probably had.

'Sebastian was just marvellous,' gushed Beatrice, totally oblivious to the conversation going on around her.

'I heard that too,' Tobias smiled. 'We'll be seeing him soon. The reviews have been fantastic, haven't they?'

'Very talented boy,' butted in Celia firmly.

'He is,' agreed Megan warmly. She thought fondly of her brother-in-law, who had given her so much support, especially when conducting the first guided tour of the Hall, dressed in sixteenth-century costume. Then an uneasy feeling started to stir inside her stomach. Oh, no, she thought, putting her spoon down. Tobias quickly turned to her.

'Are you OK, Megan?' His face was etched with concern.

Megan shook her head. 'I think I'm… going to be…' Then she quickly got up from the table and dashed to the nearest toilet.

Tobias rose from his chair. 'Excuse us, ladies,' he said over his shoulder and followed Megan.

'Huh, just as I suspected,' Celia said flatly. Beatrice looked quizzically at her sister. Oh for God's sake, thought Celia in exasperation. Did she ever cotton on to anything? 'The girl's pregnant, Beatrice,' she stated with force.

'Oh… a honeymoon baby! How romantic!' Beatrice clasped her hands together with joy.

Honeymoon my foot, thought Celia.

7

Finula took the thick, cream envelope and slid it open. Still unable to recognise the neat, bold writing on the front, her curiosity was building. Inside was a photograph. Pulling it out, she saw it was of her, as Megan's bridesmaid. Normally Finula didn't take a great picture, but even she had to admit this portrait was a good one. A very good one, in fact, capturing her coy smile and her glance cast slightly downwards, as if avoiding eye contact. The light had caught her dark red curls, and the long bronze dress, which hugged her slim build, baring one pale, freckled shoulder, complimented her figure beautifully.

Turning it round, she read the inscription: '*Best wishes, Marcus*'. Her heart stopped for a moment. Marcus. He'd contacted her. Then instantly getting cross with herself she tried to rationalise things logically. It was just a photo that he'd taken of her and he was being polite, sending her a copy. That's all. Even so, her heart had started to beat like a drum. Finula squinted her eyes to assess his writing closely. She once read that someone's handwriting could tell you a lot about the person. Marcus' handwriting was bold, solid, obviously written confidently; no hesitant, faint scribbles here. In any event, Finula thought, it was a kind gesture, which deserved to be thanked. Should she try to ring him? Then again, how? He'd left only his address, no landline number or mobile. Maybe she should send him a thank you card, then? But would that actually encourage him to contact her again? A friendly conversation would be more likely to result in their possibly meeting up, she was sure. Not quite knowing what the best course of action was, she decided to run it past Megan. She'd know what to do.

'Finula!' Her dad was calling from the bottom of the stairs.

'Coming!' she shouted back, shoving the photograph in her dressing-table drawer. Soon she was busy pulling pints, before later moving on to preparing the vegetables for that evening's dinner, and the whole while she had a spring in her step and a smile that refused to disappear. Her dad entered the kitchen, red faced and breathless.

'It's bedlam out there tonight,' he puffed. Finula shook her head; like she was ever going to be able to take that break he'd promised. 'Just to let you know, Fin, we've got full bookings next week.'

Finula looked up, surprised. 'All the rooms?'

'Yes, arranged this afternoon. A TV production team. Do you remember that chap who stayed here the other week? The producer?'

Did she ever.

'Er... Mark... no, Marcus?' She pretended vagueness.

'That's him. He rang, took all the rooms... well, what was available. Apparently they're filming a documentary here, in the village.'

Finula blinked. 'Here?'

'So he said. They'll be staying for some time,' he called, turning back to the busy bar.

Well, well, well. Marcus was coming back here, to The Templar. Finula's mouth stretched into a broad smile. She'd be able to thank him in person after all.

'You're retiring?' Connor spat down the phone.

Dylan braced himself, knowing full well how his fat, little agent would react. Although Dylan didn't particularly like Connor, finding him altogether too pushy and greedy, he had to concede that Connor had represented him very well over the years; gaining him exclusive contracts with various clothing and jewellery companies. Images of Dylan wearing the latest sports jacket or designer watch sent sales rocketing. His attending a particular gym had seen its membership soar, not to mention the aftershave commercial he had recently starred in, advertising the sexy fragrance Racer. Connor had made him money, there was no question about that, but in turn, Connor had also raked in the commissions and wasn't about to give them up lightly. On hearing Dylan's decision to retire from racing, Connor had broken out into a sweat. He couldn't let his star client slip through his podgy fingers.

'Dylan, I think you need to seriously reconsider. Think about it. Give yourself some time,' he urged, trying not to sound as desperate as he was, but Dylan saw straight through him.

'I don't need any time, Connor. My mind's made up. I need to concentrate on the racing yard.' He cast his gaze out of his office window to see his grooms scurrying about their duties. The horses were being tacked up for their early morning gallop. He longed to be out there with them, instead of catching up with all the paperwork. However, Dylan always made it a priority to oversee each horse, keen to observe any small change in performance. Each morning he assisted the yard staff with the first feeds and mucking out the stables. Each horse would be exercised for between one and one and a half hours, usually with the same groom, as Dylan wanted to make sure they got to know their horses and any habits or idiosyncrasies they may have. He was more often than not also there for evening stables too, when the horses were skipped out, groomed and checked for injuries or inflammation. The racehorses in Delany's Racing Yard lived in the equivalent of five-star hotel accommodation, always well fed, rugged up and receiving top-class care and attention. Sighing to himself, he turned his attention back to his phone call.

'But...' Connor sounded frantic to suggest a solution.

'It's that simple,' cut in Dylan with determination. 'Newmarket in November will be the last time I race.'

Connor obviously knew when he was beaten. Dylan's mind was clearly made up but, true to form, the agent's money-making brain came up with one last-ditch suggestion.

'What about a book? Your autobiography?' Connor's voice perked up, and Dylan imagined he was picturing the potential royalties stacking up. 'I could arrange it, put the feelers out. Once your retirement's announced, the publishers will come flocking.'

Dylan could hardly believe what he was hearing and he burst out laughing.

'You joking? I think I've had enough exposure to last me a lifetime, Connor,' was his reply. After reading the kiss-and-tell article of a former lover, Dylan was in no hurry to have his whole life story published.

8

Viola studied the photograph carefully. It wasn't the first time she had scrutinised a picture of Tobias Cavendish-Blake, and who could blame her? There was no doubt, he was a stunner, with his dark hair, green eyes, dimpled chin, strong jaw line and wicked grin. This was a photograph taken in his mid-twenties, when he was at his most notorious. Hardly surprising then that he had a beauty on each arm, coquettishly gazing up at him. Tobias was dressed in a black dinner suit – well, half a suit – with his white shirt slightly unbuttoned, revealing a dark shadow of hair, his bow tie hung untied, the trousers were none existent. Allegedly they had been taken off at some point in the nightclub, as a dare from Seamus Fox, his best friend. The black boxer shorts revealed firm, muscular thighs that Viola homed in on. In the background was the Fox, similarly dressed, an identical roguish grin spread across his pale face. The two best mates had opposite colouring, but both had had exactly the same attitude to life:

basically to rip the hell out of it. Which, as Viola's research had proved, was precisely what they had done.

Another picture showed a very young Tobias dressed in Eton uniform; a pristine, white shirt and black tail coat, his cold, haughty expression totally in keeping with the formality of his surroundings.

Viola sifted through the collection and picked out the one that she thought depicted him in a warmer, more natural light. It was the most recent photograph taken of him at his wedding a few weeks ago. Choosing to marry inside Treweham Hall chapel meant Tobias had not appeared publicly to the media with flashing cameras, camped outside the Hall gates and lining the village footpaths. Any rare photograph the paparazzi had managed to snap had been taken from a distance with a long lens.

Luckily, a number of discerning reporters had gone to great lengths to secure a few rounds of shots through the leafy woods that joined the back of the Treweham Hall estate. As the wedding party had enjoyed champagne and canapés, basking in the sunshine on the lawn, a few hundred yards away, cameras had feverishly clicked and flashed, recording all the day's events. They caught a radiant, young bride in an exquisite, ivory gown, holding a champagne flute, smiling with utter happiness; an older Seamus Fox, now a loyal husband and doting father to two giggling little girls, which he held in his arms, whilst his wife looked on affectionately; Sebastian Cavendish-Blake holding court, his animated face obviously entertaining the older, grey-haired lady dressed in tweed; but the absolute corker shot, or so Viola thought, was of the groom.

Tobias looked magnificent in a grey morning suit. He still wore his hair long, and those piercing green eyes shone with love and laughter. His face appeared relaxed, happy and totally at ease, a far cry from the sullen, arrogant looks thrown at the press in the past, or the defiant, devil-may-care smirks for which he was renowned. He still had 'it', though, Viola concluded. Men such as Tobias Cavendish-Blake never lost their sex appeal; it just grew with them, maturing naturally.

Viola was a man's woman. She naturally preferred men's company to women's. By and large she found women either bitchy or just plain dull. Often craving the limelight, Viola was vain enough to soak up any attention thrown her way. She was slim and attractive and her long, caramel-brown hair fell sleekly down her back. Born with sharp features, Viola had had plastic surgery to correct her hooked nose and a cute, small one had replaced it. Her thin lips had been plumped to give a full, voluptuous look, and the boob job she'd had done was her absolute pride and joy. Nobody could accuse Viola of not making the most of herself. She had totally reinvented every inch of herself. Even her name. Being christened Vera was hardly the best start in life. Maybe in the fifties, but whoever had heard of a girl being named Vera in the mid-eighties? Yet another misfortune inherited from her mother.

One thing Viola had been born with that had remained was her determination. She had true grit and real perseverance. She never gave up and she always got what she wanted. Viola's force of will knew no bounds, to the point where it was scary. Only once had she had to back down – she had had no choice; not even Viola could ignore a Restraining Order. But that was all in the past, a minor hiccup in an otherwise successful life, she liked to think. There was nothing wrong with ambition, unless you let it drive you to the brink.

She was set on a career as a producer, just like Marcus Devlin. He interested her too, though not in the same way as Tobias Cavendish-Blake. Instead she sensed her attraction to him was more kindred. Having worked with Marcus before, she had recognised instantly that he was a private man, choosing whom he socialised with on set, if at all. Often she would find him alone, deep in concentration, or quietly talking to only the one or two crew members he had known a long time. Viola suspected there was far more to Marcus than met the eye. A classic case of still waters running deep. Her instincts told her he was camouflaging his life in some way, hiding something, or maybe who he really was deep down. Why did she think this? Because she was doing exactly the same; she recognised the trait.

Viola started to read the article she had found online about 'Lord Cavendish-Blake-the-rake'. It was pure drama: the handsome, aristocratic hell-raiser finally tamed by a local, fresh-faced girl from the village. Viola's eyes narrowed. Did a leopard ever change its spots? She very much doubted it.

9

Finula steadied herself and took a deep breath. Out of the pub window she watched as two vans pulled in at the front. This was the television crew The Templar had been expecting. Would Marcus be in one of the vans, she wondered, her heart starting to thump slightly. She forced herself to get a grip and concentrate on trying to look relaxed, confident and professional.

The vans parked and three people got out and gathered together, but Marcus wasn't one of them, Finula noticed with disappointment. Moments later they came into the pub. A woman with long brown hair headed the small team. She smiled brightly and spoke directly to Dermot, who had approached their newly arrived guests.

'Hi there, I'm Viola,' she beamed, and offered her hand.

'Good to meet you, Viola,' he replied. 'I'm the landlord, Dermot, and this is my daughter, Finula.' He pointed to Finula, who smiled and waved from behind the bar.

'We're nearly all here, Dermot. Just waiting for Marcus, the producer, to arrive, but his time-keeping isn't the best,' she laughed, 'and one other, Jamie, our runner, who'll be joining us tomorrow.'

'Right you are,' nodded Dermot. 'Let's give you a hand with those cases and show you to your rooms.'

Finula quickly joined them to help. She picked up a large overnight bag from the floor next to Viola.

'No, I'll carry that.' Viola quickly grabbed the bag back, then laughed a little awkwardly. 'Perhaps you could carry Libby's case for her?' she added in a softer tone, seeing Finula's puzzled expression. A middle-aged lady with short, blond hair smiled gratefully.

'Sure, no problem,' Finula replied.

'Thank you so much. I hope it's not too heavy.'

'It's fine,' assured Finula, heaving the case up the stairs.

Dermot plonked down the luggage he had carried outside the first room on the landing.

'This is one of the twin rooms,' he stated, fishing in his back pocket for the key.

'That'll be for me and Libby,' Viola told him and took the key.

'The next room is for the single occupancy,' Finula supplied.

'That's Marcus',' Viola informed, 'so the last room's yours and Jamie's.' She looked towards an older man, probably in his fifties, with thinning grey hair. Dermot handed him his key.

'Thanks, I'm Len, the cameraman.' He shook hands with Dermot.

What a nice, friendly bunch they seem, thought Finula. 'Dinner's served between seven o'clock and nine,' she told them, 'and breakfast from seven thirty to nine thirty.'

'That's great, thanks,' smiled Viola.

'Right, we'll leave you to settle in. Just give us a shout if you need anything,' Dermot said, turning to go back to the bar. Finula followed, anticipation building for Marcus' arrival. She didn't have to wait too long.

It was early evening by the time he arrived, whilst the rest of the team were sitting choosing their evening meal. It was growing dark outside but from the window Finula could just see a figure emerge out of a Range Rover. He was wheeling a case and had a rucksack slung over his shoulder. Finula fought for composure as Marcus entered the bar and looked straight into her face, then broke into a slow smile.

'Hello, there,' he said, and his soft, Irish tones melted her insides.

'Oh, hi!' she replied, desperate to sound casual and failing miserably as her words came out rather forced and squeaky. She quickly went on, 'Had a good journey?' That was better. At least the high pitch had disappeared and her normal voice had returned.

'Not bad.' He moved towards the bar, narrowing the distance between them. Finula could see him clearly now. His dark hair had been cut shorter and his face had grown stubble, giving him an unkempt, sexy look. He had razor-sharp cheekbones and full, wide lips, which were smiling in her direction. His green eyes were glistening brightly, like emeralds.

'Thank you for sending the photograph,' she said. Now he was directly facing her. Finula's heart started to flutter.

'You're welcome.' He gazed into her eyes and for a moment everything stood still.

'Ah, Marcus, there you are!' called Viola. He turned towards the table where his team were sitting and gave them a curt nod.

'Be with you shortly,' he answered. Then, turning back to Finula, he said gently, 'Good to see you again, Finula.'

She looked at him and couldn't speak. Luckily Dermot interrupted her reverie as he came in from the kitchen.

'Marcus, welcome back.' They exchanged firm handshakes. Finula sensed real affection between the two men, assuming it was because they came from the same county in Ireland. 'Come on, I'll show you to your room.' Dermot ushered Marcus up the stairs, leaving Finula to catch her breath.

10

Flora rushed into the hallway to answer the phone. 'Hello.'

'Hello. May I speak to Dylan Delany, please?' Flora didn't recognise the female voice. It was smooth and efficient-sounding.

'I'm sorry, Dylan's not here at the moment,' she replied.

'May I leave my number for him to contact me?'

Flora was beginning to feel a little uncomfortable. Who was this? Not waiting for an answer, the confident voice continued, 'My name is Jade Fisher and I'm ringing from *Hi-Ya* magazine.'

'Oh, I see…' Flora felt slight relief. Obviously the magazine wanted to interview Dylan as the news of his imminent retirement had spread like wildfire already. After taking down the details, Flora left the notepaper with them on by the coffee machine, knowing that was the first place Dylan headed to after returning from the yard.

True to form, half an hour later Flora heard the back door slam shut and she joined him in the kitchen.

'Hi,' he smiled wearily, looking bone tired. Flora's heart went out to him. She'd be glad when he no longer had to concentrate on two jobs and just had their own yard to look after. He had left earlier that day to talk to a prospective client. 'Fancy a coffee?' Dylan's eyes squinted at the note placed by the machine. 'What's this?' He picked it up, frowning.

'Someone from *Hi-Ya* magazine called wanting to speak to you.'

Dylan rolled his eyes. Not another request. Since announcing his retirement from the racing circuit he'd been inundated, as his agent had predicted, with one journalist or another. This Jade Fisher was just the latest writer wanting a piece of him.

Flora noticed the dismissive expression on Dylan's face and pondered for a moment. 'Would you consider an interview?' she asked.

Dylan looked at her with his eyebrow raised. 'After last time I appeared in the tabloids?' He was, of course, referring to the seedy article that had been written about him, thanks to an opportunist ex-lover called Sadie Stringfellow. The incident had, not surprisingly, caused a real rift between him and Flora, which he had just about managed to bridge. No way was he going to jeopardise their relationship again.

'But what if it's on your terms? You pick the questions to reflect what you want out there.'

Dylan was astonished by Flora's words, especially after all the harm the press had inflicted. 'I can't believe you'd want me to be interviewed.' He poured them each a coffee and passed her a steaming cup.

'Thanks.' Flora blew on it and continued, 'You could always put your slant on what's happened in the past.'

Dylan looked warily at her, not sure where this was going. 'Defend myself, you mean?' He hoped this wasn't the start of any unpleasantness. He knew he had to prove himself to her. Even now, he sensed she was a little insecure, not that he blamed her. He had *been* a playboy, but convincing Flora he was no longer often proved difficult.

'In a way, yes.' Then, after taking a gulp of coffee she added, 'Could be good for business too.'

Dylan turned his head sharply and looked again at the notepaper. Flora had a point. An interview where he chose the questions may be beneficial, and coverage for his racing yard could only be good publicity. As for his private life, well, what could be more cosy than a picture of him and Flora at home together? Perhaps it was time to set the record straight and pitch a new, wholesome image, rather than the racing Romeo he was known as by the fans.

'I'll do it on one condition.' He put his coffee down and moved towards her with a playful grin.

Flora knew all too well he was up to something. She'd recognise that roguish look anywhere. 'What's that?' She too put her cup down.

He pulled her into his arms. 'That you're here with me. I want you to be part of the interview, with photographs together.'

Flora was stunned. 'Really?'

'Yes, of course. Why not?' He leant back to look at her. A smile curved her lips, any apprehensions she may have had now evaporated. 'I'll ring and tell her I'll do it, but only after my last race.'

'Are you sure about me being in it?' Flora searched his face for any regrets.

'Absolutely. We're a partnership, aren't we?' He stared challengingly into her eyes, hoping to drill home how serious he was about their relationship. As Flora looked down, Dylan caught her chin with his finger and tilted her face up towards his. 'Flora,' he whispered, 'don't doubt me.' He leant forward and kissed her gently.

Flora melted into his arms. Would he always have this effect on her? She feared he might…

11

The applause was deafening, the whole audience on its feet, clapping and cheering. Sebastian gulped back the emotion that threatened to reduce him to tears on stage. Being the professional he was, he clenched his jaw and bowed with pride. The rest of the cast bowed too, then turned to Richard III and clapped their fellow actor with admiration. Sebastian was overwhelmed. Never had he had such a reaction. Still the thunderous applause continued, making a shiver run down his twisted spine.

The restricted jacket he wore with the humped back was virtually crippling him now. Seven weeks of solid bending and crouching had made every muscle in Sebastian's back, stomach and legs cry out in discomfort. He was desperate to take a long, hot bath, sprinkled with magnesium salts, to sooth his aching body and relax his over-active mind. He had memorised each line for the role of Richard III meticulously and spoken every word naturally, with complete ease, as if it was the common, spoken language, rather than the poetic beauty of Shakespeare's play.

This had been the role that had finally made him as an actor, without question. Not one negative review had been made, which was practically unheard of in the acting profession. Each gave acknowledgement to 'Sebastian Cavendish-Blake's extraordinary talent' and yet… there was still something missing for this gifted young actor. Sebastian felt he didn't have anyone to share all this success with. Yes, he had a loving family and good friends, not to mention the rest of the cast, to whom he'd grown very close; but not that special person, the one he yearned to go home to at the end of a punishing rehearsal, or jubilant performance to talk to. To just *be* with. As the cheering and whistles bellowed from the crowd, Sebastian couldn't help but feel a little lost and empty at the thought of going back to his empty apartment. Taking his final bow, he and the cast made their departure from the stage.

Sebastian walked slowly to his dressing room. 'Still in character, Seb?' Jack, the actor who had played Buckingham, patted him on the back.

'Huh?' Sebastian frowned.

'You're still limping.' Jack pointed to Sebastian's left foot, which was dragging slightly.

'Just exhausted,' he replied.

Was it any wonder? After seven weeks of hobbling disjointedly across the stage, night after night, it was a miracle his body was able to unravel back to its former self at all. Although often teased throughout his childhood, especially by his older, bigger brother, for his slim build,

Sebastian was actually extremely toned and in good shape. He jogged most mornings (when he wasn't knackered from a late night's performance). At home, he loved running through the country estate, giving himself space to collect his thoughts and redress the imbalance in his life.

He didn't want to become a recluse, dedicated to his work and socialising with the cast only on a last night. He craved a close relationship, with all that entailed: cosy suppers, one-to-ones, meaningful sex. Instead, Stratford-upon-Avon had made him popular, but he was just attracting shallow groupies who sought friendship in the hope of sharing the limelight. It was because of this transient lifestyle, especially with the touring productions he'd done before, that he had really appreciated a solid, loving relationship back home, a safe place to return to.

Sebastian was convinced that had he not been playing the leading role, his phone wouldn't ring quite as much as it had. He was constantly barraged with invitations for lunches, parties and selective dinners. At first, he welcomed the attention and it had provided much-needed distraction. But after a while, when he realised how superficial it all was, the novelty had worn off. Actors could be a fickle bunch and Sebastian hated hypocrisy. As a result, he became choosy about who he mixed with, accidentally making himself even more sought after. If a dinner party had Sebastian Cavendish-Blake at the table, then it was 'the party'; likewise, if it didn't, it wasn't worth attending.

As this was the last night of the play, it was expected that all the cast would celebrate with drinks. Sebastian didn't want to cause offence by not joining in. He promised himself he'd stay for just one drink, then make his excuses and go. That long, hot bath was too inviting.

The roof-top restaurant and cocktail bar at the Royal Shakespeare Theatre provided the theatrical backdrop the cast enjoyed. It gave splendid views of Stratford from the balcony and it was here that Sebastian sipped his tomato juice, having escaped the raucous group at the bar.

Suddenly, he became aware of someone watching him. He turned sharply and froze.

'Hello, Sebastian.' Although it was dark out on the balcony, with only gentle lighting from the candles on tables, he knew that profile – would know it anywhere – and that voice.

'Nick,' Sebastian replied flatly, gripping his glass tightly. The figure moved closer. Now he could see his face, the one that had haunted his dreams for months.

'You don't sound too pleased to see me.' Nick was staring at him as if trying to read his expression.

Sebastian refused to give anything away and kept a neutral tone. 'I'm not,' he replied bluntly, making Nick flinch. Was this just another insincerity? Had Nick realised just what he'd thrown away? Well, tough. It was too late. Way too late.

'I just want to talk to you, Sebastian.' Nick's voice held a desperate note, making him sound needy. This wasn't the same Nick who had arrogantly cheated on him, tearing his heart to pieces.

'Well, I don't want to talk to you, Nick.' Sebastian stared defiantly into those blue eyes, which at one time could melt him. 'I *don't*,' he repeated, barging past him and back inside to the comfort of the bar.

12

Viola had booked a place on a guided tour of Treweham Hall. She had decided to get a feel for the place as a member of the public, not part of the television film crew. That way she could get an insight into the place before announcing who she was, in case she was given a frosty reception. If Jamie was right – and she thought he probably was – the moment Tobias Cavendish-Blake got wind of any media sniffing around his home she'd be whisked off the premises.

Instincts told her to befriend Finula from The Templar as best she could, hopefully paving the way for a possible interview with Tobias, as she had soon cottoned on to the fact that they were good friends. In fact, Finula had been very open about how the Cavendish-Blakes played a crucial role in the village and were thought very highly of. She had mentioned a tradition held every year, the Landlord's Supper, when the Lord of Treweham Hall held a dinner for all the residents on his estate. It dated back to medieval times, when the tenants all paid their rent to their landlord in return for supper and as much ale as they could drink. The custom was still upheld and proved a popular event in Treweham village.

Viola's interest had been particularly piqued when a nearby customer, overhearing the conversation, had rumbled with laughter over the 'fiasco' of the last Landlord's Supper. When Finula had brushed aside the remark, it had left Viola even more curious.

It was mid-October and the tours were due to stop soon, as the Hall would be closed to the public over the winter months and re-opening in early spring. As it was one of the last tours of the season, Megan had decided to take it, and she was rather looking forward to showing off the rooms for the last time that year. Her pregnancy was starting to show now. The small bump was getting more obvious, so that the couple had decided to announce their happy news to a very excited family. Beatrice had been beside herself with joy at having Celia's guess confirmed, to the amusement of Tobias. Sebastian was elated at the prospect of becoming an uncle, whereas Aunt Celia had nodded her tight grey perm in approval with a knowing look. Megan's family had been equally delighted, if not a touch surprised at the timing. Not knowing their daughter had already been pregnant at the wedding, they were a little taken aback.

'Welcome to Treweham Hall,' Megan greeted the small gathering.

Viola stood towards the back, sizing up the new Lady Cavendish-Blake. She was very pretty, in a girl-next-door kind of way, Viola conceded, admiring her thick, glossy dark hair, cut neatly into a bob. She had a beautiful, fresh complexion too, thought Viola with envy. Viola herself had often struggled with spots and forked out a fortune on expensive concealers and make-up. Megan Cavendish-Blake had style too, with a designer dress and patterned silk scarf. On further inspection, though, Viola's sharp eye clocked the slight bulge protruding from it. Was Lady Cavendish-Blake pregnant?

'So, if you would like to make your way to the Chapel…' Megan continued.

'Is that where you got married?' interrupted an excited lady at the front.

'Yes, it is,' replied Megan with a grin.

Smug cow, thought Viola with spite, but smiled with the rest of the party.

Viola made discreet notes throughout the tour, picking out points of interest for future reference. She had to admit she'd thoroughly enjoyed listening to the history of the Hall and wandering through the lavish rooms. She had been especially taken by the photographs in smart frames dotted around, depicting the Cavendish-Blake family life. Pictures of the late Lord Cavendish-Blake and his bride, two young boys riding on tricycles, one pale and blond, the other dark with a mischievous grin.

Viola was in awe of the recent portrait of Tobias, which had managed to completely capture his magnetism. To think that he had married a local village girl, when he could have had someone of much higher calibre. Viola stole another glance at the lucky woman who had bagged such a catch. She wasn't that special, was she? No better-looking than herself, surely? Viola looked down at her svelte figure tucked flatteringly into skinny jeans, showcasing her pert bum. The tight, black jumper she wore outlined her curves, making her look voluptuous, she thought, although others might think it vulgar.

'So, ladies and gentlemen, that concludes today's tour. Please do feel free to visit the tearoom.' A slight applause followed.

Megan made her way down the next flight of stairs to the tearoom where she had arranged to meet Finula. She didn't really want tea and cake in their drawing room when she could mingle with the staff in the café, and besides, Tobias was there with Dylan. Megan enjoyed the banter and was looking forward to catching up with her best friend. There she was, sitting by the window. A beam of sunlight illuminated her red hair. On noticing Megan, she waved her over.

'Hi, so good to see you!' She hugged her hard, then quickly backed off. 'Sorry, don't want to squash your bump. You're really showing now, aren't you?' Finula looked down at Megan's stomach.

Megan gently patted it. 'Certainly am.' Once seated, and with a cream tea before her, Megan was keen to hear of any gossip. 'So, the tall, dark stranger has arrived, then?' she asked with a sly smile. She was, of course, referring to Marcus Devlin, the documentary producer who had made quite an impression on her friend. Finula had excitedly filled Megan in on all the details after her dad had taken the room bookings for the film crew.

'Yes, and he's as handsome as I remembered,' gushed Finula, making Megan smile. Good, old Finula, she observed, always wearing her heart on her sleeve. She was an open book: what you saw was what you got, which was why she loved her. Megan was pleased that her best mate could have another chance to be happy, especially after being so crushed by Nick.

'He's had his hair cut shorter and grown a bit of stubble,' Finula's face was animated, 'and it makes him look more rugged and sexier than ever,' she said in hushed tones. Both girls giggled.

'So, has he made a move yet?' whispered Megan.

'Give him a chance.'

'He will. If he's any sense.'

'Bring it on,' Finula laughed.

'Well, he must be interested. I mean, why else send the photograph? I bet he's got a duplicate, framed by his bedside,' joked Megan. Finula's head went back and she laughed loudly. It was good to see her in high spirits. Megan hoped Marcus Devlin was going to come up trumps.

Two tables away, behind a pillar, Viola sat listening intently. Well, well, well. So Finula had the hots for Marcus, did she? That could prove very useful indeed, especially if they needed him to dish the dirt on the village. What was that about a photograph, though? Clearly Marcus and Finula had met before, which explained why Marcus had seemed familiar with Treweham and The Templar at the meeting. And she was dead right about the pregnancy: obviously conceived before the marriage. So it was a 'shotgun wedding'. That's how the new lady of the manor had snared such a prize. It was the oldest trick in the book.

In the south wing Tobias and Dylan were discussing plans for the training yard. 'Attracting clients from the Far East is definitely the way forward,' Tobias stated, knowing full well the astronomical sums of money they would pay.

'I agree,' replied Dylan, nodding enthusiastically. 'I'm amazed at the money they're prepared to part with. Mind you, why not? I run a top-class training yard.'

'On an ancestral country estate. That counts for a lot with some people.'

'Absolutely,' agreed Dylan, then paused. 'I've been approached by a magazine for an interview.'

Tobias looked surprised. 'You're not doing it, are you?' He had always assumed his friend's opinion of the press was the same as his own.

'Flora talked me round.'

'Really?' Tobias' eyebrow arched higher.

'Said it would be good for business. I think she has a point.'

Tobias mulled this over, his brow furrowed in contemplation. 'Hmm, maybe.'

Perhaps Flora had a point. Tobias was beginning to see how the media might actually work in a positive way for him, for once.

13

Marcus took a deep breath and ran a hand through his hair. This was a tough one. The budget was tight. He knew his role would involve editing and directing, as well as being the person who made the documentary happen. Not only was he going to be the producer, he'd have to act as manager, accountant, visionary and entrepreneur. All were talents of his – he knew that – but this time it was different. This time it was personal. Any outsider, not really knowing Marcus Devlin would assume he was an aloof character, a dark, brooding Heathcliff figure, that kept all his emotions in check, and to a degree they would be right in this assessment. But deep down, in the pit of his soul, lay torrid feelings of anger and the driving desire to correct the unforgivable injustices that had blighted the one person he had loved unconditionally, his mother.

It had been nine months since she had died. He had been there from the very beginning of her diagnosis. The cancer had raged through her body cruelly, giving him only a few short months to love and look after her, to tend to her every need. How could he cram in all he wanted to say and show her how much he cared in that short time? It was impossible. As soon as Marcus had learnt of his mother's cancer, he had tried to make time stand still. He had stopped all he was doing, backing out of a programme he had just started to make. His mother came first, it was that simple.

It had always been just him and her. Anne Devlin had been a single mother and had been fiercely protective of her only child. Being single, pregnant and from England hadn't been the best of starts in a small village in Roscommon, even though she had called herself 'Mrs' Devlin and worn a wedding ring, claiming her young husband had been killed tragically in a car accident. Anne had family in Ireland and an auntie had originally taken her in as long as Anne pretended to be a 'widow'. No one was going to bring shame to her doorstep, particularly family. As a result, Marcus grew up believing his father had been killed. It was only in the dark hours of early dawn, nine months ago, that he had learnt differently. His dying mother's last breaths had told him the truth: his father was very much alive and living in England. Marcus had been stunned, but equally appalled that he had never met or known him. Anne's faint whispers had explained why. He was married. He was well known, a somebody, with a title. Marcus strained to listen and absorb every last detail, his heart racing. The fury had started to build at that moment, and had gathered momentum ever since. His mother had been fooled, used and then conveniently disposed of. It had been straightforward to research the name she had given him, especially as he vaguely recognised it in any event. Lord Richard Cavendish-Blake of Treweham Hall.

By the time Marcus had buried his mother and recovered some form of normality, plus digested the revelation of his parentage, it was too late to pursue the matter. Exactly a month after Anne Devlin died, Richard Cavendish-Blake had followed suit. Marcus had spent restless, sleepless nights plotting how he would confront the bastard, expose him, make him pay, only to read one lazy, weekend morning, whilst poring over the Sunday papers, that Tobias Cavendish-Blake was now Lord of Treweham Hall, following the sad loss of his father, the late Lord Richard Cavendish-Blake.

Marcus had been duped, robbed of the opportunity to look his father in the eye and tell him exactly what he thought of him. He was incensed with the injustice of it all. How could people like that not be held accountable? How could he get away with it? Well, he wouldn't. It didn't matter how long it took. He was a patient man, but he would have his revenge if it killed him.

The way the resentment had eaten away at him *had* affected his health, but one day the perfect opportunity had landed right in his lap. He even wondered if his mother was helping him from above, such was the timing. He was approached by a bigwig from the BBC, wanting to make a documentary. He had an idea in his head, which Marcus leapt on. As soon as the words 'quintessential English village life' were spoken, Marcus' reaction was unusually animated, and so positive in fact that the idea had blossomed quickly into a real project. Marcus had bust a gut getting the finance together from individual donors, foundations, companies and arts funding to get the show on the road, and at breath-taking speed. It all seemed to fall into place. Having contacts with the kind of people that could make things happen had proved invaluable; that and the fact they *wanted* to help Marcus, after seeing him off the scene so long with the loss of his mother. He was both admired and respected. Then when Viola had actually suggested Treweham he was speechless, but relieved that he wasn't going to have to find a way to steer his team in that direction. Again, his thoughts turned back to his mother and how she must be looking down on him and helping him.

Marcus had researched the village for himself, hiding inconspicuously in the background, witnessing the mayhem that had surrounded Tobias Cavendish-Blake's wedding. Staying at The Templar had been ideal as it had put him right in the centre of the action – not to mention the added bonus of meeting Finula.

The thought of her made his shoulders relax and his mouth curl into a smile. Finula had been the only comfort in all of this, with her blaze of red hair and creamy, pale skin dusted with freckles. To him, she was a true Irish colleen and looked so out of place in England. The moment he had set eyes on her he had felt an overwhelming urge to pick her up and whisk her back to his homeland. Was it another coincidence that her father came from the same county in Ireland as himself? Or could it be another motherly guiding hand, leading him here to The Templar?

Sighing, he stared down at the paperwork in front of him. The bedroom he had booked this time was the largest in The Templar, with a king-size bed, wardrobe, small sofa, and a desk and chair by the bay window overlooking the velvety green fields at the rear of the building. Being at the back of The Templar meant it was quiet, giving him peace to think, as opposed to the front bedrooms, which faced the hustle and bustle of the car park and the pub entrance. Marcus stared at his notes. He was devising a list of people to interview and places to shoot. The top priority was obviously Tobias Cavendish-Blake at Treweham Hall, but how best to pin him down? Reputedly the man hated the press. Then an idea came to him. Of course. Why hadn't he thought of it before?

Later that evening, after all the guests had dined, Finula relaxed with a well-earned glass of wine in a small alcove by the bar. Marcus had eaten with the rest of the crew and was ordering a pint of Guinness when he noticed her tucked away. He smiled to himself, collected his drink and made his way over.

'Hello there, mind if I join you?'

'No, of course not.' She indicated for him to sit opposite her. 'How's the filming going?' Finula was burning with curiosity about the whole thing, relishing the prospect of being part of the documentary.

'Well, we finally start filming next week. At the moment we're getting a feel for the place, deciding who to interview and where to film.'

'Oh, I see.'

Marcus tilted his head to one side, as if the idea had just occurred to him. 'If you're interested, you could come on a day's shoot.'

'Really?' Finula's face lit up. He loved the way her eyes sparkled in delight.

'Sure,' he nodded. 'In fact, you know more about Treweham Hall than any of the team so perhaps you could advise us.'

'Treweham Hall? You're filming there?' she replied in surprise.

'We would dearly love to. The Cavendish-Blakes are local gentry, aren't they? I believe they are thought very highly of in the village, too.' He eyed her carefully, not wanting to sound too keen.

'They certainly are. Tobias is a top bloke.'

'Is that so?' Marcus' eyebrows rose mockingly.

'Yes, of course. Just because he's got a title doesn't mean he's up himself, you know,' chided Finula, looking into his deep, green eyes and feeling rather flushed.

Her pupils were dilated, Marcus noticed. He'd once read somewhere that was a sign of sexual attraction. Judging by the way she kept playing with her hair he clearly put her on edge too, though.

'I'm sure the Cavendish-Blakes are fine people,' he soothed with a gentle chuckle.

Finula loved the way his cheeks dimpled when he laughed.

'Well, don't take my word for it, judge for yourself.'

'I'd like that very much, if he'll let me anywhere near.'

'I'll ask him,' she said assertively. Bingo, thought Marcus. 'If I'm there with the TV crew at Treweham Hall he'd be more likely to agree to it.'

Marcus paused, as if in deep thought. 'Finula, that would be a tremendous help.'

She liked the way he said her name and gazed into her eyes.

'How can I thank you?' He watched her swallow nervously.

'Er...'

'How about I take you out for dinner?'

'That would be nice,' she replied hoarsely.

'Saturday? In fact, let's make a day of it.'

As luck would have it, she had a rare Saturday off, but she'd have told her dad she was off anyway, given the circumstances.

'Fine,' she squeaked.

At the end of the evening, as Marcus made his way up the stairs and crossed the landing to his room, he met Viola.

'Ah, there you are, Marcus,' she said. 'Listen, I didn't want to mention this at dinner in front of everyone, but I think I know a way to get to Tobias Cavendish-Blake,' she hissed under her breath.

Marcus smiled lazily. 'All sorted.'

'What?' spat Viola.

'I said, it's all sorted,' he replied calmly, crossing his arms.

'But...' she spluttered.

'We should be filming inside Treweham Hall by... the end of the month, I'd say,' and with that he smiled politely, passed her, unlocked his bedroom door and closed it shut, leaving Viola standing there, jaw dropped in astonishment.

Again! He's done it again, always a step ahead, she thought with annoyance.

14

Megan snuggled closer in to her dozing husband and wrapped her arms around him. He felt so solid and warm. 'Hmm,' he responded, turning to face her.

'Tobias, have you thought about what Finula asked?' she spoke quietly, hoping to catch him at his most malleable, after lovemaking and a relaxing sleep.

Megan had been excited when Finula had approached them both about the television crew possibly filming at Treweham Hall, but Tobias had been dubious, even more so when Finula had mentioned him being interviewed. Then he remembered how Dylan had agreed to an interview, thinking it would be good for business. Maybe the same applied to him. After all, publicity for the Hall, which would be open to visitors again in the spring, could only be a good thing. Plus, Treweham Hall being a possible location for television or film companies in the future made this too good an opportunity to miss. He had told Finula that he'd sleep on it, knowing full well that Megan would work on him to agree to it.

'Yes, I've thought about it,' he teased, gently running his fingers through her tousled hair.

'And?' she persisted, her eyes eagerly watching him.

'I'm not sure.'

'Oh, but, Tobias, this would mean the world to Finula. She's desperate to come with the documentary team, and watch the filming, not to mention spend time with her sexy producer chap.'

'Sexy, eh?' Tobias raised a playful eyebrow and rubbed his thumb across her lips. She kissed it and caught hold of his hand.

'Apparently so, but not as sexy as you, I'm sure.' Her eyes danced with mischief. 'Please say you'll do it and let them come.' She bent her head to slowly kiss his lips. He could feel her breasts on his chest and he began to get aroused, again. Her hand moved gently over his chest then crept under the duvet to stroke his muscular thigh, before finally coming to rest on his erection. 'Please,' she whispered in his ear, rubbing her hand delicately up and down him.

How could he deny her anything, this beautiful, intoxicating creature of his?

'Just for you, yes,' he replied huskily as she straddled herself across his legs.

15

It had been a hectic day at the stable yard. Normally Flora would have been in the office first thing, helping to deal with emails, telephone messages and delegating the team's daily rota, but today Dylan had insisted she have some time off. He'd noticed how tired she was looking and he instructed that she have a lie-in that morning as he tumbled out of bed. With Flora still recovering from the nasty virus she had got a few months ago he was anxious not to overwork her.

Three of the grooms were busy mucking out the stables as Dylan scurried about in the office trying to get through the mounting paperwork and all the entries for the upcoming races. Although he dearly loved owning a training yard, he missed spending as much time as he had with the horses. When his sole occupation was as a jockey he was racing every week and he had relished the thrill of the competition. Now more and more of his time was spent filling in forms and wading through all the red tape and, not for the first time, he realised how important Flora's input was. Without her he doubted the yard would run as smoothly as it did. It wasn't as though he didn't always appreciate her – he really did – it was just having the time to show it.

He sighed, feeling a touch guilty. Flora was only twenty and yet she had such a mature, sensible head on her, as well as being the kindest and most loving of people. She would be twenty-one in December. That would be an ideal time to show her how much he valued her. He'd take her away somewhere romantic...

Instantly his thoughts turned back to the yard. Who would cover for them whilst they went away? Again, a touch of resentment fired through him, which he quickly dampened down. What did he expect? It was early days; the yard had only just opened and the clientele was starting to build now. Once they were on their feet and properly established it would get easier. More staff could be employed, giving them better flexibility.

His thoughts were interrupted by a black BMW pulling into the yard and parking outside his office. Dylan frowned, wondering who it could be, but as soon as the driver got out and flicked back her long dark ringlets, flouncing her way towards the office door, his stomach dropped. Oh God, it was Samantha Tait.

Samantha's husband, a rich, successful architect the wrong side of fifty, but with very deep pockets, had contacted him several months ago as a prospective client. He owned two thoroughbreds and needed them in a racing yard, having recently moved them from Ireland. When Dylan had driven to seen the horses, he had had no doubt of their ability and was keen to secure Mr Tait as his client. However, his wife, Samantha, had made it perfectly clear exactly what the terms and conditions had to be. Unbeknown to her husband, Samantha wanted just as much care from Dylan as the horses, and Dylan was to service her too.

Initially it seemed a small price to pay – after all, Samantha was easy on the eye with her svelte body and daring ways – but her constant need for attention had proved too much for Dylan. He soon realised he'd bitten off much more than he could chew but, reluctant to lose a client, he had had to handle her carefully. In the end, he had managed to put a stop to Samantha's advances, and still keep her husband as a client.

Obviously, Flora knew nothing about this, and it was before they had got together, but Dylan was keen to keep it a secret none the less. So far, Samantha had melted into the background, but now it seemed she was back and, judging by the look of determination on her face, she meant business. Dylan thanked God Flora wasn't there in the office with him.

Without knocking, Samantha strode through the small corridor and into the office. She cut quite a figure in tight leggings and a brown cashmere jumper. For a short moment Dylan's gaze rested on her pert bottom, then he quickly looked up to eyes that were blazing. 'How can I help you, Samantha?' Dylan calmly asked.

'Well, you can start by telling me the truth.'

Dylan's eyebrows raised. 'Sorry?'

Samantha let out a sigh of impatience. 'Don't come the innocent with me,' she hissed. 'You tell me you can't perform...' she blushed slightly, making Dylan smirk to himself. 'Then I learn you're shacked up with the assistant trainer!' she yelled at him.

Dylan's eyes fled to the window and he noticed the staff had suddenly started to sweep up nearer to the office. Oh hell. Taking a deep breath he attempted to reason with Samantha, and calm her down.

'Listen, Samantha, it would never have worked between us.'

'That's funny, because there was no mention of that whilst you were rogering me in the hot tub, was there?' Her voice rose again, making Dylan wince. Still the stable staff brushed away, practically under the window now.

He tried again. 'Samantha, your husband is a client.'

'Well, maybe it's time he stopped being a client.' Her voice was low and menacing now. To Dylan's horror he saw Flora's car drive into the yard. He had to do something, and fast.

'What do you mean by that?' he asked in the same quiet voice.

'I mean,' she replied, her eyes narrowed and her face contorted with spite, 'that we can take our horses out of here anytime I choose.'

'It's your husband that pays the bills, I think you'll find.' Dylan's voice had an edge now, too. Outside he saw Flora get out of her car and speak to the staff. He didn't have long.

'My husband will do whatever I tell him,' Samantha batted back.

'Not if he finds out what you are up to behind his back,' Dylan retorted.

Flora was making her way to the office now, and a drop of sweat ran down his back, his heart hammering within his chest.

'He wouldn't believe you.' Her chin tilted in defiance.

Dylan rose from his desk in anger. 'I don't need clients like you, Samantha. You take your horses if you want to. I've plenty more to train. You've far more to lose than I have,' he warned.

'I'll tell him you seduced me.'

Dylan heard the outside door slam. Flora must have overheard them in the corridor. He saw her run back across the yard to her car. He gulped in panic and frustration. Samantha followed his gaze.

'Oh dear, have I made things difficult?' she chided with a sly smile.

Dylan looked at her in contempt. 'Get the fuck off my yard. I never want to see you again.'

Samantha gave him a cutting look, turned on her heel and slammed the door behind her.

Dylan sat still for a moment, trying to take stock of what had happened. *Flora.* He had to speak to her. He quickly got up and reached for his Land Rover keys. Running out of the office, he called to the three grooms still taking an interest in sweeping the spotless yard floor, 'I'll be back soon, just mind the fort!' He jumped into the Land Rover and sped off after Flora. To his deep frustration, he got stuck behind a tractor and struggled to overtake it. By the time he got home it was too late.

Flora had obviously driven at top speed to get back to his house, collect a few things and clear off. She'd taken her riding hat, boots and jacket, normally hung in the utility room, along with her toiletries and toothbrush.

Dylan looked at their king-size bed and noticed she'd forgotten her silk nightshirt. He picked it up and buried his face in it. It smelt of her, that lovely familiar faint waft of jasmine. At that moment his heart broke. He blinked back the tears that threatened to fall and told himself to get a grip. Flora would only have gone back home to her parents' house. He'd let the dust settle, then talk to her.

Then another terrible thought occurred to him. What if she didn't turn up at the yard again? What if she'd decided not to live or work with him? He doubled over, as though he'd been punched in the stomach and sat down on the edge of the bed. He was still clutching her nightgown. With a shaking hand he neatly folded it up and put it on her pillow. She'd be back he told himself. She *had* to come back.

16

Sebastian packed the last few items in his case and zipped it shut. He still had a few weeks left on the rent of his apartment, but had decided to go back home anyway. He missed Treweham Hall, and he missed his family.

After the last night of the play, when Nick had unexpectedly showed up, Sebastian felt like he needed some form of stability to secure him. Seeing Nick standing there, appearing so contrite, had shaken him up and knocked him off kilter. This showed how fragile Sebastian really was deep down. On several occasions he had contemplated seeking help, some kind of therapy or counselling perhaps, something to ease his over-active mind, which raced round in never ending circles. Sometimes Sebastian felt like he would explode with all the turmoil inside his head, forever replaying the past, wallowing in misery at what had gone on and what could have been.

In the beginning it had been great with Nick. They appeared to be perfectly suited. Both young, attractive, intelligent professionals, who made each other laugh. They lived in the same village so the relationship had soon flourished as each could easily call upon the other. Very soon they had established a loving relationship and, for Sebastian's part, had no need or inclination to look elsewhere.

Nick, however, did not feel the same. Sebastian hadn't been enough for him. Nick got tired of waiting for Sebastian to return from his touring theatre. He got itchy feet, wanting to get out and have some fun, not to be stuck inside alone.

One night he got chatting to Finula in The Templar and Nick had been surprised at how well they seemed to get on. Soon he became inquisitive; it had been years since he'd been with a woman. An urge started to grow that only Finula, it seemed, could satisfy.

Finula knew nothing of Nick's relationship with Sebastian. In fact, she didn't even know Nick was attracted to men as well as women. For a while, Nick managed to play them both at the same time. Having a dual relationship excited him, gave him contrast, as well as an almighty buzz. Then it had all gone badly wrong. Tobias had sussed out what was going on. Being Sebastian's brother as well as a close friend to Finula, he didn't take long to comprehend what Nick was up to. Finula had her own suspicions after she found certain magazines in Nick's glove compartment, when they had gone out one afternoon. Seeing a centrefold of a naked man stare up at her, whilst Nick was paying for petrol, was the last thing Finula had expected to find. In the end the truth had come out after a rather nasty drunken row, when Nick had had the bare-faced cheek to suggest a threesome! Finula had never forgiven him.

Sebastian had never forgotten. Try as he might, he hadn't managed completely to shake off all the feelings he had for Nick, but Sebastian was resolute that he would never get mixed up with him again. But why did it have to be so hard? His hands had yearned to reach out to him the other night. He longed for that warm, soft touch of his skin, to feel enveloped in his secure embrace. But it was not meant to be. Nick had shown his true colours and therefore could not be trusted. The sooner Sebastian accepted this, the better.

Taking up his suitcase, Sebastian fleetingly looked round the room to make sure he wasn't leaving anything behind. Then he climbed down the short, spiral staircase and stumbled slightly. Steadying himself, and with a heavy heart, he closed the door behind him for the last time and made for home, where he belonged.

17

Saturday had arrived and bright sunshine reflected Finula's spirits as she scurried about her bedroom preparing for the big date. She reprimanded herself for being so excited, but she really couldn't help it. She felt like she had waited quite long enough for a date with Marcus and now it was finally here she was finding it hard to contain herself. Megan had helped her decide on her outfit. Casual, yet stylish was Megan's advice, so Finula had opted for skinny jeans tucked inside brown suede boots and a cream V-necked jumper revealing just a slight hint of cleavage, and which prettily showed off her mother's heart pendant necklace that she'd decided to wear for moral support. Her brown three-quarter-length woollen jacket finished it all off nicely.

Marcus was in the bar waiting for her, chatting to Dermot.

'Ah, here she is,' Dermot said with a smile. He was pleased his daughter was taking some time off and couldn't have approved more of her company.

'Ready to go?' asked Marcus. Finula's eyes flicked over his black, fitted jeans and thick, black jumper and she thought how dark and swarthy he looked. Her heart once again started to thump.

'Yep, let's go,' she replied, trying to sound as calm as possible, when inside she was flapping with anticipation.

'Now, you two, have a good day,' chipped in Dermot, 'and don't worry about this place, Fin.'

Finula cast him a withering look, 'I won't, Dad,' she replied, making Marcus laugh. He turned to Dermot.

'And don't you worry, your daughter is in safe hands,' he said with a grin.

'I'm sure she is,' Dermot nodded.

Once inside Marcus' Range Rover, Finula relaxed a little. He seemed very calm and she reflected that he was probably used to taking charge, being a director and producer. It made her feel reassured in some way. Being the curious kind, Finula looked for clues that could tell her more about Marcus, but she struggled to find any. There were no CDs scattered about the car, indicating his taste in music, no wrappers telling her what he snacked on. In fact, apart from a few folders on the back seat, everything was pretty bare.

He saw her glancing about his car and laughed to himself. Was she trying to suss him out?

'I usually just listen to the radio,' he supplied, 'if I listen to anything.'

'Oh,' she frowned, trying to picture him sitting in silence driving. Surely everyone belted out their favourite tunes in the car?

'So, tell me,' he interrupted her thoughts, 'what would you usually be doing on a Saturday?'

'To be honest, if I'm not working, not a lot really.' Then realising how boring she sounded, she quickly added, 'I'm usually that tired, I'll have a good lie-in and probably call at Megan's in the afternoon, or go into town.'

Marcus frowned: for someone as young as Finula, it sounded all work and hardly any play.

'When was the last time you took a holiday?'

Finula was surprised by the question and had to think hard. 'Do you know, I can't actually remember.'

Marcus shook his head. 'Finula, everyone needs time out. When we've finished filming you should visit where I live. You'd benefit from the peace and tranquillity.'

Again, she was surprised. Was he inviting her to his house, that gorgeous Tudor cottage she'd seen on the internet?

Then he completely changed the subject. 'So where would you recommend we have lunch in Oxford?'

'There's a few good pubs there. I'll let you choose.'

Within an hour they entered the city of dreaming spires, rich in history and culture. After parking, they walked together through the busy pathways, with bicycles weaving in and out, until they reached a small pub tucked away down an alley. After ordering food and drinks, they sat down in a quiet alcove.

Finula noticed a flyer on the table. She picked it up. '"Lola Burrax, clairvoyant extraordinaire",' she read out loud.

Marcus rolled his eyes. 'Load of bollocks, more like,' he scoffed.

Finula laughed, but carried on reading. 'She's on tonight, at The Bear.'

'Really?' replied Marcus flatly. Did people actually believe that stuff?

'Let's go, it'll be fun.' Finula's eyes sparkled with amusement.

Marcus stopped mid-sip. 'Are you serious?'

'Oh, go on.'

'Finula, it's all a con.'

'I know, but it'll still be interesting,' she cajoled.

It was hard to say no, so full of enthusiasm and cheer was Finula, and he felt himself being persuaded.

'OK. We can go there tonight if you really want to,' he chuckled, loving the way her face lit up when he finally gave in.

Located off Oxford's High Street, the cosy little pub with low ceilings and chestnut-brown wooden panelling was heaving. Its worn oak floor had been weathered by the feet of countless generations. The first thing Marcus noticed was the ties: ties of members of renowned colleges, schools, regiments, sports clubs and long-lost establishments were assembled in serried ranks and placed in glass showcases that covered the walls. Marcus and Finula wrestled to get served at the bar and wove their way through the crowd to the snug.

'I can't believe there are so many gullible people,' remarked Marcus as he handed Finula her wine.

'Look, there she is.' Finula pointed out Lola Burrax, sitting at a corner table reading tarot cards to a young girl with eyes like saucers, evidently gripped by what the medium was saying.

Marcus smirked into his glass and suppressed a snigger. The room was crammed full of goths, hippies and long-haired drop-outs, who frankly ought to know better. It beggared belief how much money Lola Burrax would be coining in, given that each of the expectant crowd had paid £15 a ticket to watch her perform. Anticipation mounted and, in spite of not believing in anything remotely mystic or supernatural, Marcus could sense the electric atmosphere.

The young girl having her cards read gasped out loud, causing a lull and wave of whispering amongst the people in the pub.

'What do you think she's told her?' Finula hissed.

'The price of her reading probably,' replied Marcus dully. He was rewarded with a contemptuous look.

'Have an open mind,' chided Finula.

'Yeah, and an open wallet,' retorted Marcus.

The medium stood up from the table, closed her eyes and began breathing heavily. Her hands were held in a prayer-like position.

'Sounds like she's connecting with the energy,' whispered Finula, trying her best not to laugh out loud.

'Sounds like she's asthmatic to me,' batted back Marcus under his breath, making Finula double over with giggles.

Suddenly Lola opened her eyes and the crowd fell silent.

'I am about to confirm what you already know deep within you, but cannot fully access on your own. Receive higher wisdom and find your direction.'

Her dark eyes roamed over her audience. Her long brown hair was covered with a headscarf and she wore a tie-dyed kaftan. Lola started to circle around the room, creating a stillness, and each person she passed seemed dying to be picked by her. She stopped short in front of a small, grey-haired man in a colourful waistcoat. She took hold of his hand and closed her eyes again.

'I feel your vibration,' she announced, causing a faint twitter amongst the bystanders. 'I detect unrest.' The man nodded knowingly. 'You have suffered much injustice.' He nodded even more. Marcus noticed a faded band mark round his finger where a wedding ring had obviously been removed recently. 'It is a lonely path you travel, but not for long.' This seemed to brighten him up no end, judging by the big beam lit across his face.

Then Lola came to a middle-aged lady sitting down at a nearby table. Crouching down, she touched the lady's forehead with her fingertips. 'She's safe, don't worry,' Lola claimed, making the lady double over and cry. Marcus' eyes widened: what the hell was this woman playing at?

Then, as if reading his mind, she spun round to face him. Marcus stared back defiantly. 'You are in turmoil,' she said pointing a finger directly at him.

He rolled his eyes. 'Am I really?' he answered in a bored monotone.

She moved closer and searched his face.

'Your revenge will not be sweet.'

There was a stunned silence. Marcus eyed the medium with cool distaste. Speechless, Finula looked from one to the other. Suddenly, it wasn't funny any more. They both stood their ground, staring each other out. Finula gulped as she took in Marcus' steely gaze, not flinching a muscle. His hand clenched his glass so hard she could see the whites of his knuckles. Neither spoke. A still silence filled the air. One or two smothered coughs could be heard from the crowd.

Marcus remained motionless, his glare challenging. The psychic eventually moved on.

'Marcus, are you all right?' Finula could see from the look on his face he wasn't. For all his dismissive comments, Lola Burrax had clearly hit a nerve to prompt such a reaction.

'Of course I'm all right, Finula,' he replied, then gulped his drink down.

Finula noticed his hand shake slightly and regretted her insistence of coming there.

18

Viola lay all the photographs out on her bed yet again. This was more than just research, it was becoming an obsession. Since Marcus had confirmed that they would definitely be filming inside Treweham Hall, and more importantly, that Tobias Cavendish-Blake had actually *agreed* to being interviewed, Viola's anticipation had reached fever pitch. Never had she been so focused on an interviewee. *This* was the one. This was going to be the interview that made her. How many interviews had the devilishly handsome Lord Cavendish-Blake given? None. That's how many, and she was about to be the first. This was a momentous occasion – well, for her, anyway – and, she suspected, for all those ladies out there that had secretly lusted after him for years. Now they were about to see him up front and personal, if she had her way.

The interview had come at a price, quite a hefty one, apparently, but nothing Marcus couldn't deal with. The powers that be at the BBC were more than happy to meet

Tobias' demands, not only on the cost, but also on the format of the interview. Lord Cavendish-Blake was to be consulted on every question beforehand. Anything he didn't like the look of was to be deleted and replaced with one of his own choice. Hardly an open, candid approach, thought Viola with disappointment, but still, an interview was an interview, and a long-sought-after one at that. Tobias Cavendish-Blake was notorious for hating the media, after they had chased him relentlessly, and shamefully in some instances, over the years. The fact he was prepared to appear in front of a camera at all was a miracle. Viola thought that Finula had played a large part in securing this; Finula and Tobias' wet wife, she presumed with spite.

Viola homed in on her favourite picture of him again, the most recent one, taken on his wedding day. She sighed out loud at his relaxed, smiling face, green eyes crinkled with laughter, his dimpled chin and long, dark hair. Absolute perfection. She began to feel hot inside. The need to nail this interview was of paramount importance. Her career was hinging on it. If she messed up this unique opportunity, nobody would touch her again.

Marcus was in the bedroom next door. He should have been preparing the schedule for the shoot at Treweham Hall, but in truth, he was unable to apply his mind to anything but the chilling words of Lola Burrax. After all, it hadn't been just some random information she'd thrown at him. It was quite specific. *Your revenge will not be sweet.* It had hit a nerve instantly, because Marcus really did intend to seek revenge, big time. He fully meant to expose the Cavendish-Blakes for what they were: high-handed, overindulged, pompous bastards. The worst of all being the late Lord Richard Cavendish-Blake, his own father. How would the current Lord Cavendish-Blake react on learning he wasn't actually the rightful heir? That in fact he had an older brother? Not that Marcus envied Tobias his standing, and all that came with it, but the principle mattered greatly. It killed him to think of his mother being banished to Ireland carrying Richard Cavendish-Blake's child, never to be heard of again. He obviously hadn't paid a penny towards their upkeep. Even as a small child, Marcus had known that money was tight.

His hand curled into a fist. Tobias thought he was in control of the interview; well, let him think that if that's what it took to get the bastard in front of a camera. What Tobias couldn't manipulate was the way Marcus would oversee the editing and the whole production. That's where it was all won and lost. Even the saintliest of people could be portrayed as the devil incarnate with clever editing: speeches cut off to deliberately misconstrue, losing all of the positive comments and homing in on the negative, pausing over an awkward moment for emphasis, close-ups of any make-up or costume malfunction, filming before the 'action' and after the 'cut' calls to catch anything the interviewee wouldn't want to display on air. Marcus knew every trick in the book and he was going to use them all. His ultimate trump card would be to disclose his own parentage, but he was fully aware that, without proof, it was futile.

He gave a heavy sigh and turned his head towards a magazine opened out on the desk. To his shame, he had succumbed and bought a copy of *Psychic Intelligence*. As he'd flicked through the glossy pages, various adverts had leapt out at him, offering, 'personal, accurate readings', or 'guidance from the grave', or telephoned 'star sign direction'. There was even a 'white witch' selling love potions and curses. It was incredible how much business there was in this mumbo-jumbo. At the back of the magazine, there was an article warning people about fake psychics, and the irony made Marcus laugh.

> A genuine psychic will give you some personal information about yourself that is not common knowledge to prove they are truly connected with you.

He stopped laughing when he read that. Up until Lola Burrax had actually spoken to him, he had thought her a phoney. To him it was so transparent, the way she had read and manipulated her audience. Just a person's age and sex could tell clairvoyants things about their general lifestyles, interests and sometimes the status of relationships. Even where you lived could reveal a lot about a person's life, education and social background. So-called mystics would examine the way you sat, talked, the clothes and jewellery you wore, all these telltale signs offered clues in how to exploit vulnerable people who wanted some form of reassurance. It disgusted Marcus and yet... what clues had he given Lola Burrax? None. He hadn't even given her eye contact before she picked him out. It baffled him. Telling himself it was just the power of charisma and suggestion he closed the magazine with force and turned his thoughts to the far more pleasant side of his day with Finula. They'd got on well, just as he had anticipated. Finula was easy to be around. She had a natural openness about her, which he didn't often find in people. Maybe it was because of the type of characters he worked with, all of whom were a little self-centred and too ambitious for their own good. In Finula he suspected what you saw was what you got. She had an innate honesty, and it was apparent she wore her heart on her sleeve. The attraction was definitely reciprocated, of that he had no doubt.

Many women had thrown themselves at Marcus over the years and he had hated the unwanted attention. He secretly thought the interest was more due to his job as a producer than anything else, but he was wrong. Without his realising it, Marcus' quiet, reserved, almost cool exterior left many a female hungry for more. They wanted to 'crack' his armour and familiarise themselves with the inner man. The more they pressed, the more he retreated. Marcus always used his demanding career as an excuse to hide behind. If he didn't particularly fancy socialising – or, indeed, the woman herself – he would make a hectic work schedule the ideal apology for opting out.

He had married years ago when he was twenty-one, fresh out of university. Niamh had been his girlfriend of two years and, on discovering she was pregnant they both panicked and did what was expected of them. Niamh had miscarried a month after their wedding. At first they tried to carry on as normal, pretending they would have married anyway, but inevitably each found his and her own way and parted as good friends. Niamh was now a researcher for a television company in Ireland, and was married with two boys. She and Marcus still remained in contact, never having really fallen out, and their work had sometimes meant they met up.

Marcus found Finula refreshing, a far cry from the vain, go-getter girls he was surrounded by. She was happy in her own skin, without any hidden agenda.

He shifted uncomfortably in his chair. Could the same be said about him? Yes, he definitely was drawn to Finula, and yes, he'd absolutely enjoyed her company the other day, but hadn't he used her just a little? He had manipulated Finula to persuade Tobias Cavendish-Blake to take part in the documentary. Was this fair? After giving it some thought, he convinced himself it was. After all, Finula was desperate to tag along with the crew at Treweham Hall and experience the filming. He'd make sure she enjoyed herself, involve her with the team, rather than detaching himself as he usually did.

On their date, Marcus hadn't allowed Lola Burrax to ruin the evening. He had made a swift recovery after her words of doom and soon afterwards he and Finula had slipped back into cheerful banter.

On the ride home he talked about his childhood in Ireland, but was guarded in giving too much detail. Finula, having had quite a few glasses of wine, had opened up far more, telling him about her friendship with Megan, and her previous relationship with Nick. Marcus sat driving in stunned silence as she regaled him with her ex-boyfriend's antics. She finished her story off by telling him how Tobias had finally given Nick his just deserts at the Landlord's Supper. Marcus had turned sharply.

'Why, what happened?'

Finula explained the traditional event. 'Nowadays it's just a good excuse for a piss-up,' she concluded. 'Anyway, Nick turned up absolutely hammered and tried to kiss

Megan, who was working behind the bar at the time. Tobias came over and smacked him one!' She fell into giggles, then hiccupped. Marcus smirked to himself. Interesting. That story held all the qualities he was looking for: custom, tradition and the Lord of the Manor battering a villager.

Once he had pulled up outside The Templar, Finula was practically asleep. He gently stirred her.

'We're home, Finula,' he whispered.

She opened her eyes and looked into his face. 'What killer cheekbones you have. Do you know who you remind me of?'

'Who?' He laughed softly.

'That Irish actor, Ci... Cil... Cilli...' she struggled pronouncing his name.

'Cillian Murphy,' he supplied with a grin.

'Yes! That's the chap.'

'Come on, you, let's get you to bed.' He helped her out of the car and led her inside. Once in The Templar she turned to him.

'Fancy a nightcap?'

Marcus shook his head, 'No thanks, Finula, and neither should you,' he gently warned. 'Your father will have my guts for garters, returning you in this state.'

'What state?' Finula exclaimed indignantly.

'Shush!' He put his finger over her mouth. Their eyes suddenly locked. Marcus leant forward and kissed her on the lips. She tasted of dark berries from the red wine. He pulled away and smiled.

'Good night, Finula. Thanks for a great day.'

'Good night, Marcus,' she replied hoarsely, the kiss having sobered her up in an instant.

19

Dylan opened the office door and found Flora sitting at the desk, busy talking on the phone. He sighed for the hundredth time. Would she ever talk to him like that again? All pleasant and polite, with the odd tinkle of laughter? In fact, when would she start talking to him at all? he thought bleakly. He thanked his lucky stars she'd actually shown up for work.

It was two weeks now since Flora had packed her things and left his house. He missed her dreadfully. It wasn't home any more without her, just an empty shell devoid of any warmth. Everything was the way he had left it on returning home after a day's work at the racing yard. He yearned for her comforting smell of jasmine, seeing her clothes discarded at the end of the bed, her toiletries scattered haphazardly around the bathroom, her soft, warm body lying next to his. He had actually shed real tears into his pillow last night, such was the agony of his big, empty bed. But it was no good. Flora simply wouldn't listen to him.

Dylan had tried, on many occasions, to reason with her. He had endeavoured to explain what had happened between himself and Samantha Tait. To remind her that he and Flora had not strictly been an item at the time. It was at this point that Flora had coolly reminded him why that was. 'No, Dylan, we weren't together, because I'd read an explicit article about how you seduced Sadie Stringfellow.'

Dylan gave up, realising the hole he was digging himself into had just got considerably bigger. Instead he had backed off, given her space to calm down. Except Flora hadn't calmed down. If anything, her mood was getting darker by the day, well, with him anyway. With the rest of the staff she was the same delightful Flora. With the owners she was the same obliging Flora. With him she was the hard, stubborn Flora he had witnessed before.

Praying she would finally relent, Dylan attempted once more to make conversation with her. He walked over to the desk and stood in front of her, but Flora finished her phone conversation and began typing, refusing to give him eye contact.

'Flora…' He coughed awkwardly.

'What?' she asked, staring stony faced at him. He flinched.

'I'm leaving for Newmarket tonight.' Newmarket, otherwise known as the British horseracing headquarters, would be the venue of the last race he ever rode. Ideally, he wanted Flora by his side, but knew she wouldn't entertain the idea in this mood.

'Right,' she replied flatly.

'So, I won't be back for a couple of days.' He scrutinised her face for any telltale reaction. There was none.

'Don't worry. I'll be here, looking after the yard.'

'Yes... yes, I know.' He coughed again, suddenly feeling like a nervous schoolboy in front of the headmistress. 'Please, Flora—' He was interrupted by the phone.

Flora picked it up immediately, obviously glad of the distraction.

'Hello, Delany's Racing Yard,' she chirped.

Dylan sighed with impatience and turned away with a heavy heart. He might as well leave for Newmarket now. What was keeping him here? All the team were busy about their duties; Flora was so blatantly in control, he almost felt surplus to requirements. He slowly made his way to the door and quietly closed it behind him.

Once he was gone, and having finished the call, Flora sank her head into her hands. She gulped back the tears that threatened to spill. Taking a deep breath she steadied herself. This was killing her, seeing Dylan so broken, but what did he expect? He couldn't keep hurting her like this. First it was that stupid kiss-and-tell opportunist Sadie Stringfellow, now it was a bloody owner's wife, for goodness' sake! Samantha Tait's stern, controlled voice rang in her ears, cutting straight into her heart: *You seduced me.*

She cursed herself for trusting Dylan again. Flora was more determined than ever to keep their relationship on professional terms only. Living back at her parents' house whilst they were travelling round Europe meant she at least had the place to herself. At first it had proved a relaxed, quiet refuge, away from Dylan and all the emotional turmoil he evoked. Then, when she had seen how wretched he looked every morning, her resolve had waned. It was evident he was hurting as much as she was, but what choice did she have? To carry on, not trusting him, hoping he wouldn't stray again?

Flora had briefly considered getting another job, but where? To be given the position of assistant trainer, in such a prestigious training yard was amazing – she knew that – and opportunities like that didn't come by very often. Plus, at the bottom of her heart, she couldn't stand the thought of Dylan working so closely alongside anyone else. So here they were, stuck in an impossible limbo, neither happy, but both miserable without each other.

20

Sebastian breathed in the cold November air. It was bright and the sun was slowly burning away the morning mist as he gently jogged through the Treweham Hall estate. Living in a small apartment in Stratford-upon-Avon for the past months had given him a fresh appreciation for the vastness of his home. He cast a look over the green, lush acres, the reds and golds of the woods running on the east border, the clear, bubbling brook that trickled through it, and took another deep breath. This was the life.

Sebastian was in dire need of a break. Lately his life had been a constant, hectic merry-go-round of early starts, rehearsals, performances, late finishes and networking. He'd had enough. He was glad to be home. Although a tiny part of him still hankered for the attention he had received from playing the leading role at the Royal Shakespeare Theatre, he hated that streak in himself, praying he never grew into a complete 'luvvie', which he'd seen happen to so many actors. Judging by the tempo of his jogging, he assumed he was still recovering from the exhaustion. His left leg appeared to drag slightly, which was slowing him down. He needed to be patient and give himself time to recuperate properly. At least his back had finally stopped hurting, now that he no longer had to bend in a stoop day after day.

Sebastian stopped and stretched his arms in the air. The birds were singing, the sun was shining and Aunt Celia had at last buggered off home. That woman still scared the living daylights out of him. He much preferred it when it was just the three of them: him, his brother and his mother, and now that Megan had joined them it was even better. Megan was the sister he'd always wanted, and come March, there'd be another addition to the family, the future heir. The thought thrilled him and he couldn't wait to be an uncle. Yes, Treweham Hall was certainly seeing some changes at the moment.

The imminent television filming was another pleasant surprise, as was Tobias' consent to the interviews. Sebastian relished the thought of possibly being interviewed, as had been suggested. As far as he was concerned it provided the ideal platform to at last put the record straight: the Cavendish-Blakes were much more than privileged gentry, they were honest hard workers. Sebastian held his brother in high esteem, especially when he considered just what Tobias had managed to achieve on the estate. He had pulled his family out of the red and transformed Treweham Hall into a thriving business.

Despite Treweham having the positives he craved, it also sadly held one huge negative. It was Nick's home, too. Living back in the same village would inevitably mean having to face him at some point and it was no good keeping putting it off.

He decided to call in at The Templar that evening, thereby letting everyone know he was back. If Nick was there he'd deal with it. One person he knew for sure would welcome him was Finula. They had bonded last year, both having been treated badly by Nick.

Entering through the back of Treweham Hall, Sebastian was greeted by Henry the butler.

'Hi, Henry!' he called, making his way to the stairs.

'Good morning, sir. Lord Cavendish-Blake has asked to see you in his study.'

'Ah, right.' Sebastian turned and made his way along the corridor to Tobias' study. On entering he saw his brother's dark head bent over various papers on his desk. 'Hi,' Sebastian said, plonking himself on the chesterfield opposite him.

'Hi,' replied Tobias, then picked up a document and went to sit next to his brother.

'What's this?' enquired Sebastian.

'This is the contract from the BBC. It stipulates exactly what the TV crew are permitted to do and where they can go. I've approved the questions to be asked in the interviews.'

'Interviews?' Sebastian picked up on the plural.

'Yes. As I predicted, they want to interview you too. I drew the line at Mother – and Aunt Celia,' he quickly added.

'Very wise,' agreed Sebastian, 'but I don't mind talking to them.'

'Sure?'

'Yes. No problem.' Then, sensing his brother's apprehension he frowned. 'What is it?'

'I don't trust them.'

'But why? It's not some tin-pot set-up. It's the BBC, for goodness' sake.'

'I know, but... even so, it's an independent production.'

Sebastian understood his brother's reluctance, having witnessed first-hand how the media had hounded him.

'What about Megan?' he asked.

Tobias shook his head firmly. 'No way. Non-negotiable. I said right from the start Megan would not take part in any kind of filming.'

Sebastian laughed. 'Tobias, did you even ask her?'

This earned him a hard glare. 'Megan is still adjusting to a whole new life at Treweham Hall and is almost five months pregnant. I'm not having her paraded in front of the cameras.'

Sebastian stifled the chuckle threatening to escape. Megan was hardly a weak, wilting wallflower. Personally, he thought she'd shine in front of the camera, but her husband obviously did not want her to face any form of intrusion.

'OK, just you and me then. We'll handle them.'

That evening Sebastian braced himself before entering The Templar. He was greeted immediately by Finula, who was talking to a tall, dark-haired man he didn't recognise. 'Sebastian! Come and meet Marcus.' She waved him over to the bar. The man turned and smiled at him. 'Sebastian, this is Marcus Devlin, the TV producer. Marcus meet Sebastian Cavendish-Blake.'

The two men shook hands.

'No introductions necessary,' said Marcus. 'I heard your Richard III was amazing.'

'Thanks,' grinned Sebastian, a warm glow spreading through him. 'No more amazing than your documentaries, I'm sure.'

Marcus was slightly taken aback. Whilst he knew he had to be charm personified to the villagers, and the Cavendish-Blakes in particular, he hadn't expected such charisma back. He was used to being treated with suspicion, or as somewhat of an inconvenience most of the time. He eyed his brother for the first time and found, surprisingly, that he liked what he saw. Sebastian appeared down to earth, approachable, not what he had expected.

'Thank you for agreeing to be interviewed. We'll cause as little disruption as possible,' he lied.

'Fine. No problem with me. It's Tobias you've got to convince.'

Well, the fecking price he's named should help, thought Marcus tartly. Outwardly he gave an amiable grin.

'I can't wait!' interrupted Finula with excitement. Sebastian frowned.

'Finula's kindly agreed to be our second runner,' explained Marcus. He looked at her with real affection, which Sebastian immediately picked up on.

'Come and meet the team.' Marcus nodded behind him towards a table where several people sat. Sebastian looked over and was met slap-bang with two smoky-grey eyes he'd seen before. He paused for a second, then connected. It was the guy in the audience, the one who had reminded him of himself years ago.

Marcus ushered Sebastian towards the group. 'Everyone, this is Sebastian Cavendish-Blake.' They all looked up and smiled. 'This is Libby, the editor; Len, the cameraman; Viola, who will be interviewing you; and Jamie, the runner.'

Jamie shot up and held out his hand. Sebastian took it with a firm shake.

'I saw you in Stratford,' Jamie gushed, looking rather flushed.

'I know, I remember you,' replied Sebastian, looking straight into those grey eyes. This made Jamie blush even more.

Viola stood up smoothly. 'Are you looking forward to the interview, Sebastian? Please take a seat.' She offered her chair before taking another from a nearby table. Marcus watched as the small group chatted with Sebastian. There was no awkwardness, as he had assumed there would be, but just an easy, cheerful banter as Jamie asked question after question about his acting career and Libby and Len listened quietly, smiling politely. Viola seemed a tad more relaxed too, sipping white wine, but no doubt taking it all in; she wasn't a good researcher for nothing, Marcus wisely observed. He watched Sebastian totally at ease, holding court, entertaining them all with humorous tales and anecdotes.

Only once did he appear slightly ruffled, and then only for a second. It was when another man walked into the pub and stood staring at him, before eventually making his way to the bar. Judging by the way Finula glared at the man, Marcus took it to be Nick. True to form, Viola had clocked the whole incident too.

Later that evening, as Marcus was making his way upstairs, he was collared by her. 'Did you sense tension with

Sebastian when that man walked in and started staring at him?' she hissed.

'That was Nick Fletcher, the village vet, his ex-boyfriend,' Marcus supplied casually, which infuriated Viola.

'Really?'

'Hmm, apparently there was some kerfuffle with him and Tobias at a village do.'

'The Landlord's Supper?' asked Viola, suddenly remembering overhearing a previous comment made by a villager in the pub.

'Yes, the Landlord's Supper. It's time to dig deeper, Viola.' He turned to her with a steely expression.

Viola nodded in agreement. 'Leave it with me, boss.'

21

The day had finally arrived. Newmarket would be the last course that Dylan would ride at in the aptly named 'end-of-term' race meeting. Newmarket was truly special, rich in royal history due to Charles II spearheading the development of the town some three and a half centuries ago, when horseracing became 'the sport of kings'. Newmarket is affectionately known as the global headquarters of racing today and considered its home. So, where better place for Dylan Delany, champion jockey, to close his racing career?

At home, in his own training yard, with Flora, he thought miserably as he slowly made his way to the starting line along with all the other jockeys. A few called out to him, wishing him all the best. He waved and smiled back, but inside his heart wasn't in it. Flora had knocked all the enthusiasm completely out of him. He didn't feel whole without her by his side. Try as he might the adrenalin refused to rise. Instead of this being his last memorable chance to bask in grandeur, he simply wanted the race over and done with so he could get back home.

This was a far cry from the competitive glory-seeker Dylan, who stopped at nothing to win. He was stunned by the effect Flora had had on him. Never in his life had he let a woman get to him like this. But there she was, under his skin the whole time. She was there in his mind as he woke up, throughout the day, and she was the last thing he thought about as he turned off the bedside light. He wasn't eating properly, he just had no appetite and he certainly hadn't slept much. When he did, his dreams pictured Flora and her accusing, hurt eyes boring into him.

He hadn't prepared for this race, mentally or physically, and he felt the relentless attention he was receiving was undeserved. He glanced upwards, towards the Millennium Grandstand, where he knew Tobias had booked an executive box. He imagined them all – Tobias, Megan, Seamus and Tatum – quaffing champagne on their private balcony, enjoying a spectacular view of the course, and watching him now with baited breath and expectation.

Dylan turned his head to the packed crowds in the stands. The atmosphere was celebratory and jovial, except he wasn't. A lump formed in his throat as he wondered if Flora was watching too. He pictured her in the racing yard office, hunched over the small TV. Or did she even care? Perhaps she was riding, or busy talking on the phone to an owner.

Flora was actually in front of her parents' huge widescreen TV, barely containing herself. Her nerves were stretched to a frazzle as she watched Dylan ride to the starting stalls. For the hundredth time that day she cursed herself for not relenting and wishing him good luck before he left. Instead she had remained poker faced and given him nothing but a cold, hard glare. Now she hated herself for it and wanted more than anything to turn the clock back. With a shaking hand she turned the volume up on the remote control. Flora knew that Tobias and Megan were there supporting him, along with Seamus and his wife, but what must they be thinking of her? Choosing not to go and cheer on the very man who had so tenderly nursed her back to health a few months ago. Weighed down with guilt, she swallowed and tears started to fill her eyes. Blinking them quickly away, she leant forward to watch the race start.

Dylan's horse was distinctive: ironically called Last Chance, he had a white streak on his muzzle. Dylan was wearing black and pink striped silks. Flora noticed the dark curls peeping out from his riding hat, which for some reason made her heart clench even more. And then they were off ...

Dylan got a good start and was towards the front of the main pack of runners bunched on the inside. He was well aware of the horse directly behind him, Chequered Flag, which was the one to watch. Dylan was steering Last Chance wide, to stay out of trouble and to avoid the worst of the ground, now badly churned up from the afternoon's racing. Chequered Flag was keeping pace just to his rear, Last Chance ahead of him by a couple of lengths. Dylan kept an even rhythm. Last Chance was performing foot-perfect, overtaking the two leading horses. He was galloping towards the finishing line when suddenly Dylan caught Chequered Flag making a move on his inside. Chequered Flag shot past, making Dylan react in a split second: go for it, now! It was an automatic reaction rather than a conscious thought.

'Go, Dylan!' screamed Flora at the television, jumping up and down.

Meanwhile, in the executive box, Tobias and Seamus cheered their mate on with gusto, making Megan and Tatum smile with affection.

'Come on, Dylan!' called Tobias, his hands clenched tightly; he and Seamus had rather a large wager on Dylan's last race.

Then, just as Dylan was approaching the finishing line, Last Chance lost his footing, firing Dylan headfirst onto the ground. The horse untangled his limbs with a snort of indignation and shot off, leaving Dylan to curl into a ball, being kicked as he rolled beneath the hooves of the horses thundering past. The moment Dylan stopped rolling through the grass, he did the first thing he was trained to do, check for movement in his legs. Feeling them twitch he allowed himself momentarily to black out.

'Dylan!' screeched Flora at the telly, tears pouring down her cheeks.

'Jesus, he's fallen.' Seamus gave Tobias the binoculars.

Tobias took them with a trembling hand, whilst Megan and Tatum screamed with fright. Tobias watched the medics lift Dylan onto a stretcher, then into the ambulance by the white railing. His heart was pounding in his ears as he saw he friend's motionless body whisked urgently away. Turning sharply, he directed, 'Tatum, you stay here with Megan for now. Seamus, we'll go to the hospital, quickly.'

Seamus had already sat Megan down and was pouring her a drink of water. Tatum stood nearby, looking helpless with tears in her eyes.

'Yes, of course,' she replied. 'You two go now, we'll follow later.'

Seamus and Tobias rushed away to be with Dylan.

Back at her parents' house Flora was hysterical, not knowing what to do. Her immediate reaction was to try to get to Newmarket, and quick, but how? What about the training yard, could she just leave it? No. She needed to speak to the staff. Hastily she set off there.

Dylan became conscious of voices. Opening his eyes fully he could see he was surrounded by white coats and concerned faces. His chest hurt, but at least he could feel his legs and move his feet.

'Hello, Dylan. You've had quite a nasty fall,' said one of the white coats.

Blinking his eyes clear, he could see the doctor was an attractive blonde with brown eyes the colour of chocolate.

'I know,' replied Dylan matter-of-factly, then winced when he tried to move.

'Try to keep still, Dylan. I'm afraid you've broken a couple of ribs.'

'Anything else?'

'Most likely concussion, after the bump on the head and several cuts and bruises, but apart from that, you should be OK.'

'Great,' said Dylan flatly, then silently reprimanded himself. He'd got off lightly. He'd known jockeys dumped into ditches at thirty miles an hour, dragged face down through birch fences, break collarbones and even necks, never to walk again. Paralysis was the fear of all riders.

'You've two visitors waiting patiently to see you,' said the blonde doctor.

Flora? Could Flora be here? Dylan's heart leapt, then hit rock bottom when his rational brain kicked in. Of course not. How could she have got here that fast? Tobias and Seamus, waiting like caged tigers at the hospital room door, were finally allowed to enter.

'Dylan, how are you?' Tobias was pale with worry. Seamus pushed back his copper fringe with an unsteady hand. Dylan was touched by their obvious concern.

'I'll live,' he gave a shaky grin. Then an idea struck him, which lifted his spirits considerably. 'Flora. I need to see Flora.' He looked intently at Tobias, urging him to respond.

'Don't worry. I'll get in contact with her.'

'Now, Tobias. Do it now,' pressed Dylan.

Tobias frowned and looked at Seamus, who was signalling him to go and use his phone.

'Give her a ring, Tobias,' he gently advised, sensing Dylan's desperate need.

Outside, in the corridor, Tobias took out his mobile and scrolled through his contacts to find the training yard's number. Hopefully, Flora would be there. On the second ring it was answered.

'Delany's Racing Yard,' said a voice he recognised as Flora's, but he could hear clearly that she'd been crying.

'Flora, it's Tobias—'

'Where's Dylan? Is he all right?' she interrupted, hysteria setting in again.

'Yes. He's in the hospital. Flora, he's asking for you.'

Thank God. Thank God. Thank God. 'I'm coming,' she replied immediately, sobbing uncontrollably now.

'Not in the state you're in, you're not fit to drive. Listen, I'll arrange for a car to come and pick you up.'

'Thank you,' Flora replied with relief.

'Just sit tight, Flora. Everything with be OK.'

'Thank you,' she gulped again.

It was late in the evening by the time Flora arrived at the hospital. Dylan had only managed soup at dinner time, then slept solidly, in the sound knowledge that Flora was safely on her way. Tobias and Megan had booked into a local hotel for the night and arranged a room for Flora to stay in too. Seamus and Tatum had reluctantly made their way home to pick up the children.

Outside the hospital, the press was gathered in force already, desperate to catch any glimpse of celebrity visitors, or Dylan actually leaving. A short statement had been made by Dylan's agent, Connor, informing them all that Dylan was now in a stable condition and badly needed rest.

Tobias met Flora outside the hospital gates as arranged and together they were driven through the main entrance with a flurry of flashbulbs and cameras chasing after them. Flora took a deep breath, ducking her head as a bright light suddenly blasted through the car window.

'We're nearly there, Flora,' Tobias tried to sooth, knowing full well the effect all this was having on her.

At last they were ushered into the hospital. Tobias took Flora to Dylan's room, a small, private haven tucked away from the main ward.

'I'll leave you alone,' Tobias told her. 'I'll wait outside here.' He pointed to a row of chairs nearby.

Flora nodded then looked through the window. Dylan was asleep. She quietly pushed the door and crept inside and immediately Dylan stirred. Flora rushed to his bedside.

'Dylan,' she whimpered, and swallowed hard to stop herself from crying. She clutched his hand and he curled his fingers round hers tightly.

'Hey,' he smiled.

'Oh, Dylan...' Then her shoulders started to shake with emotion.

'Flora, don't cry,' he said quietly.

'How... how are you feeling?' she choked.

He attempted humour. 'Well, I certainly went out with a bang, didn't I?'

'I'm sorry, Dylan. I'm so sorry...'

'Listen,' he gently interrupted, 'it's me that's sorry. Sorry for hurting you, but please believe me, we weren't an item when Samantha Tait—'

'I know,' she butted in, not wanting her name to be mentioned, especially not here, not now.

'Flora, I'm lost without you. Please come back. I... I... love you.' There, he'd said it. Three words he'd never, ever uttered to another human being. He'd stunned himself, as well as Flora. She gaped at him.

'You've never said that before.'

'More fool me. It doesn't mean I've never felt it, though.' His blue eyes twinkled, looking straight into hers. Flora swallowed, then nodded.

'Yes, of course I'll come home. Someone needs to look after you, don't they?' She attempted humour now too, making Dylan smile. He loved the fact she called his house 'home'.

'Come here, you,' He gave her his most seductive look, making her melt. Leaning carefully over him, she closed her lips over his. It was the sweetest kiss they'd ever shared.

'I love you too, Dylan Delany,' she whispered in his ear.

22

Marcus strode to the far end of the dining room. He had arranged with Dermot to have a private area screened off to hold a meeting. As usual the team sat waiting patiently for their producer to arrive. Viola was brimming with information after being directed to delve further, which she had with gusto. Jamie was still in awe after his audience with Sebastian Cavendish-Blake, while Libby and Len had quietly and reliably got on with the job in hand. As was his way, Marcus slammed down his clipboard, sat down abruptly and stared at the team expectantly.

'Well, where are we up to?' he asked, almost accusingly, casting his sharp eyes round the table.

As always, Viola was the first to speak. 'I've spoken with a few prominent members of the community. The vicar, tenants of the Treweham estate, a councillor, local farmers and the vet, Nick Fletcher.'

'And?' Marcus' eyes narrowed.

Viola tilted her head to one side, as though considering, all to build tension, of course.

'Some of it could prove interesting,' she hinted.

Marcus never had the patience for Viola's mind games.

'What?' he asked sharply.

'Well, Nick Fletcher certainly has an axe to grind. He couldn't spill quickly enough about how Lord Cavendish-Blake practically beat him to a pulp.'

'On camera?' butted in Marcus, looking towards Len.

Len nodded. 'Yes. Viola contacted me the moment Nick agreed to be filmed. I also took shots of his veterinary practice: him tending to animals, and a couple of the staff who work there.'

Marcus smiled in approval. Good, let Nick Fletcher come across as the kind, caring vet who was victimised by Tobias.

'Did he mention his relationship with Sebastian?' he asked.

'Yes,' interrupted Viola, who didn't quite care for the way Len was getting all the praise. 'According to Nick, Tobias put a spanner in the works, splitting them apart when he learnt about their relationship.'

'Really?' This was all music to Marcus' ears, even though he knew it wasn't quite the truth; far from it, in fact, but what the hell? It was a good story and, more importantly, portrayed Tobias in a bad light.

'There's also a couple I'd like you to meet – lottery winners, apparently – who moved into the village.' Marcus didn't look too impressed. 'They bought the Gate House on the Treweham Hall estate. Rumour has it that didn't go down too well with Lord Cavendish-Blake.'

Marcus rolled his eyes. 'Why's that? New money, I suppose?' he asked sarcastically.

'Exactly,' chipped back Viola, sensing his growing interest. 'A reliable source tells me Tobias Cavendish-Blake basically blanks his neighbours, although he was happy enough to exploit their winnings. It's believed they overpaid for the Gate House. They're from the North and he took advantage of their unfamiliarity with the area.'

Absolute perfection. This was going better than expected.

Marcus turned to Libby. 'I'd like to go through the rushes with you.' The last thing he needed was Libby editing anything without his consent.

'Yes, no problem. I've sorted, labelled and put them in some form of sequence. I'll let you look at it before reordering the footage to tell the best story, or making any cuts.' Marcus nodded in agreement.

'One other thing,' said Viola, making them all turn to face her. 'Have you heard of the Straw Man Festival?'

There was a slight pause before Marcus sighed, again his impatience evident. 'Elaborate,' he said curtly.

'It's held here in Treweham every year on the first Monday after Twelfth Day. It marks the traditional start of the English agricultural year.'

'What happens?' asked Jamie.

'A local chap dons a five-stone metal and straw costume and parades through the village, accompanied by a motley crew of morris dancers and a decorative plough.'

Marcus spluttered, his mind spinning back to their first meeting, when he'd mentioned *The Wicker Man*. This wasn't a wicker effigy used in human sacrifice, but more a symbol, a talisman, celebrated by farmers. Viola continued,

'The straw man is then ceremonially burnt at the end of the festival, or the costume is.'

'Sounds a bit creepy,' Jamie said. Subconsciously he was associating it with the horror movie too.

'Hmm, burnt by the Lord of the village,' finished Viola with satisfaction at seeing Marcus' eyes glitter. She knew he was concocting his own spin on this.

'OK. Let's include it. Len, we'll need you back here in January. Let's get the whole festival, especially when Lord Cavendish-Blake sparks the straw man.' He looked at his clipboard. 'Right, we film in Treweham Hall at the end of the week. Finula will be joining us, and,' he paused looking at each one in turn, 'I want you to make her as welcome as possible. She's done us a great favour getting us in there. Show your appreciation.'

Bet you're showing her plenty of appreciation, thought Viola tartly. Everyone agreed politely, before Marcus strode off as abruptly as he'd entered.

Marcus was practically bouncing, buoyed up on adrenalin with the way things were nicely stacking up into place. He caught Finula's eye behind the bar and made his move.

'Hi there.' He gave his most charming smile. Finula blushed.

'Hi,' she replied, her heart started to thump.

'Fancy that nightcap later this evening?' he asked, slowly looking her up and down. Did she ever, with him looking so devilishly handsome in his black fitted jumper, showing off his broad shoulders and biceps.

'Why not?' She tried to sound casual, but felt anything but. 'I finish here in a few hours.' She turned to face the multi-coloured bottles stacked neatly on the glass shelves. 'What are we drinking?'

'Jameson always goes down well,' replied Marcus with a grin. He really fancied an Irish whiskey tonight, amongst other things.

'Jameson it is, then,' said Finula, reaching for the green bottle.

'I've got glasses in my room, just bring the bottle.' He looked into Finula's eyes, challenging her to object. Was he being too forward? His high spirits were encouraging him.

'Will do.' She gave a wink, then instantly regretted it. Why couldn't she just be cool for once? Because it wasn't in her, she dully acknowledged. Marcus' face creased into laughter. He loved her openness, finding it amusing.

An hour later and Finula discreetly made her way to his room, choosing to go the back way, used for staff only. She tapped quietly on the door and it was immediately opened. Marcus stood there grinning broadly.

'Come in.'

He'd set the scene flawlessly, with just the lamps on his desk and bedside warmly glowing. The Corrs were playing softly in the background. Finula handed him the bottle of Irish whiskey.

'Ah, lovely,' he smiled.

Finula went to sit on the small sofa at the side of the room. She watched the back of him, his slow, confident movements as he smoothly poured generous measures into the two glass tumblers on his desk. He turned, holding both glasses, and met her stare.

'There you go, that'll put some hairs on your chest.' Finula giggled, half with nerves. He sat next to her and raised his glass. 'Cheers.'

'Cheers.' She clinked her glass and took a sip. Gulping back the potent liquid made her eyes water. Once it had finished burning the back of her throat she wheezed, 'Pretty strong, isn't it?'

Marcus laughed. 'Sorry, I assumed you'd had it before, being a landlord's daughter and all.' His eyes twinkled with mischief in the dim light.

Finula couldn't tear her gaze away from him, taking in his defined cheekbones and full lips. His eyes found hers and for a second neither of them spoke, they just appreciated the moment. Marcus admired the shape of her elegant, creamy neck and shoulders sprinkled with freckles that her silk, strappy top exposed, and he had a sudden impulse to bury his face in them. Knocking back most of his drink, he faced her again.

'Finula, can I kiss you?'

'Do you always ask first before kissing a woman?' she replied with laughter.

'I don't often kiss women,' he replied straight-faced. She frowned. 'I'm considered to be somewhat prickly,' he told her with a wry grin.

'You're not!' Finula protested indignantly.

He looked off into the distance over her shoulder, as if considering. 'No,' he agreed, 'I'm not with you. You obviously bring out the best in me.'

Finula was touched. She understood what he meant, though, after seeing how he acted round his film crew. She put it down to the stress of the job. For a moment she sensed a more vulnerable Marcus and wanted to wrap her arms round him.

He read her thoughts; her expression was so telling. Finula really was an open book. Again, he thought how out of place she appeared here in the Cotswolds. Finula would blend in seamlessly in his home town. A part of him wanted to pick her up and run all the way back to Roscommon.

'You haven't answered my question,' he softly reminded her with a glint in his eye. Finula put down her glass and looked him straight in the face. The whiskey had given her Dutch courage. Then she moved closer to him and tilted her head towards his.

'Yes,' she whispered.

His lips joined hers in an instant, gently at first, then more forcefully as his tongue probed her mouth. Finula's head swayed, her hands clung to his shoulders to steady herself, and they felt firm and solid beneath the fine, black wool. His arms encircled her closer into him, and she inhaled his delicious scent of citrus limes and bergamot.

'Finula,' he murmured thickly, as his hands ran through her long, red curls, loving the silky feel of them.

Finula was on fire with the sensation of his touch and she needed to feel him too. Her hands ran up his jumper and stroked his muscular back. The feel of his warm, smooth skin heightened her desire. His kiss plunged deeper as he leant forward, leaving her in no doubt of his arousal. He pushed further into her, whilst Finula feverishly ran her hands over his body.

There was a knock at the door. They both froze. For one dreaded moment Marcus thought it may be Dermot. 'I'll get it,' he whispered, getting up from the sofa. He pulled his jumper straight and opened the door slightly.

'Marcus, can I run something past you?' It was Viola.

'Not at the moment. We'll speak tomorrow.'

'Oh, but—'

'Good night, Viola,' he said firmly and closed the door.

Finula's mouth twitched and Marcus shook his head with exasperation. 'Bloody woman never knows when to switch off,' he muttered with a frown.

Finula sat up, still a little hazy from the passionate kiss. She had suspected that he would be passionate; cool on the outside, yet burning hot underneath.

'Let's have another,' she sighed. Marcus raised his eyebrows and gave a wicked grin. 'Drink, that is,' she replied, handing him her empty glass.

23

Viola was fuming. How dare Marcus be so dismissive, and judging by the look of his flushed face, ruffled hair and creased jumper he was obviously up to no good. Evidently someone was in his room. Three guesses who, she thought with spite. Slamming her bedroom door shut, she decided to have a glass of wine to help her calm down. Instead of phoning for someone to get one for her from the bar, she pulled a bottle of Pinot Grigio out from under her bed and unscrewed the top. She tilted her head back and took a great swig. Then another. That was better.

Then she reached for her notebook. A list of questions lay neatly written on the front page. Questions either approved or predetermined by the interviewee. What a joke. Deciding there and then, Viola clicked her pen and began to add a few notes of her own. If Marcus was too preoccupied to speak to her, she'd take matters into her own hands. It wasn't live television, after all. If Libby thought it inappropriate then it would end up straight on her cutting-room floor, wouldn't it? Viola's blood was up. She was on a mission, and with her that was dangerous. Once she became focused, her mind ran wild and knew no boundaries. She lost all rationalisation, becoming either fixated or neurotic.

The sad scenario regarding her ex-boyfriend epitomised this precisely. Refusing to accept the relationship was over, she totally ignored his pleas to leave him alone. Being in denial meant it became normal for her constantly to ring, text, email and follow him. When he acquired another girlfriend, Viola upped the ante. She took stalking to a whole new level, till in the end the poor girl reported her to the police. Well, having dead animals sprawled over her car and death threats posted through her door left her with very little option. Viola was prosecuted and a restraining order was imposed to protect the girl. Luckily for Viola, she was given a suspended sentence. News hit the local newspapers, so she moved away, far enough for nobody she now knew to have any idea of her sinister past. Changing her name to Viola by deed poll helped, too. In every sense she had reinvented herself, changing her name, address, hair, dress style and career. The only thing that she had kept, unfortunately, was her disturbing nature.

24

'Hey, Tracy, look at this!' Gary called.

'What is it?' His wife came to look over his shoulder at the letter he held.

'It's from them telly people, you know, the ones doing the documentary about the village.'

Everyone living in Treweham couldn't fail to notice the television crew's presence. Certain villagers had been affronted that they hadn't been directly asked to be involved, especially when they heard who had been selected to be interviewed. Now it looked like the Belchers were to be approached next. Gary whistled. Just wait till the shooting club hear about this, he thought, picturing their faces when he told them he was going to be on the telly.

Gary and Tracy Belcher's lives had changed dramatically when they had won three million pounds on the lottery over nine months ago. Being a young, working-class couple from Lancashire, they had chosen to move from their Northern roots and settle in the Cotswolds, having honeymooned there and fallen in love with the area. It seemed like fate was lending a helping hand when the Gate House had suddenly come on the market, just as they had begun their search of the area. Despite the Gate House being a Grade II-listed building and having rustic, period charm, it was the location that proved the main pull for Gary and Tracy. For the Gate House was set in the tranquillity of the Treweham Hall estate, far away from any prying eyes. Privacy had been key for the Belchers, particularly after having received threatening letters demanding a share of their money – or else. In the end, Gary and Tracy had had no choice but to relocate, far away from their 'friends' who had started to take advantage of their fortune.

Gary had settled immediately and, he being a larger-than-life character, his affable, good humour had gained him many friends at the local shooting club. The stiff, refined set in tweeds and waxed jackets found Gary-from-the-North rather amusing. They would chuckle into their hip flasks as Gary regaled them with stories and anecdotes with animation; and of course, he had money. In many ways he was an enigma to them. Gary had been inundated with various invitations, not just to shoot dinners, but select drinks parties, where inevitably he would supply the entertainment. He was hilarious and once he had downed a few pints, any inhibitions he may have had totally vanished.

Tracy, however, was a complete contrast to her husband, and she suspected that maybe people were laughing *at* Gary, not *with* him. She didn't like the way their northern accents were often mimicked, and therefore had chosen to say as little as possible. As a result, Tracy was considered shy, especially compared to her loud, gregarious husband. It had taken a while for Tracy to get accustomed to the high life, having worked in a care home since she was eighteen. She found it hard to adjust to being a lady who lunched. It was boring. More importantly, it was idle, and totally went against everything she believed in. Tracy had a hard-work ethic and had been thought very highly of in the care home where she had worked. In the end, she decided to offer voluntary service in the local home for the elderly just outside Treweham village. Not only had it given her purpose, but she had met a lovely bunch of people whom she felt more in tune with than the pompous, mickey-taking set at the shooting club.

Tracy took the letter from Gary and read it. Should they agree to be interviewed, or not? After all, the reason why they had moved here in the first place was to keep a low profile. But when she voiced her concerns to Gary he just laughed.

'We're hardly likely to receive any begging letters here, Trace.'

This, she had to concede, was true. Gone were the days when those around them stared with envious eyes, eager to get hold of their money.

'Go on, it'll be fun,' coaxed Gary, putting his arm round her. 'What have we to lose?'

'Hmm... all right then,' she relented. It couldn't do any harm, could it?

25

Dylan drowsily opened his eyes. The painkillers he'd been taking had dulled most of the agony in his chest, but had left him in a permanent state of weariness. Dylan wasn't used to keeping still. He was a doer, always on the go, especially as the training yard was still in its infancy, which meant he had been running at full pelt, with very early starts, long, strenuous days and late night finishes. He felt riddled with guilt that Flora was now handling the bulk of running the yard, due to his incapacitation. Thankfully, Tobias had kindly lent them two grooms from the Treweham Hall stables, which had alleviated some of the workload.

Dylan sighed again, watching the early dawn gradually emerge through the bedroom curtains. He desperately longed to saddle up and canter through the sunrise, feel the fresh air on his face and the warmth on his back. This was the longest stretch he had been without riding and he missed it terribly.

He turned his head to look at Flora, lying peacefully asleep next to him. She was an angel, he thought, his heart swelling with love. He watched her chest gently rise and fall. He admired her soft, young flesh, her blonde waves spread across the pillow, her delicate eyelashes and rosebud lips.

Flora had fussed and spoilt him ridiculously since he left hospital, and he had revelled in it, lapping up all the attention. Well, it had been a while since anyone had showed him this much interest, hadn't it? He was going to milk it for as long as possible. Flora had been a bloody good trouper, coping with the yard as well as nursing him. However Dylan, being Dylan, had urges. He was in dire need of some TLC, and not just the Florence Nightingale kind either. Knowing his acrobatics in the bedroom were somewhat limited at the moment – he could barely move without searing pain shooting through him – he coughed quietly. Flora stirred, having not allowed herself to fall into deep sleep in case Dylan needed her in the night. His hand covered hers.

'What is it, Dylan?' she whispered. 'Do you need your painkillers?'

'Hmm... no.'

'Oh.'

'Flora?'

'Yes?'

'Er... would there be any chance of a blowy?'

There was a moment's pause. 'Dylan! You're supposed to be recuperating!'

They both fell silent, then Flora started to giggle uncontrollably, making Dylan join in, then stop instantly as it hurt too much. After a few minutes Flora turned on her side to face him. He looked into her eyes with adoration.

'Thanks, Flora, for everything.'

She understood him. It was one small sentence, but it carried so much. He was thanking her for much more than just looking after him. Flora smiled mischievously and turned back the bedcovers to reveal Dylan's bruised and broken body. Despite his injuries he was still in fantastic shape. Flora's gaze ran over his wide shoulders, dark chest, strong arms, muscled thighs to his enormous, pulsing erection. Dylan caught his breath as she lowered her face to kiss the dark hair running down below his stomach. She hovered over the tip of his shaft, teasing him with butterfly kisses round his hips. He groaned and shifted slightly. Still Flora tantalised him with light kisses, then finally she allowed him satisfaction as her lips covered his throbbing end and her tongue circled the sensitive nib. Dylan let out a cry of ecstasy as her mouth sucked and released him.

26

Sebastian woke feeling tired again. Back at home, in Treweham Hall, meant being looked after very well. He'd had a healthy, balanced diet (even cutting out alcohol), plenty of exercise and early nights. Yet despite this he still felt completely knackered. The other day he'd stumbled and almost tumbled down the long, sweeping stairway. Deciding to play it safe, he'd rung the family doctor and arranged an appointment. Perhaps Dr Giles would prescribe a course of vitamins? He certainly needed something to pick him up out of this lethargy.

Sebastian flung back the covers and put on his dressing gown. He was starving and wanted to make his own breakfast this morning, rather than have Henry bring it to him in an hour on a silver tray. He entered the quiet kitchen and quickly made himself toast and tea, before any of the staff arrived to scurry about their duties. Taking his breakfast, he made his way back to the stairs, when he noticed Megan wandering through the corridor with Zac.

'You're up early,' he commented with raised eyebrows.

'Couldn't sleep,' she replied. 'Just about to do the same.' She nodded towards his hands.

'Come through to the drawing room when you've done,' he invited, whilst whistling to Zac. Zac followed, wagging his tail. Soon Sebastian and Megan were both sitting munching warm, buttered toast and sipping Earl Grey tea.

'Still being sick?' asked Sebastian, watching Megan eat with gusto.

'Not every morning now,' she replied with a weak grin.

'Oh, darling, has this pregnancy been so frightfully awful?'

Megan couldn't help but smile to herself. Her brother-in-law was such a character, a true thespian, using flowery vocabulary, peppered with 'darling' and 'frightfully'.

'It's not so bad,' she assured him. 'It'll be worth it.' She patted her bump, which seemed to be getting bigger by the day.

'I'm sure it will,' agreed Sebastian, and looked into the distance.

Megan eyed him thoughtfully. She noticed his hand quiver slightly as he lifted his cup to take a sip. He looked pale and drawn.

'Sebastian, are you feeling all right?'

He appeared startled by the question for a moment, then sighed. 'Not really. I've not been sleeping very well lately.'

Megan nodded. 'Is there anything worrying you?' she tentatively asked. Megan wasn't accustomed to seeing Sebastian so subdued. He was usually the life and soul of the party. It felt strange, seeing him so downcast. He paused, as if considering the question.

'Just tired, that's all.' He gave a tight smile and bent down to stroke Zac, lying at his feet.

Megan wasn't convinced and said as much to Tobias later that evening whilst they were snuggled up together on the settee.

Tobias had been to see Dylan that afternoon. They'd discussed the short-term plans for the yard whilst Dylan was still recovering. Tobias had been impressed by Flora, not only by her ability to manage the business so well, but with the love and care she was showing Dylan. He'd watched him lap it all up with a wry smile. Then the image of his friend's still body being stretchered into an ambulance flashed through his memory and he shivered with dread. Thank God that was Dylan's last race. He'd been lucky never to have experienced something that frightening before. Now he was listening to Megan's concern over his brother.

'What do you think's wrong?' He looked into his wife's troubled face and stroked the side of it. She was more beautiful with every passing day. Pregnancy gave her complexion a rosy glow and made her eyes shine. Her figure was swelling with his child and he couldn't possibly love her more.

'I'm not sure. Do you think Nick Fletcher's been on the scene again?'

Tobias let out an impatient sigh. He'd wish that man dead in a heartbeat, the trouble he'd caused his brother, not to mention Finula.

'It's highly likely. He does live in the same village, after all.'

'I wish Sebastian would meet someone special.'

'So do I, Megan. So do I.' Tobias leant forward and kissed her softly on the lips.

27

'They're here!' called Gary, peering out of the window, rubbing his hands together with anticipation. Tracy was a little more restrained. Whilst she had agreed to be interviewed, she still felt a touch anxious. Not for the first time, Tracy wished she had some of her husband's enthusiasm. Life must be so much more enjoyable if one can breeze through it without a care. She often envied Gary's *joie de vivre* and was left feeling like a wet lettuce in comparison.

Truth be told, Tracy had been happier before winning the lottery. A part of her felt guilty owning so much, without having earned it. But there was no turning back now. Even if by some miracle Gary agreed to go back home to Lancashire, it wouldn't be the same. They wouldn't fit in. Things had changed. Tracy remembered the look on her so-called best friend's face when she told her she was moving away. She'd wanted to believe it was because Sharon would miss her, but deep down she knew the real reason for her crest-fallen expression. No more gravy train: Tracy was going and taking her money with her.

'Shall I get the door?' Tracy asked, watching Gary fidget impatiently by the window.

'No, no, I'll get it.' He sped off into the hall. Tracy went to the window and watched Gary march down the pathway to greet their visitors. There was a slim, attractive woman with long, brown hair, a middle-aged man carrying a camera, and a young, trendy-looking man wearing faded jeans and a combat jacket, who was also carrying some form of equipment. She grinned to herself, watching Gary pump everyone's hand enthusiastically.

'This way, come through!' called Gary, ushering them through the hall and into the lounge. The film crew weren't expecting the rather brash interior, with its gaudy abstract artwork glaring from the walls on large canvases, and the floors covered with thick shag-pile carpet. A huge plasma television stood in the corner, opposite a black, leather sofa. Not what one would imagine for a listed gatehouse.

Tracy stood waiting for them, nerves starting to edge in. Choosing to appear smart but casual, she had opted to wear red Capri pants and a white and red striped shirt. She had finished the outfit off with red ballet shoes. Tracy cringed when she realised Gary still had his slippers on.

'So,' he slapped his hands together, 'sit down, make yourselves at home. Do you want a brew?' There was a pregnant pause, until Tracy intervened.

'A cup of tea?'

'That would be lovely, thank you,' smiled the lady with long hair. 'Let me introduce the team.' She turned to the two men standing next to her. 'This is Len, our cameraman, and Jamie, the runner. I'm Viola.'

'Pleased to meet you,' returned Tracy, her stomach beginning to tighten. 'I won't be long.' She hurried into the kitchen to put the kettle on. As she was busying herself with making the tea, the sound of Gary's laugh boomed through the doorway.

'So, in the blink of an eye, I went from stacking freezers at Iceland, to moving into the Gate House on the Treweham Hall estate!' she heard him exclaim.

Tracy decided to use the hostess trolley instead of a tray, in case her nerves got the better of her and she dropped it. She'd picked up the trolley in a local vintage shop because it reminded her of the one her gran had had years ago. Unfortunately, the casters squeaked a bit, making her feel somewhat self-conscious wheeling it into the lounge.

Luckily she didn't see Jamie suppressing a giggle, the image of Julie Walters' Mrs Overall springing to his mind.

'I've made some parkin,' Tracy smiled, leaving everyone staring at her in wonder. Gary's laugh echoed round the room again, making Jamie jump.

'It's ginger cake!' Gary cried. 'Nobody's heard of parkin round here, Trace.' He winked in his wife's direction.

Viola managed a feeble laugh. 'Oh, I see. Yes, please, we'd love a piece of parking cake, wouldn't we?' She looked at Len and Jamie, who nodded their heads willingly.

After the niceties were over, Viola explained the procedure. Gary and Tracy were to relax and enjoy the experience, just answer a few simple questions and appear as natural as possible. 'Easy-peasy,' she encouraged with a warm smile that didn't quite reach her eyes, Tracy noticed.

'Bish, bosh, bash,' replied Gary, rubbing his hands together again.

Tracy wished he'd stop doing that, suddenly finding it highly irritating.

Len set the camera in place. Jamie was adjusting the lights, standing on tripods, to Len's requirements. He then held a huge, furry microphone near to Gary and Tracy. Viola took out her clipboard and cleared her throat.

'Sound check,' Len said.

'Testing one, two, three,' answered Viola, 'testing one, two, three.'

'Good to go,' said Len.

Jamie's hand moved closer to Tracy and Gary with the microphone.

'Well, what a lovely home you have,' beamed Viola.

'Thanks,' said Tracy with a smile.

'We'd all love to know, how does it feel, living on the Treweham Hall estate?' she asked in clear, concise tones.

Gary jumped in. 'Smashing. All this space is a far cry from where we came from, innit, Tracy?'

'Yes, we're very fortunate to be living in such a beautiful part of the country.'

'What brought you to the Cotswolds?' enquired Viola.

'We came into money—'

Gary was interrupted by Tracy. 'Yes, and we decided to return to Treweham after honeymooning here a few years ago.' She didn't want Gary to talk about their unpleasant experience back home. 'When we saw the Gate House was up for sale, we couldn't resist it.'

'Is that why you paid over the odds for it?' asked Viola innocently.

Gary and Tracy stalled. Had they overpaid for it? They didn't like being ripped off – who did? But being made to look foolish made it worse.

'Well, we paid the asking price,' Gary finally replied. His voice was quieter, calmer now.

'The price Lord Cavendish-Blake asked for it?' Viola still spoke matter-of-factly.

'We didn't like to haggle,' Tracy answered.

'You mean you felt uncomfortable?'

'Well… you know…' Gary stumbled.

'Do you find Lord Cavendish-Blake intimidating?' Viola pressed.

'He's… a bit…' Tracy tried to explain.

'Yes?' Viola responded quickly.

'Well, maybe he was a bit standoffish at first. We invited a few people round when we first moved in.'

'A house-warming party,' Gary supplied.

'Yes, and he seemed…' Tracy trailed off.

'Unapproachable?' Viola offered.

'Er… just a bit aloof, I'd day,' finished Tracy hesitantly.

'Even though he was happy to take your money,' concluded Viola.

Gary coughed with unease. 'Yeah, but he did invite us to his wedding.'

'And made us feel very welcome,' Tracy conceded.

Viola gave a quick nod and moved onto the next question.

After a shaky start, Viola rounded the interview off on a positive note, asking about their future, possible children, and telling them how lucky they were to have such a beautiful home. All in all, the experience had gone relatively OK.

Although Gary wasn't as jubilant when seeing the television crew off, he returned to the lounge looking fairly optimistic.

'How do you think it went?' Tracy asked.

'I think we came across quite well, don't you?'

'Hmm, I hope so.' She had a very uneasy feeling about the whole experience now.

28

Flora was shattered. Running around after Dylan as well as taking care of the training yard was taking its toll. Dark circles hung below her eyes. Dylan was now managing to get up and about a bit, but he hadn't returned to work full time yet. Instead, he did as much paperwork as possible from home, leaving Flora to attend to the staff and horses.

She had just ridden a horse at full pelt down the all-weather woodchip gallops and felt invigorated. She passed the stables, which were being mucked out by the busy grooms. Fresh hay and buckets of water stood outside, ready to replace yesterday's.

Marching into the office, she heard the phone ring. Quickly picking up the receiver, she was just about to speak when a voice barked at her. 'Is that Delany's Racing Yard?'

'Yes, it is.'

'Where's Dylan Delany then?' Affronted by the sharp tone, Flora decided to tread carefully.

'He's unavailable at the moment. Can I help you? I'm the assistant trainer.'

'Suppose you'll do.'

Charming. Flora paused, waiting for the rather angry voice to continue, which it did without any prompting.

'I need someone to look at my horse. It's a bloody waste of space and costing me a bloody fortune.'

'Who's speaking, please?' Flora asked, her instincts started to ring warning bells.

'Roper, Graham Roper. I own Phoenix Rising, but the only thing that horse is rising is my blood pressure, plus the fees it's costing me to keep it!' he thundered.

Flora knew this horse. She'd seen Phoenix Rising run a few times. The reason Flora remembered the poor horse was because he had trailed in last every time, and received a good thrashing from each frustrated jockey who had ridden him. Flora's heart went out to the beautiful horse, with its rich brown coat that shone like French-polished mahogany. Instantly she acted on her gut feeling. Where horses were concerned, Flora's intuition was invariably spot-on.

'We'll look at Phoenix for you,' she smoothed, trying to sound professional, as well as calming the irate owner down.

'You will?' He sounded surprised as well as relieved.

'Yes. Where is he at the moment?'

'Here, in my stables. It's been in a few training yards. The last one was Fox's, but I've just had a blazing row with that idiot Sean Fox and told him where to go.' She could imagine. Seamus' dad, Sean Fox, was renowned for his fierce temper. Graham Roper would have made a fine match for him. Meanwhile, a horse was suffering, thought Flora bleakly.

'Can you deliver him tomorrow?' she asked.

'I can deliver the lump today,' retorted Roper with a snort.

Flora closed her eyes. She hated any kind of cruelty to an animal but knew a conversation with Dylan was necessary before agreeing to take the horse that day.

'I need to speak to Mr Delany first—'

'Tell him, he either takes my horse, or it's heading for the knacker's yard,' cut in an ice-cold voice.

Flora's eyes filled. 'Tomorrow. Bring Phoenix tomorrow morning, first thing.'

'Right you are.' The phone slammed down.

Flora took a deep breath and decided to head off home early. She desperately needed to speak to Dylan.

Dylan was propped up by his bureau, papers spread out before him. He'd been busy contacting owners and chasing up fees, plus arranging for all the horses' six-monthly blood tests.

He half turned to Flora, not expecting to see her this early. 'Everything OK?' he asked, still looking at his paperwork.

'No.'

Dylan stopped what he was doing. She had his full attention now. 'What is it Flora?' He frowned at the worried expression on her face.

'We've had a call from some owner called Graham Roper.'

Dylan shook his head. 'Grim Reaper more like,' he muttered.

'You've heard of him?'

'Too right. He makes Sean Fox look like Father Christmas. He's owned a few horses in his time, but he's no horse lover.'

'I gathered that. He wants us to train Phoenix Rising.'

Dylan sucked in a breath; he too had seen this horse run. 'Have you seen its form?'

Flora sighed. 'I know, but, Dylan, you should have heard the way he was talking. He sounds a complete ogre. That poor horse is going to suffer unless we take it on. Sean Fox has tried.'

Dylan gave a harsh laugh. 'I bet he has,' he replied, knowing full well just how Sean Fox would have dealt with it.

'I said he could drop him off tomorrow morning,' Flora stated quietly.

'What?' Dylan's eyes widened.

'Please, Dylan, he says Phoenix is for the knacker's yard otherwise.'

Dylan could see how upset she was, but they were running a business, not a charity.

'Flora, I'm sorry, but I really don't think this is viable.'

'I'll sort him. I've the patience,' she countered, hope in her eyes.

Dylan swallowed. This was hard. It killed him to see her like this.

'Just give me two weeks. If you don't see any improvements then… then we'll have to let him go.' Her voice cracked as she finished speaking.

And this was before the horse had even got here, thought Dylan dubiously. He couldn't fault Flora's reasoning, though; two weeks wasn't a lot to ask. He admired her passion, which was why she was his assistant trainer, he reminded himself. He also reminded himself of Flora's hard work and commitment towards the yard and felt he couldn't deny her this one request. With a heavy sigh, he relented.

'OK. Two weeks.'

Flora went to hug him. 'Oh, thanks, Dylan!'

He winced in pain as she squeezed his broken ribs.

The next morning, as arranged, Graham Roper pulled up at the training yard with Phoenix Rising in a trailer. Dylan chose to be there with Flora, not trusting Roper to do business decently with Flora. They both flinched at the way he was handling his horse, pulling roughly at the reins, tugging at its mouth. Flora couldn't bear it. She rushed across and offered to take over. Immediately he flung the reins at her.

'Help yourself,' he said flatly. Dylan wanted to punch his arrogant face. 'So, Delany,' Graham Roper stared squarely at Dylan, 'think you can do something with it, then?'

Dylan eyed him coolly. 'We'll do what we can.' He was keen not to make any promises.

'You're its last chance,' Roper replied, almost accusingly.

Dylan didn't care for his tone or his attitude, and he was glad Flora had talked him into taking the horse. He looked towards Flora, who was gently stroking Phoenix. Even now, the horse was slightly trembling. Dylan also spotted the scars that the excess of whipping had caused and clenched his jaw.

'I said, we'll do what we can. He's in good hands,' Dylan reiterated in a steely voice.

'Pah! Good luck with that.' Roper flicked his hand dismissively. 'Right, I take it there's something to sign then?'

'My office is this way,' directed Dylan. He turned to speak to Flora, but she'd already gone. No doubt she'd taken the horse quickly away in case this monster changed his mind, thought Dylan wryly.

Inside the stables, Flora continued to sooth Phoenix's jumping nerves. She softly massaged the horse's strained muscles and back, then gently rubbed wound gel into the long, thin risen welts from the whip. Flora could see his hind legs were swollen. This could be for a number of reasons, but judging by the horse's size and shape it wasn't down to obesity or lack of exercise; more like trauma, she concluded with anger. She hosed the inflamed legs with cold water and applied liniment before bandaging them. Phoenix loved the way she pacified his tired flesh and butted her gently to carry on.

Flora laughed quietly. 'You're not used to this, are you, old boy?' The horse neighed in reply and butted her again. Flora flung her arms round his neck. 'It's all right, Phoenix. You're safe now.'

Sebastian was feeling anything but safe. He took a steady breath and prepared himself as he walked into the doctor's surgery. He hadn't had to wait long before his name was called to go through.

'Hello, Sebastian,' Dr Giles smiled. 'Take a seat.' Once Sebastian was sitting opposite his desk, he asked the usual, 'So, what can I do for you?' He'd noticed Sebastian's slight limp as he'd entered, plus the pale, tired face.

Sebastian coughed slightly, 'I feel exhausted all the time and my leg appears to be dragging sometimes.'

Dr Giles nodded. 'I see. When does it seem to drag?'

'After about forty minutes' walking or jogging. Also, when I'm really tired.'

'Do you suffer any cramps?'

'Yes. At night my leg often spasms.'

'Have you experienced any other symptoms?'

'No, not really. Just the tiredness and dragging leg.'

Dr Giles rose from behind his desk. 'I'll just take a look at you.' He reached for a small, silver torch and shone it in Sebastian's eyes. Then he asked him to sit on the side bed and tested his reflexes by tapping below his kneecaps. All the while his face was set in concentration, giving very little away. Sebastian tried to read any signs at all, but the doctor's expression remained impassive. Finally, after examining him thoroughly, Dr Giles directed Sebastian back to his chair.

'Do you think I should consider physiotherapy?' he asked.

The doctor looked squarely at him. 'You could try physiotherapy. It certainly wouldn't do any harm,' Sebastian sensed a 'but' coming, 'but, I think we need to delve a little deeper.'

Sebastian gulped. 'How deep?'

'I'm going to refer you to a neurologist.'

'A neurologist?' he squeaked.

Dr Giles nodded slowly, 'Yes, Sebastian, a neurologist.'

29

It was the evening before the television crew's visit to Treweham Hall and Marcus' stomach was in knots. Now that he had finally got what he had craved for, the prospect was rather daunting. He reminded himself exactly why he was in Treweham. He had orchestrated the whole thing: the documentary, the location and the subject. For months he had been planning and plotting this moment, when he could expose the Cavendish-Blakes for what they really were.

He badly needed more information on the late Richard Cavendish-Blake (refusing to think of him as 'Dad'). In order to dismantle the man's reputation and good name Marcus had to learn more about him. All he knew was that apart from siring him and not supporting his mother, Richard Cavendish-Blake had left two other sons, a wife and his ancestral home. Again, the notion of revealing himself as his bastard son passed through his embittered, cynical mind, but without proof – which he didn't have

– it was futile. The last thing he wanted was to appear foolish or, even worse, a fraud. Marcus had a reputation, a professional high standing, and he most definitely didn't want that being sullied in any way. Plus, he had his pride, and his pride for his mother, he thought fiercely. There was no way his mother's memory was going to be tainted either.

His reverie was interrupted by a knock at the door. Hoping it wasn't Viola, he was relieved to hear Finula's voice.

'Marcus, are you there?' Instantly his restless mind calmed and he opened the door with a relaxed smile. She never failed to cheer him up. The sight of her creamy, white complexion, bright eyes and riotous red curls dissolved any feelings of anger.

'Come in,' he opened the door fully.

'I'm so excited about tomorrow,' Finula gushed. 'Are you sure there's nothing I can do to help?' She searched his face for an answer.

'Just be your usual, lovely self,' he assured her, with his hands in his pockets, leaning against the wall. His gaze travelled over her svelte body and his need for her started to grow. He could feel a slow, burning sensation start to rise from within. All of a sudden he didn't want to be here, in this room, in The Templar, with her father under the same roof. He yearned to take her someplace else, away from everyone.

'Finula, after we've finished shooting at Treweham Hall, I'm thinking of going home for a quick break. Do you fancy coming along?'

She looked at little startled. 'You're going back to Shropshire?' Again, that charming, black and white Tudor cottage sprung to mind and her heart leapt.

'Only for a couple of days. There's things I could be doing at home.' He had renovated his cellar into a studio, with all the necessary screens, recording and editing equipment he needed to work from home.

'I'd love to come,' she answered with enthusiasm. Something told him she was never going to play it coy and he wasn't disappointed.

'Good, because I'd love you to come.' Wouldn't he just.

He moved forwards, staring intensely into her eyes. Finula's heart started to pound as he advanced towards her. Marcus was looking dangerously handsome in black jeans and an olive-green shirt, which revealed a touch of hair at the opening. His eyes glistened with mischief, inches away from hers. Then he lowered his face and gently kissed her. His lips were soft and probed hers, then his kiss became stronger and more forceful as his tongue slid across hers, making her jolt in delight. Her arms reached round his neck, pulling him further in to her. Finula could feel his heart hammering against her chest. He tugged her closer still and his kiss became deeper. Her hands ran into his short, dark hair and he groaned with pleasure.

'Finula, I want you so much,' he whispered thickly into her ear.

His throbbing erection pressed hard against her. She was melting under his touch. His fingers traced the outline of her chest, his thumbs circling the stiff nipples. Finula cried out in desire, then ran her hands down his body to rest just below his jeans waistband. She delved lower and brushed the tip of his pulsing shaft.

'My God, Finula,' he growled with lust, feverishly unbuttoning her blouse to reveal a white, silk bra bursting with two heaving breasts he ached to taste. He dipped his head to lick the rosebud tips protruding from the edge of the silk, then stopped abruptly at hearing another knock on the door. Finula gasped, the two of them urgently separated and she hurriedly fastened her buttons back up. Cursing under his breath, Marcus strode over to the door, whilst Finula quickly hid to the side of the room. 'This had better be good,' she heard Marcus mutter as he opened the door, then froze as she listened to his next words. 'Ah, Dermot, what can I do for you?'

'Have you seen Finula? I've been looking for her everywhere.'

'Er... no.'

Finula stifled a giggle. It was the first time she'd heard Marcus uncertain of himself.

'Well, if you do, tell her *she's needed at the bar*!' Dermot spoke the last few words loudly, clearly for her benefit, not believing Marcus one bit.

'Yes, will do,' Marcus replied. Dermot eyed him with a knowing look and disappeared.

Finula doubled over laughing at Marcus' face.

'It's not funny,' he said in exasperation. 'The sooner we're in Shropshire, the better.'

30

Tobias was waiting patiently in his study. It was 10.30 a.m. and he'd been up since the crack of dawn giving strict instructions to all the staff. He reiterated to them all, including Henry, how they were to be fully aware of the visitors from the film crew who would be invading the Hall. He stressed discretion. He also informed them where the boundaries lay for the filming. Anyone seen beyond these areas had to be reported immediately to him. Basically, the television crew were allowed in all the rooms that were already opened to the public, plus the library, which was where he was to be interviewed. Sebastian had chosen to be interviewed outside in the grounds, so Tobias had given permission for them to shoot there too. All the other private rooms, especially their south-wing suite, were strictly forbidden territory.

Megan was overseeing the tearoom. She had asked the kitchen staff to provide refreshments there for the documentary team. It seemed the ideal place, as Tobias was so keen to keep them at arm's length. She was now approaching her sixth month of pregnancy and was as radiant as ever, in a dark, plum dress with a matching cashmere pashmina. Megan was at pains to look elegant and business-like, whereas Tobias had stubbornly chosen to wear casual jeans and a check shirt, determined not to make any effort. Sebastian, too, appeared completely relaxed in combat trousers and a grey, long-sleeved T-shirt as he threw Zac's ball up and down the Great Hall, encouraging the black Labrador to scurry across the tiled floor, much to Henry's distaste.

Lady Cavendish-Blake was at fever pitch. Badly put out at not being included in the interviews, she had decided to wow the film people with a floaty, lilac creation she had bought especially for today. The accompanying fascinator seemed rather over the top, but was totally Beatrice. Tobias had rolled his eyes at the vision of layered lilac that was his mother, whilst Megan and Sebastian had exchanged amused looks.

Tobias heard the doorbell and then the commotion that followed. Zac ran at full pelt to the hallway, pursued by Sebastian. Meanwhile, Henry and Beatrice raced to answer the door. Henry won, making Beatrice stand to the side patiently on tenterhooks.

'Darling, shouldn't you have worn a suit?' She ran her gaze over Sebastian, who was now covered in dog hair.

'They can take me as they find me, Mother,' he replied with a grin.

Henry showed the film crew in and Beatrice introduced herself and Sebastian, who was clutching an overexcited Zac.

Jamie immediately knelt down to stroke the dog, catching Sebastian's eye. 'Hello again,' he said with a charming smile.

Sebastian smiled back. 'Hello, Jamie.' Jamie flushed, flattered that Sebastian had remembered his name. Tobias strolled nonchalantly down the hallway, looking cool, calm and collected. Marcus took in what he perceived to be an almost arrogant swagger, and a flash of contempt crossed his face. Halting before the small crowd, Tobias spoke in a clear, firm tone.

'Henry, please show our visitors to the tearoom.' Henry bowed, then Tobias turned to Marcus. 'Mr Devlin, a word in my study, please.'

'Certainly,' replied Marcus, equally confident.

Marcus' eyes ran wildly over the portraits hanging from the walls as he walked down the corridor. He was desperate to seek out Richard Cavendish-Blake, but didn't have the chance before they reached Tobias' study.

Turning coolly to face Marcus, Tobias picked up the document from his desk. 'I take it you've read and digested this contract, Mr Devlin?'

'Yes, I have,' Marcus replied, then added, 'Lord Cavendish-Blake.' To think, this jumped-up eejit was his actual brother; *younger* brother. Whilst he was busy lording his great ancestral home and position over him, Marcus stood in defiance, knowing he was the first-born son.

'Good. Then we all know where we stand.'

'Absolutely,' agreed Marcus, staring Tobias in the face, refusing to be intimidated.

'Under no circumstances do any of your team… wander or pry, or approach any member of my family or staff unless they ask me first.'

Marcus nodded. 'Of course not.' What an absolute jackass, he thought. Then he saw him, Richard Cavendish-Blake, bold as brass, hanging majestically above Tobias' head. His title and name were engraved on a small, gold plaque at the bottom of the frame. He had the same green eyes as Marcus himself, speckled with amber; then he noticed with sickening realisation that Tobias had them too. He peered into his face for any other likenesses. Tobias was frowning.

Marcus coughed and spoke quickly. 'May I take this opportunity to thank you, and reassure you of our good intentions,' he lied with poise.

'Hmm, I'll have you shown to the tearoom,' Tobias replied, clearly unconvinced, making Marcus smirk to himself. 'I'll be ready in the library in an hour.'

'Thank you,' Marcus replied.

Inside the tearoom he found Finula chatting to a woman he assumed was Megan. He caught the tail end of the conversation, '... his house in Shropshire.' He saw Megan's face light up just before he joined them. 'Ah, Marcus, meet Megan,' Finula introduced them.

'Pleased to meet you, Lady Cavendish-Blake,' he smiled.

'Oh, call me Megan,' she smiled back.

Marcus was taken aback by her informality. She seemed a natural, pleasant girl, without any airs or graces, as one might expect. But then, she was Finula's best friend, so why wouldn't she be lovely? he reasoned with himself.

'Have you met the team?' he enquired.

'Yes, everyone seems to be getting along fine.' Megan nodded towards Sebastian chatting to Jamie, Viola, Len and Libby. Marcus looked towards the group. Jamie was mesmerised by what Sebastian was saying, whilst Len and Libby were nodding politely. Viola seemed a touch distracted.

He turned back to face Megan with a grin. 'He's quite a character, your brother-in-law, isn't he?'

Megan threw her head back and laughed. 'Very much so.'

'I believe you were recently married here?' Marcus asked.

'Yes, that's right, in the chapel. Come, I'll show you it.' Finula and Marcus followed Megan up the grand, sweeping staircase, along the corridor and into the pretty chapel.

'It's stunning,' said Marcus, who genuinely seemed impressed by the stained glass, arched windows, small, ornately carved altar and pitch-pine pews.

'It is, isn't it?' agreed Finula, reminiscing about Tobias and Megan's wedding day and all the excitement it had encompassed.

Marcus had noticed another room opposite the chapel. The door had been open to reveal rows and rows of books.

'May I ask what this room is used for?' Marcus pointed inside it as they exited the chapel and passed it again.

'Oh, that was my husband's late father's study,' Megan casually threw over her shoulder. 'He recorded everything since time immemorial apparently.'

Marcus frowned.

'You know, all the incomings and outgoings of the Hall, every member of staff who ever worked here, all the social functions the Hall hosted, that kind of thing. He was keen on diaries, too,' she added.

Marcus took in a sharp breath. Diaries, in that room. He *had* to get access to them. But how?

'How interesting,' he replied calmly, following behind Finula as they climbed back down the stairs and headed into the tearoom. Viola was waiting for them, clipboard at the ready with a determined look on her face. This was a big day for her and she wanted everything to go just so, as did Marcus.

'Should we set up in the library?' she asked him.

'Yes, you all go.' He turned to Megan and Finula. 'Megan, on reflection, I would like to take a few pictures of the chapel. Would that be possible?' He took out a small camera from his jacket pocket.

'I don't see why not.'

'That's great, thanks. I won't be long.' He then called out to Libby, 'Libby, why don't you decide on the location in the grounds for Sebastian's interview?'

'Will do,' she called back.

Sebastian joined her. Megan and Finula sat down at a nearby table with another cup of tea.

Marcus pelted up the stairs. He quickly took a few random snaps in the chapel, then hot-footed it across the landing to the study full of ledgers and books. The smell of old parchment filled the air. Marcus had to squint to read the writing on the spines lining the shelves. They were all meticulously dated and labelled, which was highly convenient, he noted, as the specific period of time he was interested in was the year in which he was born, or just before, 1985. Scanning the leather-bound ledgers, he eventually came to a spine marked *Treweham Hall Accounts – 1985*.

Marcus seized the book off the shelf and hastily opened it. He got his camera ready to photo anything that caught his attention. Flicking through the yellowing pages of writing in blue fountain-pen ink, he saw rows and rows of names in alphabetical order. They were the staff employed at the time. Each name had the area or position in which they worked, either kitchens, stables, housekeeping, grounds, butler or valet. Marcus' eyes quickly ran over the names, then stopped dead when he saw 'Anne Devlin – kitchens'. There she was, his own mammy. So that's how she had met Richard Cavendish-Blake. She had *worked* for him. His mouth curled at the classic archetype: lord of the manor having his wicked way with the scullery maid. He bent over the page and took a photo of it, then hastily put the ledger back.

If only he could find the diaries, but where would they be? All the shelves appeared to have the same size books, so he assumed they must all be similar accounts to what he'd just read. Surely the diaries must be locked up? Marcus looked to the glass cabinet at the far side of the room. There were books in there too, smaller and unlabelled. Could these be them? He tried to open the glass door, but it was obviously locked. Then he heard footsteps coming up the stairs.

'Marcus!' It was Finula's voice. He dashed out just as she appeared at the top of the stairs. 'All done?'

'Yep, let's go,' he smiled as naturally as he could and joined her. He put an arm round her shoulder and kissed her cheek. Megan, waiting at the bottom of the stairs, saw the affectionate gesture and smiled to herself. It was good to see Finula so happy; she deserved it.

'Megan, could you show me to the grounds? I just need to check on Libby?'

'Sure, this way.' Megan walked them through the stone-floored hallway with dark, oak panelling, leading them into the kitchens. Marcus drank it all in, knowing his mam would have been in there too at one stage in her life, scurrying around like the staff today. Somehow it comforted him to know she had been there. They went out through the back doors.

'Treweham Hall supplies fruit and vegetables to local businesses,' explained Megan, which accounted for all the greenhouses. Marcus nodded. They found Libby and Sebastian in the knot garden towards the side of the Hall, sitting chatting on a wrought-iron bench.

'This is a perfect spot,' said Marcus. Not only did it showcase the garden, bursting with aromatic plants and culinary herbs, but it gave a spectacular view of the Hall, which the public wouldn't normally see. Marcus breathed in the scents of rosemary and lemon balm. Would his mother have cooked with these herbs years ago?

'I thought so,' agreed Libby. She too had appreciated the backdrop of Treweham Hall from this angle. Having worked together many times, the two were often in tune with the other. Their personalities made for a good working relationship; Marcus' impatience for perfection was always tamed by Libby's pragmatic, reassuring approach, and the job always got done. Marcus and Libby's roles often blended together, especially when working on a tight budget with limited resources.

'OK, I'd better check on Viola.' Marcus turned to Megan again. 'Can you show me to the library?'

'This way,' she replied with a smile.

Once again Marcus thought how nice Megan seemed and wondered how she had ended up with a husband like Tobias.

The library proved every bit as impressive as the rest of the Hall, with its mahogany panelling and endless rows of books. A mobile stepladder was suspended from the highest shelf. The dark wood floor was covered with Persian rugs and the whole space was illuminated by the light streaming through the large stained-glass window at the bottom of the room. The pictures showcased the Cavendish family lineage through marriage from various earls and possible royalty, judging by the crowns that were worn.

A fire crackled softly in the large, tiled fireplace. Above it hung a portrait of Tobias, recently painted, by the look of it. Viola was standing staring at it. Her anticipation was palpable. Never had an interview meant such a huge deal to her. The fact Viola had been 'researching' Tobias Cavendish-Blake for weeks had added even more fervour. I probably know more about Tobias than his own wife does, she thought sardonically as she continued to gaze at his portrait. Those piercing green eyes were mesmerising, and as for that dimpled chin... hell, he was hot.

She looked at her watch: not long to go now before she actually sat down and talked to the man himself. Her eyes flicked over the agreed questions, give or take one or two extras she'd slipped in. She so wanted to make an impression on him. Not just an impression – she wanted him to be attracted to her. Why not? She was just as good-looking as his wife, wasn't she? And in better shape, when comparing her large breasts, tiny waist, long slim legs and pert bum, all tucked inside a figure-hugging sweater dress. She pictured his wife's bulging belly and sniggered to herself. All she had to do was let him know she was available; ready, willing and available.

31

The library was set for the interview. Jamie and Len had placed all the lights and microphones in position. Viola sat with her back to the camera, so only Tobias would be visible, centre stage. The rest of the crew were seated behind all the equipment at the far end of the room. Finula had joined them, waiting with excitement for it all to begin. As instructed, only the film crew and Finula were allowed in the library.

Finally, Tobias' footsteps could be heard along the hallway. Viola took a deep breath. Marcus' stomach clenched. Tobias walked in, about to give his first ever interview. The atmosphere was electric. He strode over to the chair waiting for him, sat down with utter composure, looked evenly at everyone and spoke.

'I'm ready.'

Jamie shot up and fed wires around him before attaching a microphone to his shirt. After tapping it and checking for sound, Len asked Jamie to move one of the lights closer to Tobias. Tobias sat regally, waiting for the onslaught. The lights felt hot and he could feel himself start to burn under them. Marcus stared intently for a few seconds, then after signalling Len, shouted, 'Action.'

'Lord Cavendish-Blake, may I start by thanking you for agreeing to be interviewed, exclusively?'

Tobias gave a rather bored look; he hated any form of grovelling. 'You may.'

Arrogant shite, thought Marcus.

'What made you decide to finally face the cameras?'

This was slightly off track, Tobias noted immediately, but answered the question with ease and honesty.

'Money, basically. This estate costs a fortune to run, many people's livelihoods depend on it and opening up Treweham Hall to the TV cameras will bring in much-needed revenue.'

Won't it just, the money-grabbing swine, thought Marcus, remembering the eye-wateringly large sum of money the Cavendish-Blakes had demanded.

'So, you personally take responsibility for your staff and tenants?'

'I like to think I have a good working relationship with them, yes.'

'By providing for them and upholding old, family traditions, such as the Landlord's Supper?'

This was veering further off track. 'Yes,' Tobias replied with caution.

'I believe you very generously settle the bill for quite a… raucous night?'

'Yes, I think it's money well spent and I like to see my tenants enjoying themselves.'

'Wasn't there some… altercation at the last Landlord's Supper?'

Marcus didn't intervene. He'd suspected Viola would pull this stunt. She was asking questions on the agreed topics, but twisting and pushing a little too close for comfort.

Tobias paused and stared coolly into her. Viola's heart thumped uncontrollably. She found him so dangerously attractive, yet still wanted her interview to make an impact. In a way, pushing him like this turned her on.

Finally, he answered. 'I objected to having my wife manhandled and so I reacted like any other husband would.'

'By knocking a man out, flat on the floor?'

'No. By knocking a man out, flat on the bar,' corrected Tobias straight-faced.

Finula giggled, Marcus shot round with a stern 'keep-quiet' face, making her hold up her hands in apology.

Viola gave a light tinkly laugh. 'I see. Could we talk about your wedding here at Treweham Hall? I understand it took place inside your charming chapel last September?'

'Yes. We wanted a small, private affair.'

'And I believe congratulations are in order, as Lady Cavendish-Blake is due to have your first child in March?'

The implication was clear: it had been a shotgun wedding. The dig certainly wasn't lost on Tobias. This woman was seriously starting to piss him off. Any hint of trying to cast Megan in a bad light made his hackles rise. Then, just as he was about to tell her in no uncertain terms what he thought, Viola sat forwards in her chair slightly, tipping her pelvis, then uncrossed her legs languidly, leaving Tobias in no doubt she was a true brunette. He blinked with disbelief. All the while the camera rolled, catching his expression. It looked for all intents and purposes like he was stalling for time, when in reality he was actually stunned. Nobody but Tobias could have seen Viola's lurid act because they were all behind her, facing him. He took a deep breath and steadied himself.

'My wife and I are extremely happy to be bringing our first child into the world. We consider it a blessing.'

Marcus was delighted he'd been clearly knocked off kilter.

Finula shifted uncomfortably, suddenly not finding this exciting or amusing any more. The questions weighed heavy with insinuation and undertone, making her feel uneasy. She looked towards Marcus, who was still staring in concentration. Did she notice his lips twitch slightly? After what seemed an excruciating thirty minutes for Finula, the interview concluded and Marcus called it a wrap.

Tobias stood up, untangled his microphone and threw it on the chair, before walking out of the library stony-faced without a backward glance.

32

Viola watched Tobias storm off and a spark inside her ignited. On impulse she quickly got up from her chair and discreetly followed him whilst the rest of the team were tidying away the equipment and chatting.

Finula sidled over to Marcus, who was sitting talking to Libby in hushed tones. Interrupting them, Finula said, 'Marcus, can I have a word with you?' Marcus looked a tad annoyed at being disturbed, but stood up to join her. 'Marcus, I don't feel comfortable about the way Tobias was interviewed,' she whispered, her eyes full of concern.

Marcus put a hand on her shoulder. 'I know how it must appear to you, Finula. Viola's technique can be somewhat—'

'Harsh?' butted in Finula with force.

'Direct,' Marcus reasoned. He saw the anger in Finula's face and quickly added in a soothing tone, 'Listen, don't worry. The interview will be edited. Libby will give it the best possible angle and nothing gets in the final cut without my consent. I'll make sure Tobias is portrayed in his true light.'

Too right he would. This seemed to placate Finula and her shoulders relaxed a little. Marcus tilted her chin up and kissed her mouth. 'Looking forward to Shropshire?' He spoke flirtatiously, his eyes dancing with devilment. Finula couldn't help but melt. He was irresistible with his sparkly green eyes and the soft Irish tone of his voice.

'I've just realised who your eyes remind me of,' she said, smiling as it suddenly dawned on her. Marcus froze, waiting for her to finish. 'Tobias!' Still he stared, speechless. 'Don't you see?' She pointed towards the portrait of Tobias hanging above the fireplace. Marcus turned to look.

'Can't see it myself,' he shrugged casually, whilst his heart raced.

'Surely, you must! Your eyes are exactly the same: green with speckled amber.'

Marcus smiled. 'If you say so.' He quickly changed the subject. 'Listen, I'd like an early start at the weekend, if that's all right with you?'

'Yes, no problem. What time?'

'Let's set off early, about 7 a.m.?'

'Fine. I'll be ready.'

Down the hall, Viola quietly followed Tobias from a distance. Once he entered his study she hovered outside for a moment to collect herself. Glancing in a nearby mirror she fluffed her hair, drew her shoulders back, stuck her chest out and knocked on the door.

'Come in!' Tobias called, fully expecting to see Henry standing in the doorway, not that vile woman who had just interviewed him. Looking her up and down with dislike he waited for her to speak. Viola took in the mean, moody look aimed her way and again, it set a trigger off. He was certainly going to be a challenge, but she revelled in a challenge.

'Lord Cavendish-Blake, I've just come to thank you again. It really is appreciated.' She moved forwards to his desk. Was he imagining it, or did she just lick her lips? Viola was standing right in front of him now.

'How did you find this room?' he asked in an ice-cold voice.

'I followed you,' she answered, leaning forwards with her hands on his desk, giving him a good view of her cleavage.

Tobias moved his chair further away and stared directly in her eyes.

'In fact, you could say I've been following you for some time.'

Tobias, recovered now from her stunt in the interview, was beginning to get this vixen's measure.

'Really?' he replied in a bored voice, but still this didn't deter Viola.

'Yes,' she gave a throaty laugh. 'I know all there is to know about you, Tobias.'

Still he just stared with repulsion. This woman had some nerve, coming in here like this, after having just interviewed him in the most provoking way.

'I think you've revealed rather too much to me too,' he stated in a flat voice.

Again, Viola gave a husky laugh. 'I could reveal so much more, especially as your wife must be somewhat… indisposed.'

Tobias resisted the urge to throw this bitch out of his home, instead calmly playing the game by raising an eyebrow. Viola leant further forward; he could smell her perfume, a heavy, potent fragrance. Was there anything subtle about her? He doubted it.

'I can be very discreet. Just say the word.' She licked her lips again.

Enough was enough. Tobias stared into her face. 'Out. That's the word. Out of my study. Out of my home and I don't want to see your face again. Understand?'

Viola's eyes narrowed. Nobody spoke to her like that, nobody.

'Be careful, Tobias. I can make your name mud,' she replied in a low, threatening voice.

'It's Lord Cavendish-Blake to you.' He cast her a look of contempt.

'Well, *Lord Cavendish-Blake,* I know people who would be only too pleased to dish the dirt. Ex-girlfriends? I'm sure there's one or two with axes to grind, aren't you? The last thing you need is your little wife getting upset, hmm?' she spat under her breath.

Tobias pulled a lever behind him, making a bell ring. Within seconds Henry arrived.

'Henry, show this woman out immediately.'

'How dare you!' she hissed.

'This way, madam, if you please.' Henry ushered Viola out of the study.

Tobias was shaking with rage. He *knew* it was a mistake letting the fucking media in. Experience told him hell hath no fury like a woman scorned, and Viola's threatening words could cause real harm. The last thing he needed right now was for Megan to get upset by any scandal.

Viola wasn't wrong when she mentioned ex-girlfriends with axes to grind. What he needed was his own ammunition. What was the saying, fight fire with fire? He picked up his mobile phone and scrolled through the directory until he came to the name he needed. David Lombard, ex-police, who had worked for him before. Lombard owned his own security business and also had contacts in the private detective field. He had organised the security for Tobias and Megan's wedding, plus looked over the hotel in France where they had honeymooned.

'David, it's Tobias. Listen, I need you to do some digging on…' he scanned the BBC contract for her name, '…a Viola Kemp.'

33

Sebastian was sitting waiting for his name to be called again. Yesterday had helped take his mind off things, but he knew there was no escaping today's appointment with the neurologist. He glanced down at the reading material on the coffee table. It was mainly gardening magazines and holiday brochures. Maybe that's what he needed, a good holiday. But who would he go away with? He sensed that sad, lonely feeling seeping into his soul again and tried to force it out. Why was life so tiring, he pondered bleakly. He looked round the waiting room. Everyone had someone with them for moral support. Where was his back-up, his shoulder to cry on? He blinked back the tears that were threatening to fall. At last he was summoned to go through.

Sebastian wasn't there long. The appointment was a repeat of the previous one, the same tests were done on his reflexes and his eyes were examined. He was asked to walk in a straight line, putting one foot in front of the other.

After the second step, the doctor waved his hand and said, 'Enough.' Sebastian sat back down with a heavy heart. 'I'm going to request a brain scan, Sebastian, and a scan of your neck too,' the doctor told him matter-of-factly.

'A brain scan?'

'Yes, plus a lumber puncture.' The neurologist looked into his eyes with compassion.

'Will... will it hurt?' Sebastian swallowed. His mouth had gone dry.

'Lumber punctures are not pleasant, but you will be given an anaesthetic.'

'I see.' Sebastian's eyes started to fill.

The doctor coughed and spoke gently, 'Sebastian, have you come here alone today?'

'Yes,' he whispered.

'Don't you think it would help to have a little support?'

'Maybe.' But who? He hadn't told anyone about this.

'You won't have to wait long. A letter will be sent next week advising you of the appointments.'

'Thank you.' Then Sebastian paused. 'What are we looking at?' He scanned the neurologist's face for any clues.

'Let's not speculate at this point. Let's get the results of all the tests back first.'

Sebastian left the surgery and drove home in a state of numbness. Desperately wanting to talk to someone, he considered telling his brother, then ruled it out. Tobias was happy for the first time in a long while, newly married and expecting his first child. The last thing he needed right now was his brother bringing the mood down.

Then there was his mother, but bless her, she was neither use nor ornament, with her head in the clouds. She didn't even know he was gay.

Megan was a possibility – she had gently asked if there was anything wrong not long ago – but no, she would only tell Tobias. So that was that. There was no one.

Deciding to put off going home, he pulled into the car park of The Templar. He was in dire need of a drink. On entering the bar he was greeted by Dermot. He asked for a pint of real ale then sat down in an alcove. He glanced around the pub, hoping Nick wasn't there. He wasn't, thank God.

Then he became aware of someone watching him. It was Jamie. He smiled and called him over, glad to see a friendly face. Jamie was there in an instant.

'Hi, Sebastian, are you OK?' Jamie noticed Sebastian's quiet demeanour. He was not being his usual flamboyant self.

To hell with it, thought Sebastian, why not offload for once? It would be easier to talk to someone he hardly knew, instead of being careful not to upset those he was close to.

'Do you know what, Jamie? No, I'm not OK.' His voice cracked.

Jamie's face fell. He moved closer. 'Whatever's the matter?' he asked, genuinely concerned. His smoky-grey eyes searched Sebastian's face with worry.

'How long have you got?' replied Sebastian sardonically.

'As long as you need,' Jamie answered softly.

34

Flora arrived at the training yard earlier than usual, eager to see Phoenix. The past week had seen her rising early, working relentlessly all day with the horse, then dragging herself home, late, to an irritated Dylan. Dylan considered himself dedicated to his yard, but Flora was something else; and whilst he applauded her commitment, he didn't particularly appreciate being cast aside on the back burner, playing second fiddle to Phoenix. As ridiculous as it sounded, he rather resented the endless time Flora was spending with the horse. Since Phoenix's arrival Flora had spent every waking hour on him, from dawn till dusk, leaving her far too tired for any quality time with him. Even her day off was whiled away tending to Phoenix.

Last night, when she'd crept into bed next to him, he'd waited to see if she'd cuddle into him like she used to, but within a few minutes he'd heard her gentle snores, obviously out like a light. Charming. Gone were the days when she couldn't keep her hands off him. 'Flora…' He'd softly tried to rouse her, giving her a slight nudge, but there was no response. Sighing with frustration he'd turned away.

Flora entered Phoenix's stable. As always, the horse's eyes darted towards her and he neighed in delight at seeing her.

'Come on, old boy, let's get started.' Flora stroked Phoenix's mane, whilst he nuzzled into her neck. The bond between them was strong and had been formed immediately. Flora hadn't connected so quickly with any other horse before. She instinctively gauged his every move and he in turn responded to her every command. It was a perfect match, a flawless partnership.

In the week since Flora had begun working on him Phoenix had made remarkable progress. She'd started not only with tending to his whip scars and swollen legs, but by massaging and stretching his tired limbs. Following the horse's body with her probing hands along and across the muscle fibres had told her Phoenix had tension throughout. Flora had exercised him with gentle schooling to increase his relaxation and suppleness, which should then have a positive effect on the horse mentally and emotionally. Just speaking to him in a soothing manner was helping. After only a few days, Phoenix felt wonderfully loose and pliable underneath her. His paces were becoming more relaxed, without stiffness or tension in his back or muscles. He had an easier action and greater balance, not to mention he was starting to build strength and confidence. Flora soon learnt that by not forcing or restricting the horse in anyway, allowing him elasticity throughout his back, shoulders, knees and hips, letting him move freely, she was starting to get the best out of him. She suspected he had previously been forced into an unnatural shape that hadn't suited him.

Whilst watching him being ridden up the all-weather woodchip gallop, Flora noticed the horse's stride. He had a high knee action, which meant he was hitting the ground hard. This didn't bode well for a flat-race horse. What a horse with high knee action needed was a 'soft ground', a turf that was damp from the rain, instead of the hard and dry going it would face in the summer months. It was perfectly clear to Flora that Phoenix was built to run in the winter: he was a jump racing horse, not a flat racer. *That's* why he wasn't winning. It certainly wasn't because of any lack of strength, talent or agility. He'd been trained to do the wrong thing!

Totally convinced of this, Flora had gone a step further and looked up Phoenix's pedigree from the paperwork Graham Roper had left with Dylan in the office. She'd seen that both the sire and dam side had been flat racers, but the dam's sire was in fact a jump racer. Obviously Graham Roper and the previous trainers hadn't thought to look at the lineage of the mother's father. Recognising that Phoenix wasn't a loser after all, but could almost certainly be a winner, had made Flora even more resolute about keeping him. But how? One thing was for certain: she would do everything she could to keep him away from Graham Roper.

Dylan pulled into the yard. He didn't expect to see Flora in the office, knowing full well where she would be. He quickly flicked through the post and turned on his computer. As always, a list of emails glared up at him. He noticed one was from Graham Roper and his jaw tightened. His eyes narrowed at the tone of the message, which was every bit as conceited as the man was in person:

Any results? I'll be there at the end of the week.

Dylan closed his eyes. If Roper decided to take his horse back, how the hell would Flora handle it? He got up and made his way to Phoenix's stable. For a moment he stood and watched her. She was an absolute natural, that was for sure. He could see the bond between her and the horse and his heart was pulled. Phoenix saw him and snorted, as if objecting to his presence, making Dylan laugh to himself.

Flora turned and smiled brightly. 'Hi.'

'Hi,' he walked over to stand next to her and put his arm round her waist. Phoenix snorted again, making them both giggle.

'He's jealous,' she said, 'aren't you, old boy?'

'Hmm, don't see why. He's the one you spend every waking hour with,' Dylan replied with a smile, then patted the horse.

'Dylan, I want you to watch him down the wood-chip gallop.'

'Why?'

'Just look. Tell me what you see,' she replied.

After tacking Phoenix up and setting off to the gallop, Dylan stood at the side and watched closely through his binoculars. He observed the horse's knees rise high in the air, then slam down with force to the ground as he pelted down the strip. The penny dropped. Clever Flora for noticing it. He couldn't help but admire her as she came trotting back with a look of hope on her face.

'What do you think?' she panted, dismounting.

'He's got high knee action.'

'Exactly! Phoenix isn't meant for the flat. He's a jump horse.'

Dylan frowned.

'Look at his pedigree,' urged Flora.

'I have,' replied Dylan.

'But the *dam's* sire was a jump horse,' she insisted.

Dylan nodded and thought for a moment. What was he going to tell Roper? 'Flora, Graham Roper is coming at the end of the week.' His heart broke to see her face fall.

'Don't let him take him, Dylan,' she pleaded.

'He owns him, sweetheart. I can't stop him,' he spoke gently.

'Please, Dylan,' she begged.

Dylan sighed. What in God's name was he to do?

35

Finula stifled a yawn. Getting up so early to be ready for the 7 a.m. start after a late night working was taking its toll already. She glanced to the side of her. Marcus was busy concentrating on his driving, and soon they would be off the motorway and entering Shropshire. The journey hadn't taken too long and it had passed particularly quickly as they chatted and laughed comfortably together. It occurred to Finula again how at ease he was when it was just the two of them, compared to his more serious, intense side when working. She wondered who else he could relax with, when he wasn't amongst his colleagues.

Finula longed to learn more about Marcus. So far, he had been a closed book, never talking about his family or his past, and it had started to intrigue her. She only really knew what she had gleaned from looking him up online months ago; about his career and that he had been married once, briefly. He had talked a little about his mother, who had died last year, but there had been no mention of his father.

Instinctively Finula had refrained from probing, sensing his need for privacy, but now she *did* want to know. After all, he knew all there was to know about her, didn't he? He'd been living in her home for the past few weeks, got to know her dad, her friends, and was pretty hands on with her, she reflected happily. This weekend would bring them closer together. She hoped he'd really unwind and switch off, giving her his full attention.

She looked again at his profile. Hell, he was handsome, in a dark, brooding way that appealed to her. His forehead held a slight frown, as it so often did. Why? What was going on in that complex mind of his? Surely, it couldn't always be work. He had once chastised her for being 'all work and no play' so he must appreciate a decent work-life balance. So, what exactly did he have on his mind? The words of the clairvoyant sprung into her head: *Your revenge will not be sweet.* What a strange thing to say and yet… it did seem to have had an effect on him at the time, for some reason.

'Nearly there,' he said, turning off the motorway junction. He glanced at her and smiled. It felt good having Finula by his side as he made his way home.

She was the only girl he'd brought back there. Usually he would date in London, where he frequently worked, and chose to keep his house as the safe, private haven he had bought it to be, tucked away in the Shropshire hills. But with Finula, it had seemed the most natural thing to do, to bring her back to share his world. His emotions for her had taken him by surprise. He had never expected to feel like this about anyone, especially so soon after his mammy's death.

'I must confess to having a peep at your house on the internet.'

Marcus grinned to himself; she was so open and honest. Many a girl wouldn't have admitted to that, even if they had had a sneaky look.

'Now, why am I not surprised to hear that, Finula?' he chuckled, pulling onto a roundabout signposted 'Deacon's Castle'.

'Deacon's Castle, that sounds so quaint,' remarked Finula.

'It is. There's lots of history to it. The village once had a castle owned by a rich deacon and when it was destroyed, the stones from the castle were used to build many of the surrounding buildings. The local pub, for one.'

'Really?'

'Yeah, we've picked a good time to come. There's an arts festival here this weekend. It's always a great atmosphere. There are flags hanging from the shops and bunting across the streets. There's lots going on, with dance, music, singing, workshops and films, in all kinds of venues.'

'Fantastic! When you say venues, do you mean shops and pubs?'

'Not just that. Churches, libraries, hotels and galleries open up, too. The festival's a big deal in Deacon's Castle.'

'Marcus, it sounds amazing!' Finula could hardly contain herself.

Then, he carefully turned down a rural side road.

'It's a bit bumpy,' he warned as the 4 x 4 jostled up and down the uneven dirt track, which ran up into the hills.

Eventually he pulled into a cobbled driveway and parked outside his home. Finula's eyes widened with delight. It was every bit as pretty as she'd remembered from seeing it online, with its black timber frame, the white walls covered with ivy. The windows were leaded and had boxes underneath them containing bright winter pansies. The garden, although quite void of colourful plants, with it being November, was still perfectly maintained.

Together they carried their luggage to the front porch and, once inside, Finula was struck by how neat and tidy Marcus' home was.

'Who looks after your house when you're not here?' she asked. Clearly someone was keeping the place shipshape.

'A couple from the village come once a fortnight to clean and garden.' He smiled to himself again: she didn't miss a trick. Her eyes were darting about the place, taking everything in, from the wood burner nestled inside an open brick fireplace, embedded with a driftwood mantle, to the wooden beams running along the ceiling, to the stone floor covered mainly with rag rugs. A rocking chair stood under a window, which looked out on to the lush jade hills. There was no television, nor any kind of music system that she could see, just bookcases crammed full of books, and magazines piled high on a coffee table. As if reading her thoughts Marcus explained.

'I don't like any form of distraction when I'm here. It's strictly chill-out territory. In fact, you'll struggle to get a signal for your phone, or internet connection.'

'Is that why you bought this place?' she laughed, 'so no one can contact you?'

'Yes,' he replied, looking deep into her eyes. He moved to stand in front of her. Finula's heart started to beat faster. 'It's just you and me now,' he said quietly, and Finula's legs went weak.

They spent the day exploring the many stalls, open studios and the artisan market that Deacon's Castle Festival had to offer. Finula was captivated by the place. She loved wandering among the artists and crafts people selling their wares of furniture, jewellery, ceramics and silk. Inside the Public Hall, oil paintings, watercolours, textiles and cards were exhibited, whilst the Women's Institute served afternoon tea under gazebos in the vicarage garden. Circus acts performed along the steep, narrow streets: jugglers, stilt walkers and unicyclists. A bake-off was taking place in a nearby café and a banquet was laid out in the restaurant next door. Classic films were played in the top room of the Deacon Castle Inn and a brass band could be heard playing from inside the church. All in all, it was magical and Finula was totally spellbound.

'Oh, Marcus, it's just wonderful!' Her eyes shone with excitement.

'I thought you'd like it,' he replied, passing her a cup of mulled wine from a nearby stall. Dusk was falling now and the old Victorian streetlamps had started to glimmer, giving the little town an even more enchanting feel.

'Let's get something to eat.' She pointed towards a spit roast on the side of the street.

'Yeah, but let's take it back.' They'd spent all day at the festival and Marcus wanted a sit down, plus an Irish whiskey in front of his wood burner.

Within the hour the pair were munching their hog roasts, sipping whiskey in Marcus' cosy lounge. He never drew his curtains, preferring to look out at the dark sky, scattered with stars like diamonds. Only the light from the fire filled the room. Finula hadn't felt this relaxed for a long time and suspected Marcus hadn't either.

Once they'd finished eating, Marcus refilled their glasses. She was sitting leaning against him on the sofa, totally at ease.

'Marcus, tell me about your ex-wife,' she asked quietly.

Although a touch taken aback by the question, he answered without hesitation.

'I met Niamh at uni. We were together for two years, then married when we found out she was pregnant. Unfortunately, Niamh miscarried our baby and then… well, we drifted apart. We're still good friends, though. I see her occasionally through work. She's a researcher.'

'Oh,' Finula replied flatly. Marcus again smiled at her transparency.

'I'm good friends with her husband, too. In fact, I'm godfather to their eldest son, Callum.'

'Oh, right.' She sounded a little perkier, making Marcus laugh out loud.

'What?' She looked up at him, bewildered.

'You. You're such an open book, Finula.'

'I am not!' she replied indignantly.

'You so are.'

'To be sure, I am not Marcus Devlin,' she mimicked his Irish voice, badly.

'That, darlin', has got to be the worst Irish accent I've ever heard,' he spluttered.

She loved the way he'd called her 'darling'. Suddenly they caught each other's eye and sat completely still until Marcus put his glass down. 'This way,' he said huskily.

He led her up the creaky, wooden stairs, ducked under the low beam on the landing and into his bedroom. It was small, containing only a double bed covered in a pale grey bedspread, and a bedside table. The room was filled with moonlight shining through the large, leaded window. Marcus took her in his arms and his mouth sought hers. Finula responded instantly, kissing him back urgently. She breathed him in, that sexy, tangy citrus fragrance he had, and pulled him closer. Marcus took a gentle handful of her hair and tugged her head further back to deepen his kiss. Finula's hands moved over him, encouraging him out of his clothes. In moments he was stood naked in front of her. Her eyes devoured his broad, dark chest, hard, muscular thighs, slim waist and swollen erection.

'I want you,' she whispered as Marcus pressed his lips to the hollow at her throat and to the freckles that dusted her shoulders.

Feverishly he yanked her top off and unbuttoned her jeans. Soon their bodies were entwined on the bed. He eased back a little to savour the moment and ran his hands down the length of her naked, alabaster-white body, over the curve of her breasts, the swell of her stomach and the round of her hips. She felt soft and warm beneath his touch. He cupped her breasts as his lips and tongue sucked and licked them. He heard her moan. Then he slid his hands between her thighs and pushed them apart, feeling the slick heat and smoothness of her. 'Finula,' he groaned, easing himself between her legs. He edged into her, with infinite slowness and unhurried strokes. Her hands brushed his toned back as he thrust deeper, making her arch in pleasure. He started to move harder and faster, taking Finula into ecstasy, and she cried out his name as he finally exploded inside her. They held each other tightly. Marcus blinked back the tears in his eyes, which took him by surprise. He hadn't felt this close to another person for such a long, long time. He rolled to one side and pulled her onto his chest. 'Finula, you're amazing,' he said gently, kissing her head. Finula hugged him.

'So are you,' she whispered back.

Together they fell into a blissful sleep.

36

The next morning Finula woke to the sound of church bells ringing. Rubbing her eyes, she turned to see an empty space next to her. Frowning, she listened carefully, to see if she could hear Marcus in the house but all was silent. Then she noticed a note on the bedside table.

I'll be back by 10 a.m. Help yourself to breakfast, or enjoy a lie-in and I'll make it when I return. x

Where had he gone? Deciding to shower and get dressed, Finula got up from the crumpled bed. No wonder it was so creased, the action it'd seen last night, she giggled to herself. Then, curiosity got the better of her and she decided to take a peep inside Marcus' bedside table. Opening the drawer reminded her of when she had opened Nick Fletcher's glove compartment and found that rather incriminating evidence of his bisexuality. The drawer was empty, apart from one envelope and Finula couldn't resist taking it out and looking. Inside was the same photograph he'd sent her two months ago. The one he'd taken of her as a bridesmaid. A warm glow tingled inside her. He'd kept a copy for himself. How flattering, she thought with glee, carefully placing it back inside.

The church was fairly busy as Marcus slid quietly into the back pew. He had just lit a candle and offered up a prayer. Marcus felt closest to his mammy in church, she having been a devout Christian. Marcus did have a faith deep down, but he also had some burning questions that needed answering. Like why did his mammy have to die? She was all he had. No other family except an aunt, a scattering of cousins and a father he'd never known. His eyes misted over at the injustice of it all. Stark, vivid images of her fading away from him in pain swamped his mind. Her sallow, sunken skin and dark, bruised eyes haunted him. Then, as always, his memories inevitably cast back to her last words, telling him in breathless gasps, but with utter determination to finish, who his father really was. Marcus often wondered how it would have unfolded if Richard Cavendish-Blake hadn't died and he had been given the opportunity to actually meet him. What would he have said? Would his father have believed him? He turned to watch the candle he'd just lit flicker. How fragile life was; how easily it could be snuffed out, just like that flame.

A little later, driving back, Marcus' mood began to lift at the thought of being with Finula again. It felt warmly comforting returning to a home that wasn't empty for once. Entering through the back door into the kitchen, he was greeted by the smell of bacon and eggs cooking. Finula was there, hovering over the hob, bright eyed and smiling.

'Ah, good of you to make it, Marcus.'

Marcus laughed and kissed her lips. 'Hello, you. I've been to Mass,' he explained.

Finula's eyebrows raised, 'Really?' She didn't have him down as a churchgoer.

'Hmm, I do occasionally. It feels good for the soul,' he smiled.

Finula couldn't work out if he was serious or not.

'I'd have gone with you, if you'd mentioned it.'

'Would you?'

'Sure. Now, sit down and enjoy.' She'd laid the small table in the kitchen and placed two English breakfasts down.

'This looks delicious, Finula. Thanks.'

They chatted over a leisurely breakfast and Marcus couldn't remember when he'd ever felt this relaxed. Finula, too, seemed less stressed, just spending time at her own pace, instead of rushing round The Templar at top speed. It was times like this that made her reflect a little on her own lifestyle. Would she always want to live with her dad in a busy pub, permanently on call?

As if reading her mind, Marcus looked into her eyes and said, 'Finula, let's stay another night. We can head back tomorrow morning.' He reached his hand out over the table and she held it.

'Let's,' she replied.

They spent the day wandering around Deacon's Castle again, only this time it was a lot quieter. The festival had finished and packed up, leaving the narrow cobbled streets bare. Only a few shops were open. One of them was a book and record shop, which also doubled up as a café. Marcus was obviously well known to the shopkeeper as they sat down and ordered coffee and cake.

'Good to see you, Marcus,' said an elderly lady with a twinkle in her eye. 'And who's this young lady?' She turned to Finula.

'Margo, meet Finula,' he answered with a grin.

'Oh, what a pretty name,' said Margo.

'For a pretty lady,' replied Marcus, still smiling at Finula, who was by now blushing slightly.

'Please to meet you, Margo.'

Finula loved Deacon's Castle. It had a vibe all of its own, in a vintage, quirky kind of way. Again, thoughts of leaving The Templar crossed her mind, and she realised she wasn't in any hurry to go home. She liked the idea of being hidden away here with Marcus. She looked at him as he chatted comfortably with Margo. Gone was the frown that so often etched his brow, and the tension that radiated from him frequently. Here, he was just Marcus, just one of the locals, not an award-winning documentary producer with the stress and worries that involved. What was that comment he'd made this morning about good for the soul? He did seem a tortured soul at times and it was starting to concern her.

Later that evening, after eating a stir-fry that Marcus had rustled up, they sat by the wood burner again, sipping red wine. She made him laugh with stories of her childhood.

'How old were you when you lost your mammy, Finula?' Marcus asked quietly.

'Eleven.'

He hugged her into him, 'Jeysus, that's no age.'

'I know, and I miss her every day. How about you, Marcus, do you have any contact with your dad?'

He stiffened suddenly and she could see he was trying to stay calm. 'He's dead,' he replied flatly.

Finula was startled by the coldness in his voice, which was completely devoid of any filial emotion. 'And I never met him,' he finished with a firmness that closed the conversation.

Finula took the hint and remained silent. Marcus, realising how abrupt he must have sounded, put his wine glass down. He ran his hand through her silky hair and kissed her neck, then made his way to her mouth and kissed her deeply, running his tongue over hers. Finula responded by clutching him nearer, suddenly wanting to feel his skin against hers. Their kiss grew more urgent. They tugged and pulled at each other's clothes impatiently until they were both naked, lying on the rag rug by the wood burner. Marcus closed his mouth over her creamy breast and flicked his tongue over the jutting nipple, whilst running his hand between her soft thighs. His finger slid into her warm parting and slowly circled her core, making Finula gasp in pleasure. 'Have you any idea what you do to me?' he asked huskily, looking into her face as his finger probed inside her.

'Marcus,' she gasped again, arching her back upwards towards him. He increased the pressure of his touch, intensifying her desire. Then, just when she thought she'd burst, he thrust himself firmly into her. His strokes were hard and rapid, he was pent up with emotion and passion and needed a release; it came within seconds, leaving them both dizzy. He sunk his head into her neck and took deep breaths.

Finula felt wetness on her shoulder. 'Marcus,' she whispered, 'are you crying?'

He lifted his head up and tears were streaming down his face.

'Marcus, what's the matter?' she asked, her face etched with concern. She wrapped her arms round him, like a mother would her child. Gently she rocked him, whilst his sobs finally came to a halt.

'I'm sorry, Finula, you shouldn't have seen that.' He unwrapped himself from her embrace and wiped his face.

'Don't be silly, Marcus. It's never wrong to show your feelings.' He looked away, embarrassed. 'Do you want to talk about it?'

He turned and stared into her. Should he? Could he? No. 'I can't,' he simply replied, leaving Finula at a complete loss.

37

Tobias eyed the report with utter satisfaction. When he'd asked David Lombard to do some digging, he never expected a find like this. As Lombard had told him, his contact had only had to scratch the surface, and the results were startling.

Viola Kemp – or Vera Kemp, to be more precise – had led quite an eventful life, and not in a good way. From what the PI had discovered, she'd left a trail of destruction behind her wherever she went. Although described as intelligent and ambitious, there was no camouflaging the dark, sinister streak running through her. Viola had been born into humble surroundings, but had undoubtedly made the most of her brains, as her impressive qualifications proved. She had also made the most of her looks, undergoing extensive plastic surgery. But for all that she had achieved, the brushes with the law remained the most telling part of her story. Viola had been labelled a 'troubled teenager' and had been arrested for shoplifting. In her early twenties she had been stopped by the police for driving whilst under the influence of alcohol.

However, the most chilling turn of events had left Tobias wide eyed with shock. Viola had been convicted of stalking an ex-boyfriend and, more alarming, had taken to drastic, frightening measures to warn his, then, partner away. Viola had left dead animals on the girl's car bonnet, squashed hedgehogs, birds, mice. Then came the relentless hate mail, phone calls and text messages full of scorn and threats. Eventually, Viola had had a restraining order issued against her with – and this is where Tobias' interest was really piqued – a suspended sentence. Basically, if Viola Kemp ever stepped out of line again, she'd likely face imprisonment.

Well, it seemed I've struck gold, thought Tobias, smiling to himself. He could very easily report her for harassment; she'd admitted to 'following him around for some time' to the point that she claimed to know more about him than his own wife, plus she had exposed herself to him, then trailed after him to his study, propositioned him and then threatened him. If this wasn't enough ammunition to keep Viola quiet and out of the way, what was? In fact, he would demand more than just her silence. The interview she had conducted was a travesty. He was in no doubt just how it was intended to portray him, given the nature of the questions, insinuations and allegations thrown at him. He should have trusted his own instincts and kept the media away, even though Treweham Hall wouldn't have benefited from the hefty fee paid. After a few moments' consideration he decided on a plan. The film crew had taken enough footage inside the Hall and the grounds, plus they had the interview with Sebastian – they could use that. His interview had to go, though: wiped clean, deleted. Was it his fault if it suddenly went missing? After all, he had kept his side of the bargain, hadn't he? And he knew just the person to clear this mess up.

Tobias was in his drawing room with Zac at his feet. The dog's ears pricked up when he heard Megan enter the room. 'Ah, there you are.' She was wearing dungarees and carrying a paint brush, which made Tobias smile, reminding him of his pot-bellied workmen. Megan caught his expression and laughed. 'I know I don't look very glamorous, but they're *so* comfy.'

Getting up from the sofa, he went and put his arms round her. 'You look beautiful,' he said, smiling, 'but I'm not sure you ought to be painting in your condition,' he gently warned.

'Don't fuss. I'm fine. Come and see what I've been doing.' Megan led him into the future nursery and Tobias stood back and admired his wife's handiwork. She had painted a mural on the far wall containing every children's character imaginable. There was a forest with Hansel and Gretel's gingerbread house, together with Red Riding Hood walking through the trees, followed by a wolf, the Pied Piper played his flute with children dancing around him, Jack and Jill were tumbling down a hill in the distance, whilst Humpty Dumpty sat on a stone wall. Rapunzel's plait dangled from a tower, whilst a frog floating on a water lily waited patiently to be kissed into a charming prince. It was enchanting and Tobias was bowled over by Megan's talent.

'What do you think?' she asked.

'Megan, it's absolutely fantastic.' His eyes took in all the detail. He shook his head in amazement. 'How do you do it?' he asked in awe.

'I just let my imagination run riot,' she laughed.

'Come here, you.' He hugged her warmly. Nothing and nobody would ruin this precious time in their lives, he'd make damn sure of it.

38

Well, this wasn't one for the claustrophobic, mused Sebastian, as his body, laid flat on a trolley and head strapped into a moulded hard pillow, was slowly manoeuvred into the narrow tunnel of the MRI machine. Trying to relax and, most importantly, keep still, Sebastian projected his mind to happier times – standing ovations, thundering applauses, after show celebrations – then his mind moved warmly to Jamie's face, full of compassion and care. Those smoky-grey eyes had willed him to disclose all and to totally offload the mountainous worries that had gradually built up over time. He had sat and listened, never interrupted, but instead let him finish. After Sebastian had completely shared just about everything that was on his mind, Jamie finally spoke.

'If you need any form of support, I'd be happy to help. Let me drive you to the hospital. Don't be on your own.' Sebastian was touched and the relief Jamie's kind words gave was huge.

'Thank you, Jamie,' he had replied, and truly meant it.

Now, here he was, getting his brain scanned, while Jamie was sitting patiently in the waiting room. It was to be a full day at the hospital, making Sebastian even more grateful for Jamie's company. After the brain scan in the morning, a lumbar puncture was to be performed late in the afternoon. This was the more daunting for Sebastian, especially after having read all the leaflets about the procedure. Willing himself to have courage, he had signed all the necessary paperwork first thing on arrival, before giving himself any chance to change his mind. It was for his own good, he kept telling himself, blocking out the side effects and possible consequences, which the doctors had had to explain. It threatened to be a frightening experience, and one that he had dreaded facing alone. Thankfully he didn't have to any more.

Sebastian closed his eyes and tried to ignore the noise and vibrations of the machinery as it clicked and scanned inside his skull. What would it find? He gulped away the fear and concentrated once more on positive thoughts.

Outside, in the waiting room, Jamie flicked through the *Filmmaker* magazine. One day his wishes would be fulfilled and he'd be as successful as Marcus Devlin. Jamie was tenacious, he had drive, and was resolute in his ambition to climb up the career ladder to reach the same dizzying heights of those he had admired: Sebastian, for one. Who would have thought that just a few, short months ago, whilst he had so eagerly admired his performance at the Royal Shakespeare Theatre, he'd be here, giving him moral support in a hospital? For all Sebastian's fame, confidence and joviality, he was, deep down, the same as him: somebody who needed somebody. Jamie appreciated Sebastian's honesty, and the way he had trusted him with very private matters. It was a privilege to listen to his innermost fears and be there for him. Sebastian would have his absolute discretion, something he didn't think Sebastian had enjoyed with other friends or lovers. Right now, all Jamie wanted to do was comfort Sebastian, to take away all his troubles and anxieties, if he'd let him.

After what seemed an age, the noise stopped. Sebastian was able to speak to the nurses standing behind a glass screen. 'Is that it?'

'Almost, Sebastian. We're just going to move you further inside to scan your neck now. You're doing really well,' they encouraged.

Moments later Sebastian felt another vibration and his body edged further down the tunnel. Then the noise started again.

At last it was over. He had a few hours' reprieve before the lumbar puncture. Sebastian walked back into the waiting area to see Jamie there, face etched with concern.

'How did it go?' he asked as Sebastian took a seat next to him.

'Fine, all I had to do was keep still. It's this afternoon I'm worried about.'

'You'll be OK, I promise.' Jamie laid his hand over Sebastian's.

'I'm glad you're here, Jamie.' Sebastian looked into his eyes. 'I don't think I could do this alone.'

'Well, you're not alone,' replied Jamie firmly.

'Sebastian, we need you to lie on the bed and curl up your legs to your chin as high as possible. This will spread open your spine, making it easier to insert the needle between the discs.'

As the doctor had explained, she was to give him two injections in his back. The first to numb the surface area, then a second to allow a deeper anaesthetic, enabling the long, thin needle to pass right into his spine and extract brain fluid.

This time Jamie was allowed to sit next to the bed. He held Sebastian's hand, as the first injection entered his back. After a few minutes the second anaesthetic was inserted. Sebastian flinched slightly and gripped Jamie's hand tightly. 'Now, Sebastian, I'm going to gently place the lumbar puncture needle into your spine. The fluid may flow out, or it could come drip by drip, so bear with us.' Luckily the fluid was collected into test tubes pretty quickly. All the time Jamie's hand clasped Sebastian's. Within twenty minutes it was all over.

'Do you want to look?' asked the doctor.

'Yes.' Sebastian turned his head to see two test tubes of what looked like water.

'It's nice and clear, not cloudy, which is a good sign,' remarked the doctor.

'Thanks,' replied Sebastian rather lamely. It had been a long day and he wanted to go home.

Knowing the results would be imminent, Sebastian wanted to take time out and reflect before facing the onslaught of what his life had in store for him. As Jamie drove them back to Treweham, he suddenly didn't want to just say goodbye to him at The Templar.

'Jamie, let's go for something to eat, somewhere quiet, just the two of us.'

Jamie turned and smiled. 'Sounds like a good idea.' He patted Sebastian's knee and once more Sebastian was filled with an unfamiliar warm reassurance.

39

Phoenix took off at pace over the fence and landed perfectly with ease and balance. Flora patted his neck. 'Good boy,' she gushed, swallowing the cold, frosty air. Her gut feeling had been proved well and truly right. There was absolutely no doubt in her mind: Phoenix was a jump racehorse, not a flat racer, as he'd been previously trained. After he'd seen how the horse could hurdle the fences Flora had set up in the paddock, there was no hesitation in Dylan's mind either. In fact, all the yard staff couldn't help but be impressed by Phoenix and how naturally he had adapted to flying through the air with effortless strength and poise. They were all thrilled with him, and Flora was ecstatic.

Dylan, however, was dreading the impending visit from the horse's owner, Graham Roper. The fact that Flora had been so right about Phoenix had left him with a terrible dilemma. Phoenix had real talent, but not the kind Roper was after. As far as Roper was concerned, his horse couldn't win a flat race to save itself. However, if he discovered

Phoenix's enormous potential as a jump racer, would he decide to take him elsewhere? And how would Flora cope without Phoenix? Christ, he couldn't bear the thought of Flora's reaction. He'd never seen her connect so well with a horse; the two worked together flawlessly. The problem was really playing on his mind. What he really needed was time – time to put Roper off and give himself a chance to think of a solution – but Dylan didn't have that luxury. As he saw Roper's car in the distance through his office window, driving down the track, he quickly ran to the paddock and warned Flora to put Phoenix in his stable, well out of the way.

Slamming his car door shut, Graham Roper marched towards the office. Dylan caught up with him, after returning from the paddock.

'Hello, Graham.'

Roper turned abruptly, 'Well, any news?'

Once again Dylan resisted the urge to punch the arrogant swine's bloated face. 'This way.' He guided him into his office. Dylan certainly didn't want any of the staff to overhear this conversation. Dylan took a deep breath as Roper stared into him, obviously expecting results. 'It's not good news, Graham. Phoenix is never going to win a flat race,' he told him directly.

'What?' Roper spat. 'You mean I've wasted a shed-load of money on that fucking animal for nothing?'

Dylan winced; the compulsion to hit this bastard suddenly increased. 'He's not going to perform the way you want.'

'Well, I've gathered that!' Roper's face was flushed in anger. He sat down on the chair next to Dylan's desk and stared into space. Dylan moved to sit opposite him. He opened the desk drawer to get the necessary paperwork. Then hesitated. He looked at Roper who was sitting still, speechless.

'I suppose…'

Roper's face shot up sharply, 'What?'

'If you don't want to spend any more money on the horse—'

'Too fucking right,' he snorted, then searched Dylan's face for an answer to his mounting problem.

'Well,' sighed Dylan, desperate to sound convincing, 'I could try and find a buyer, someone to take him off your hands.'

Roper gave a harsh laugh. 'Like who? Who in their right mind would want that?'

Dylan paused, then shrugged for effect. 'I'll put the feelers out, see if there's any interest.'

Roper looked beaten. His tone suddenly lacked anger, or any emotion at all. He shook his head in defeat. 'You do that, Dylan.' He got up from the chair and looked out of the office window. 'Which stable is he in?'

Dylan had to think on his feet. The last thing he needed right now was for Roper to see what good shape his horse was in. 'Er… Flora's just taken him out for some exercise. She'll be a while yet.' Then he quickly added, 'You can leave him here until I find a buyer.' Roper turned and looked quizzically at him. 'It'll save time if someone's interested in him, to come straight here,' Dylan added.

'Whatever,' Roper replied, totally lacking any interest by this point. 'Just get rid of it quick, Delany,' he threw over his shoulder, as a parting shot before slamming the door behind him.

Dylan watched him rev up his car and speed off, churning up a trail of dirt behind him. Dylan sat back in his chair and expelled a sigh of relief. With his hands behind his dark curls, he narrowed his eyes and thought long and hard. To be fair, he hadn't actually lied to Roper, had he? He'd just been economical with the truth. He'd told him that Phoenix would never win a flat race, and he wouldn't. The fact that he could jump like a dream and was more suited to soft ground he had kept to himself – and with good reason. Roper was no horse lover. He merely saw them as a means to make money. His whole attitude repulsed Dylan. He had no guilty conscience whatsoever, knowing he had acted in Phoenix's best interest, not to mention Flora's, whom he would protect at all costs.

His feelings for her grew stronger by the day and he simply couldn't imagine life without her. This was alien to Dylan, who had, up until now, woven his way in and out of relationships, refusing any form of commitment. Now the tables had turned. He did want Flora, more than anything, but was she ready to commit? After all, she was only twenty. Her twenty-first birthday was in two weeks' time, just before Christmas. He so wanted to make it special for her, especially as her parents were still away on their travels round Europe in a campervan, and her brother had decided to stay with his friends over the holidays. A party, that's what he'd do, throw a fabulous twenty-first birthday party for her. She deserved to be made a fuss of, after all she'd done. Flora had single-handedly kept the show on the road when he'd been recovering from his fall. His idea gathered momentum. He pictured a marquee dressed with a winter wonderland theme, guests laughing over mulled wine, glowing candles, tables decorated with holly and ivy, a small band playing festive music, maybe a hog roast... His thought were interrupted by the phone. 'Delany's Racing Yard.'

'It's me. Is the coast clear?' hissed Flora, making Dylan smile to himself.

'Yes. He's gone.'

'Good.' There was a pause. Knowing her stomach would be in knots, Dylan spoke.

'Phoenix is staying, for the moment.'

'Oh, thank God for that!' His heart melted. Now all he needed to do was stump up the money and try to buy a top-class horse from under the owner's nose.

40

Tobias was getting tetchy. It was always the same in early December. Treweham Hall was thrown into total chaos, as his mother insisted on the traditional festive decoration of the Hall. This was no mean feat, and resembled a military operation, rather than a family preparing for Christmas. A fir tree of gigantic proportions was always ordered and delivered from Norway. Getting the huge tree securely in place in the hallway was a mammoth task, as was climbing the ladder and balancing from the staircase and landing to decorate it. Megan was strictly forbidden to go anywhere near it, not even to lift a bauble. Poor Henry had been given the onerous task of placing the angel right at the top and, given his lack of head for heights, he was hardly the ideal candidate. Aunt Celia had landed on them again, much to Sebastian's despair. Beatrice was on full alert, ordering the whole household about.

In the end, Tobias had quietly slipped away and headed for The Templar. He had unfinished business with a certain person to be found there. The television crew only had a few more days in Treweham, according to Megan. Finula had told her that Marcus and his team would be leaving shortly, after filming the village's yuletide preparations, and after that, they'd be gone. Tobias strode into the village with purpose, the report he'd got from David Lombard tucked neatly inside his woollen coat. On entering The Templar he was greeted by Dermot.

'Hello there, Tobias, what can I get you?'

'Just an orange juice, please, Dermot.' He waited for Dermot to pass him his drink before taking a sip, then asked, 'Where can I find Viola Kemp?'

Dermot looked a little surprised. 'I've not long served her lunch. She'll be at the far end of the dining room.'

'Thanks.' Tobias nodded and went in search of her.

What did he want with Viola? Wondered Dermot.

Viola had just finished her meal and was sipping a tonic water whilst going through her notes. The interviews she had conducted were labelled and in chronological order. All her research was neatly stored and easily accessible. The contact details of every person contributing to the documentary had been stored, in case they needed to be approached again. She was just finishing when a shadow fell across her laptop. Looking up, she saw Tobias glaring down at her. Well, well, well, what could he want? Second thoughts, perhaps? Hardly surprising, judging by the size of his wife. He must be gagging for it by now. Viola sensed triumph, and a warm glow rose through her.

'I'd like a word, in private.' Tobias sounded firm and in control. But then, he would, wouldn't he? Somebody like Tobias wasn't likely to come contrite, full of regret and remorse. That would be so unlike the aristocratic playboy he was at heart. Viola smiled smugly: how the mighty crumble.

'So where would you like to go, in private?' She arched an eyebrow.

'Your room.' That way no one would overhear him.

Hell, he really was desperate for her. Basking in her victory, Viola shut her laptop. 'This way,' she said, the conceited laughter in her voice evident.

Tobias was thankful that nobody saw them as he followed her up the stairs. She had composure, he'd give her that, with her straight back and shoulders, head held high. It would be interesting to see if she still had the same composure once he'd finished what he had to say.

Closing the door behind him, he reached for the envelope inside his coat.

Frowning, Viola asked, 'What's that?'

'I decided to do a little research myself,' he replied, staring her in the face. Did he detect a slight flicker of apprehension? 'And it uncovered some things that were most interesting.'

She stood and watched in silence. This wasn't going at all to plan.

'It appears you've led quite an... eventful life, haven't you, Viola? Or should I say, *Vera?*'

She gulped, her eyes growing wide like saucers.

Tobias continued, 'That's quite a list you've racked up: drink driving, shoplifting, *stalking*. I take it your employers are unaware of your past? But how would it look if it was all resurrected, just like you threatened to resurrect my past?' Viola's eyes darted to the brown envelope in Tobias' hand and she swallowed again. 'Especially with a suspended sentence hanging over you,' he finished with force.

'I... I've done nothing wrong,' she croaked weakly.

'Nothing wrong? You came into my home, admitted "researching" me to the point of obsession, you exposed yourself to me, propositioned me, then threatened me.' His glare bored into her, making her tremble slightly. She licked her lips nervously.

'So, what are you going to do?'

'Here's the deal. You are going to delete all the footage of my interview.'

'What? I can't do that!' she rasped.

'Oh, I think you can, Vera. Your reputation and career depend upon it.'

'How? I can't just erase stuff like that. It's with Len and Libby, probably Marcus, too, by now.'

'Then you'd better gain access to it all somehow and destroy it. The interview with my brother and the filming inside the Hall and grounds you can keep.'

'Oh, thanks,' she replied with sarcasm.

'You're welcome,' he nodded back with a tight smile.

He threw the envelope at her. Inside was a copy of the report, but he'd kept the original. 'Read it for yourself. Don't be a fool. You do as I say and keep well away from me and my family, or else I'll have you slammed behind prison bars. Got it?'

Viola took the envelope with a shaking hand. Tears threatened to spill, tears of shock, anger and frustration; not of regret.

41

Finula had never been so happy. She'd always loved Christmas, ever since she was a child, and watching her dad haul out the decorations from the loft, her excitement grew. She was standing at the bottom of the ladder, being passed each of the dusty boxes full of trimmings.

'I think that's everything,' said Dermot, as he shone his torch round the dark, musty loft cavity.

'Let's get cracking then!' Finula picked up a couple of boxes and made her way down to the bar. She'd need to start decorating in there first, ready for that night's Christmas Cocktail Evening. Every year The Templar would celebrate the first weekend in December by having a cocktail evening when, for the first hour, the drinks were half price. It was always a huge success, bringing the village together at the start of the festive season.

Finula's imagination had spun into overdrive, inventing cocktails with a Christmas theme. Obviously, there would be the old favourite drinks of sherry and mulled wine, but her more creative Christmas cocktails were notorious, from the Sexy Santa's Snowballs, consisting of cognac, almond milk, double cream and crème de cacao, or the Ding Dong Merrily, with oranges, cloves, cinnamon, bay leaves and gin, to the Templar Tipsy Tipple with cranberry juice, citrus vodka, syrup and prosecco. It was an evening full of fun and laughter, and her favourite time to work. Tonight would be extra special as Marcus had volunteered his services behind the bar.

'Are you sure?' Finula asked him, not convinced he fully knew what he was letting himself in for.

'Sure. I've worked in a bar before. How do you think I survived as a student?'

'Good man, yourself,' butted in Dermot, overhearing, and he slapped Marcus heartily on the back. So that settled it. Marcus would be joining them, serving drinks to a packed pub.

It pleased Finula that her dad clearly liked Marcus, and she loved it that the two of them chatted easily together. Dermot had approved of Finula staying with Marcus in Shropshire, glad that she'd taken some well-deserved time out. Christmas was playing on his mind slightly, though – would his daughter choose to go to Shropshire again? The thought of spending Christmas alone wasn't a comforting one, but he'd never let his feelings show. Finula had a life of her own now and she deserved to be as happy as she evidently was. Secretly, he was also pleased that the centre of Finula's attention was Irish, and even from the same county as himself. The link made it extra special.

'So, what time do I report for duty?' Marcus asked.

'At 7 p.m. sharp,' replied Finula with a grin, then waved a set of antlers at him that she'd dug out from a box, 'and don't forget to wear these.'

'Really?' Marcus looked horrified, making Finula chuckle.

'No. Not if you don't want to,' she reasoned.

'You can wear one of my Christmas jumpers instead,' Dermot called over his shoulder, as he went back up the stairs for the rest of the decorations.

Once alone, Marcus grabbed Finula to him and kissed her long and hard. 'I've been dying to do that all morning,' he whispered huskily into her ear.

Finula giggled. 'Any other urges?'

Marcus nuzzled her neck. 'You bet. Is it your bed or mine tonight? I've no intention of sleeping another night alone with you under the same roof, darlin'.'

Finula had been wondering how that might pan out, picturing either herself or Marcus creeping clandestinely into the other's room. She wouldn't want to be caught red-handed by Viola or any other of the crew. Then again, how would her dad react to Marcus slinking into her bedroom?

Deciding for her, Marcus said, 'I'll come to you. I can be very discreet when I want to be.'

Finula believed him, and he could be secretive, too. On the one or two occasions when she'd tried to raise the issue of him crying in front of her, he'd brushed it away, refusing to talk about it, and it was beginning to worry her. There was evidently some problem he refused to share. He was obviously hiding something but what? When she had asked openly about his dad, the response was hardly what she had expected. He had simply clammed up. It was patently clear how close he must have been to his mother and the devastating affect her death had had on him. She imagined him caring for her towards the end of her life and her heart cried out for him. He'd done it all alone, with no brother or sister to support him. Despite his cool and calm outward appearance, his successful career and controlled poise, he was underneath a vulnerable man, with, she believed a troubled mind.

Dylan had just filled the bath with hot water, glistening with bubbles. He was looking forward to having a good soak after a hectic day at the yard. He heard Flora in the adjoining bedroom and poked his head through the door.

'Hey, come and join me.' His blue eyes were twinkling with mischief.

They were getting ready to go to The Templar that evening. Flora, too, found the thought of relaxing in a long, hot bath tempting.

'You know, I think I will,' she smiled back.

Within minutes she was lying between Dylan's muscular legs, having her back gently scrubbed.

'Hmm, that's lovely,' she purred, loving the soft feel of his hands against her skin. He pulled her hair to one side and kissed her neck.

'We should do this more often,' he said, as his kisses reached her shoulders. Flora closed her eyes in bliss.

'We should,' she agreed.

'Flora, I've been thinking about your birthday.'

'Yes?'

'How would you like a big bash to celebrate your twenty-first?'

There was a silence. Dylan frowned. Had he said the wrong thing?

'To be honest, it wouldn't feel right, with my parents being away.'

'Oh...' Had he been tactless?

'I'd rather celebrate, just the two of us.'

Whilst flattered, he couldn't help but feel she deserved more. Then he dully realised that what she *really* wanted was to keep Phoenix. That would be the icing on the cake, not some booze-up without her family. Once again, his mind mulled over the predicament. He pulled her onto his chest and hugged her.

'Fine, just the two of us then,' he murmured, whilst his hands began to wander over her breasts.

Back at the Hall, Megan was wearing a black dress that hid her bump rather flatteringly. She rounded it off with a fine silver woollen shawl. Tobias was waiting for her in the drawing room, sipping a brandy. He wasn't particularly looking forward to going to The Templar that night. He usually enjoyed the Christmas Cocktail Evening, but this time there would be company there he could well do without – the television crew. Good riddance to them when they finally left Treweham in a few days' time. It couldn't come soon enough for him.

'Right, I'm ready.' Megan entered the room.

Tobias looked towards his wife and all his worries and unhappiness evaporated. Megan looked radiant in pregnancy. She was positively glowing and he could burst with pride when seeing her beautiful, round belly, swelling with his child.

'You look wonderful.' He stood up and drained his drink. 'Let's go. Sebastian said he'd drive tonight.'

'Really? Won't he want to drink?'

'Apparently not.' Tobias agreed, it was a little strange that his brother had volunteered to take them all to The Templar, when usually he'd be downing the cocktails. Come to think of it, Sebastian had been rather subdued for a while now.

As expected, The Templar was packed to the rafters. Slade were belting out their Christmas hits, as Dermot, Finula and Marcus served drinks at break-neck speed to all the merry locals. Despite being made to wear a ridiculous reindeer sweater, Marcus was actually enjoying himself. The pub was trimmed with holly and ivy, a Christmas tree sparkled in the corner and the inglenook fire crackled invitingly. The atmosphere was buoyant and the cocktails were being knocked back with cheer and gusto.

'Hey, glad you made it!' called Finula to Megan, Tobias and Sebastian as they entered the bar.

'Wouldn't miss it for the world,' replied Megan. She turned to Marcus and smiled. He smiled back, then nodded towards Tobias standing next to her. Sebastian had gone off to join Jamie further down the pub. Tobias nodded back coolly. Arrogant shite, thought Marcus, not for the first time. Then he noticed how warmly he greeted Finula and Dermot. The contrast was almost embarrassing.

'Busy then?' he grinned at Finula.

'It's a madhouse! But I love it,' she laughed.

Marcus turned away to serve someone at the end of the bar. He was glad to go, feeling uncomfortable watching Tobias, Megan and Finula chat closely together. He suddenly felt an outsider and, to make matters worse, Dylan and Flora had just joined them. It was obvious how well they all got on, judging by their easy chatter and laughter. Marcus caught sight of Finula out of the corner of his eye as he poured another cocktail. There was no denying her contentment, being here with her friends. Then it dawned on him, like the warning of a death knell. How was Finula going to react once she'd seen the documentary? She had been angry enough just listening to Tobias' interview, so what would she make of the editing? He had reassured her that only he could endorse the finished film. His mouth went dry. He glanced again at the girl who had come to mean so much to him and he considered for the first time the pain of losing her.

Finula was fiery, passionate but, above all, loyal. Look how faithful she was towards her dad and The Templar, always putting herself last. How would she respond to someone casting her close friend in such a bad light? Then another dark thought struck him. What would Dermot think? This was the first time Marcus had allowed himself to stop and taken stock of his actions. The adrenalin of revenge had now disappeared and a sad, empty feeling had replaced it, making his eyes mist over with emotion.

'You OK, son?' Dermot asked, looking concerned.

Marcus' head shot up. 'Yeah, fine.' He quickly finished mixing the drinks and handed them over the bar.

Further down the bar, Viola was on her guard. Closely watching her colleagues enjoying themselves drinking back the cocktails, she told herself this was the time to make her move. She urgently needed to gain access to Len, Libby and Marcus' rooms. If Tobias had truly meant what he had threatened – and there was no doubt in her mind that he did – then she had to move fast.

Luckily Viola could be extremely resourceful when she needed to be. That morning she had noticed the cleaning staff were using a skeleton key card to enter each room. She had cunningly followed one cleaner after she'd finished all her duties and looked where she had put it, in the reception desk, second drawer on the right. Waiting till after the first cocktail hour, when everyone was getting nicely sozzled, she hastily made her way to the desk and got the key card.

Quickly, she made her way up the stairs. She knew her actions could cost her her career, but then again, if she didn't delete the interview footage from the cameras and laptops, she could end up behind prison bars, and her career would be ruined then anyway. Fortunately, the team shared passwords to access one another's work, as they were using laptops allocated to them, not personal ones. With a pounding heart and trembling hands, Viola did what she had to do.

Dylan noticed Gary and Tracy Belcher enter The Templar. He'd always liked them, finding their down-to-earth ways endearing. Several months ago they'd hosted a dinner party, which he'd been invited to and had thoroughly enjoyed their company. Dylan called them over and Gary shook hands with him.

'Hiya, mate, how you doing?' Gary's northern accent stood out, making Dylan smile.

'Fine, thanks, Gary, and you? Tracy, you look lovely as always.' He kissed her cheek, making her blush slightly.

'How's the training yard going?' she asked politely.

'Good, thanks.'

'Don't you ever miss racing?' Gary asked.

'Sometimes, yes,' nodded Dylan.

Gary, who was always up for a party, suddenly suggested, 'We should arrange a day at the races. It'd be fun.'

'Oh, yes!' cheered Tracy.

Dylan laughed. 'The next big meeting will be the Tingle Creek Chase at Sandown.'

'Sounds great. I really fancy going. What do you say, Dylan?'

'Why not?' Dylan replied, loving his enthusiasm.

'Do you know, I wouldn't mind learning to ride.' Gary looked thoughtful.

Dylan burst out laughing. 'You might want to lose some timber first.' He looked over Gary's bulging waistline.

'What you saying?' Gary pretended to look offended.

'That you're too fat to ride a horse,' cut in Tracy drily, making the two men laugh out loud.

It had given Dylan an idea, though, one that could just be the answer to his problem.

42

Sebastian had received another appointment to see the neurologist, to discuss the results of his brain scan and lumbar puncture. He knew the letter was coming, but seeing the facts there, in black and white, made it all the more real – and daunting.

Some Christmas this is going to be, he thought bitterly, shoving the letter in his jeans pocket.

Megan entered the drawing room, looking fresh faced and rosy cheeked. She'd just taken Zac for a walk round the grounds, and as always, Zac came thundering towards Sebastian full force.

'Hello, old boy.' The dog's tail thrashed against him as he bent down to stroke him.

'You've certainly got a friend there,' laughed Megan.

'Haven't I just,' he replied, smiling as Zac had now slumped onto the floor, belly up, wanting even more of a fuss. If only people were like dogs, reflected Sebastian, so open, honest and loyal, showing nothing but love and devotion. How much nicer the world would be. Was he getting cynical? But surely he had every right to be? He felt sure he was soon to receive some life-changing news and he didn't feel ready for it. He was ill equipped, too young, at the top of his career and not ready for it all to be over. It was all wrong.

'Sebastian, are you all right?' Megan's voice was quiet and full of concern.

He looked at her. She was the epitome of vitality, with her glowing, flawless complexion, thick, shiny brown hair and bright eyes. Life itself was growing steadily inside her, while he was feeling anything but vibrant at the moment. He felt drained, perturbed and on the brink of depression. If it wasn't for Jamie's support, mentally he would probably have sunk into a quagmire.

'Sebastian?' her voice was more urgent now.

He blinked. For a moment he considered telling her everything, then resisted. Instead he just sighed. 'Just exhausted. I'll be fine after a good night's sleep.'

Megan didn't look convinced. 'Listen, Sebastian, if there's anything wrong—'

'Ah, there you are!' interrupted Beatrice, dashing into the room. 'Look what I've found!' She held two large books covered in dust.

'What are they?' frowned Sebastian.

'Photograph albums, darling,' she replied with glee. 'I've had Henry retrieve them from Daddy's study.' She sat down next to Sebastian and beckoned Megan to join them.

Opening a page, Megan grinned at the first photograph. It was a large black-and-white picture of a young wife, holding her first-born. Beatrice had been a looker, no doubt, with shoulder-length blond hair swept back off her pretty face. She smiled elatedly into the camera, showing off her beautiful son and heir, wrapped in a pristine, white shawl. Behind her stood the doting husband and proud father, tall, dark and utterly handsome. Just like Tobias, thought Megan. There was no denying the likeness.

'This will be you soon,' chirped Beatrice, tapping Megan's lap. Then, turning to Sebastian, she said, 'And you too, darling, in time.'

Sebastian's eyes caught Megan's and they both suppressed a sigh. Dear God, did anybody truly know him? he thought bleakly.

The following day Sebastian once more made the journey to see the consultant. Jamie had wanted to accompany him, but the film crew were having their last meeting and he couldn't miss it. Sebastian didn't mind, feeling the need to be alone, unsure of his own reaction to the neurologist's findings.

Once settled in front of the consultant, Sebastian braced himself and, sitting straight backed, with cool composure, he listened carefully to what he had to say.

'Sebastian, your brain and neck scan showed two areas of inflammation.' He turned his computer screen to show him the scan images.

Sebastian's eyes homed in on the grey-white picture before him. It was a strange sensation, looking into your brain. The consultant's finger pointed towards a small, white blur to the upper right side of his brain, the size of a fifty-pence piece.

'As you can see, there is a slight sign of inflammation here, and,' he then flicked the screen to another picture, 'one here, at the base of your neck.'

'I see,' whimpered Sebastian, not really understanding at all.

'This inflammation has caused scarring, or legions, known as sclerosis.' Sebastian's eyes widened, recognising the term immediately. Multiple sclerosis. Oh my God. Seeing his alarmed face, the consultant nodded his head understandingly.

'Sebastian, you do have multiple sclerosis, but it is not the end of the world. Believe me.'

'But... nobody in the family has it,' he replied faintly, swallowing down the panic.

'It isn't hereditary.' The consultant pointed again to the screen, 'You have just a *very slight* sign of inflammation. I'm used to seeing scans with half the brain inflamed.' The doctor was trying to sound as reassuring as possible. Sebastian looked up at him, and the consultant's words gave him a little more confidence.

'Will I... will I end up in a wheelchair?' he gulped.

'You have primary progressive MS. Your symptoms are likely to progress *very* gradually. In some cases, MS sufferers' symptoms don't increase at all.'

'But... but I thought it was a compressed nerve, in my back, that's what I'd been told in the past,' insisted Sebastian, somewhat accusingly.

The consultant nodded, completely understanding how he must be feeling right now.

'My advice is this,' he said, and Sebastian's head shot up, willing to take any advice offered. 'Carry on as normal. You could have gone for years believing you had a compressed nerve. Unfortunately, you met me.'

'How have I got this? What's caused it?'

'In truth, we don't fully know. There are various theories. Have you ever been involved in an accident? Bumped your head?'

'No.'

'Stress or emotional trauma are other considerations.'

Well, he'd had plenty of that.

'How long have I had it?'

'The proteins in your brain fluid taken from the lumbar puncture tell us that you've had this quite a long time. I'd say about seven or eight years.'

Sebastian was dumbstruck. He'd been living his life with this for approximately eight years! It beggared belief.

Again, the neurologist attempted to calm him. 'Sebastian, I know this is a lot to take in, but there is plenty of support out there. You're not alone. You will remain in my clinic and I'll see you every six months, if necessary. Remember, you've had MS a long time, so you're actually doing remarkably well.'

He was right. This wasn't going to define him. With a steady breath, Sebastian stood up, shook the consultant's hand and made his way home.

43

For the last time on this project, the television crew sat patiently waiting for their producer to arrive. This time, however, there was a light, jubilant atmosphere of a congratulatory kind, as opposed to the tense, nervous ambience from the very first meeting. The final meeting was one that consisted only of last checks, thanks and farewells, so they didn't have anything to worry about. These meetings were notoriously upbeat and with it falling at Christmastime, there was an extra joyful lift.

Until, that is, Marcus came in, looking moody as always. It had an immediate effect on the rest of them. Viola sat up straight. She was particularly wary, not knowing yet if the deleted footage had been noticed. Judging by Libby's usual pleasant demeanour, she suspected not. Marcus, however, looked a little temperamental, but then again, that was nothing new.

'So,' Marcus threw his clipboard down on the table, 'let's take stock.' He looked straight at Viola. 'I'll need all the research, notes, contacts and details sending to me.'

'You have most of it already, but I'll make sure you get everything,' she responded.

He then turned to Len. 'All the rushes gone to Libby?'

'Yes, Libby has it all.'

Libby confirmed, 'I've reordered all the visual and audio material collected on each shoot to tell the best story. I've also assembled scenes for you to view.'

'Good. We'll start work on the rough cut after Christmas. I aim to get the first cut finished by early February.'

Libby's eyebrow rose. This was asking a lot, but wasn't unachievable. Marcus' talents lay in the selection and sequence of each scene, from its proportions, structures, rhythms and emphasis. From that would evolve the fine cut, paying attention to the details of each and every shot. Once that was agreed between Libby and Marcus, the sound designer, music composer and title designer would join them. Sound effects and music would be created and added to the final cut. Once everyone was happy with the final cut, an exact copy would be made.

It was a long and comprehensive process, one that would normally give Marcus a buzz, but a niggling doubt was holding him back this time. What had started as pure revenge was now morphing into something that could change everything. The words of that clairvoyant taunted him once more: *Your revenge will not be sweet.* Choosing to ignore his reservations, he carried on. 'Right, we're done here then.' He glanced round the table. 'Thanks, and have a great Christmas.' Turning to Libby again, he finished, 'We'll meet at the studio early January.' With that he marched out of the dining room and walked straight into Dermot.

'Can I have a word, Marcus?' Dermot looked serious. Jeysus, he hadn't seen him sneak into Finula's bedroom, had he?

'Er... yes.'

'This way.' Dermot led him over to a nearby alcove. 'Let me come straight to the point. The thing is, Marcus, I'd like you to stay here, with us, for Christmas.'

'Oh... right.' Marcus was touched. In truth, he had hoped Finula would join him in Shropshire, but realising she would never leave her dad, he was grateful for the invitation. The last thing he needed was a Christmas all alone. 'Well, that's very kind Dermot. I'd love to stay.'

A look of relief crossed Dermot's face. 'Good, that's settled then.'

44

It was a cold start to the day. The bright sun was slowly clearing the fog hovering over Treweham village. Dylan straightened his tie and pulled out the navy woollen jacket hanging in the wardrobe. Flora was busy rootling under the bed.

'They must be here somewhere,' she said in exasperation as her hands felt for any sign of the newly purchased suede boots.

Since arranging to go to the Tingle Creek Chase with Gary and Tracy, she'd been deciding which outfit to wear. The dress code for Sandown Park was smart, but not too showy. In the end, Flora had opted for a chocolate-brown dress, matching brown suede boots and a dusky pink pashmina. The effect was simple, classy and fit the bill perfectly. Dylan watched her through the mirror on the wardrobe. Hell, she was pretty, in a totally natural, unspoilt way. Her good nature meant she was just as nice inside as out. She caught him looking at her, as she eventually managed to find the boots and sat on the edge of the bed tugging them on.

'What are you smiling at?' she asked.

'You.' Dylan turned to face her. Flora stood up.

'How do I look?'

'Wonderful,' he replied, pulling her into his arms. 'Looking forward to the races?'

'Yes, course I am. It'll be fun with Gary and Tracy.'

'It will.'

Originally, Tobias and Megan had been invited to join them as well, but they'd declined. Or rather Tobias had answered for them both, not wanting Megan standing in the cold at six months pregnant. Finula and Marcus had also been invited, but with The Templar so busy at the moment, Finula didn't want to take any more time off. So, it was just the four of them. Secretly Dylan was pleased: it would give him a better chance to speak to Gary alone. There was something he was eager to run past him.

Tracy Belcher sat waiting by the lounge window, looking out for Dylan and Flora to arrive. She, too, was pleased that it was just the four of them today. Tracy had always felt somewhat intimidated by Lord Cavendish-Blake and since that interviewer had commented on them overpaying for the Gate House, her unease had grown. She begrudged being taken advantage of.

Gary, on the other hand, had never let it bother him. He could take or leave Tobias Cavendish-Blake and he was more than happy with where he lived, even if he had paid slightly over the odds for it. So what? They could afford it, and it was a damn sight better than where they'd been. Not that he didn't miss Lancashire – he often did – but not the so-called 'mates' that, in his eyes, had ripped them off even more. At least with Tobias it hadn't been personal. With his friends in Preston, it had been, and it still stung that as soon as he had mentioned moving away they'd all practically dropped him. Apparently, him going (and taking his lottery winnings with him) was all it took to completely disown him. Even Finchy, his best mate, had never got in contact, which he could have done quite easily, as Gary had purposely kept the same mobile phone number. But no, not a word. It was as if he had never existed. That was why he had made such an effort to settle in the Cotswolds. Gary was a larger-than-life character, but there were reasons behind his full-on bonhomie. He wanted friends and he craved the same camaraderie he thought he'd had back home.

'They're here!' called Tracy, jumping up from the chair with excitement. She'd been unsure of what to wear, so had looked up the dress code online. Still feeling a touch self-conscious in her short tweed skirt and matching jacket (especially as Gary had laughingly called her Miss Marple) she answered the front door.

'Hi, ready to go?' beamed Flora. 'Hey, loving the outfit.'

'I'm not sure. Do you think it's the right thing?' Tracy chewed her bottom lip anxiously.

'Of course! You look great, really,' assured Flora.

There was no such reservation with Gary, as he ushered them all to the car, where Dylan sat waiting behind the wheel.

Dylan couldn't help but smile to himself, watching Gary in his dark suit and bright pink tie, bellowing with laughter at something Tracy had said. Once again, he was glad it was just the four of them.

They all enjoyed the trip, chatting together amicably about the prospect of the races. Dylan tried his best to keep a straight face when he'd noticed Gary studying a map for Tingle Creek village.

'Tingle Creek Chase is named after a horse that had a particularly good record racing at Sandown Park,' he explained.

'Oh, right. I thought it was the name of the village it's in,' said Gary, not at all embarrassed or offended by the correction.

Dylan smiled. 'No, it's in Esher.'

As Dylan pulled into the racecourse car park, Flora's anticipation rose. She loved the races and seeing horses perform at their best. Her thoughts turned to Phoenix; she knew he was every bit as capable as the horses here. She imagined him taking part, lining up with all the other thoroughbreds, ready to chase and glide through the air over the fences.

Dylan had booked them into one of the Imperial Boxes, to experience the thrill of the races, situated above the winning post. This would provide the perfect environment to entertain them all. The box had an ideal view of the live racing action with direct access to a private balcony. There was also a champagne reception, buffet and complimentary bar. Dylan had pulled out all the stops. Today was about impressing Gary and Tracy, and ultimately getting them on board. He had a plan, and it required their co-operation.

The lavish spread had had the desired effect and Gary and Tracy had been gripped by the whole experience. Gary proved to have a winning streak and Tracy forgot any inhibitions she may have had in the excitement of it all. Flora chatted easily with her and the two had gelled well. Seeing them huddled together, deep in conversation, Dylan made his move.

'Having a good time?' he grinned at Gary.

'Bloody brilliant, mate. I think I'm a natural,' he bellowed, patting his inside jacket pocket, which was bulging with all his winnings.

'Still thinking about learning to ride a horse?' ribbed Dylan with a smirk.

'Nah, but it's good watching 'em race.'

Dylan paused; now was the time. 'Ever thought about owning one?'

Gary turned to him. 'What, a horse, you mean?'

'Yes. Maybe in a syndicate, or partnership?'

'Why? Do you fancy it?'

Dylan nodded. 'I'd like to buy a horse for Flora, one we're training at the moment. It's got great potential; could end up somewhere like here.' He pointed towards the race track. Gary's face lit up. Sensing he'd grabbed his attention, Dylan continued, 'I'd want a partnership, joint owners.'

'Why not just buy it yourself?'

'Basically, the current owner is a nasty piece of work. If he knew I wanted the horse, it could make things difficult. If an outsider who he didn't know bought it, then he wouldn't bat an eye… and believe me, he wants rid.'

'Why? If it's got potential?'

'Because it's not the potential he wants, or can even see. He's not a horse lover, just a businessman.'

Gary warmed to the idea of part-owning a horse. He pictured himself in the winner's enclosure, basking in all the glory. Dylan could see he'd caught his imagination.

'This could be a regular thing for us.' He nodded towards the girls chatting animatedly. Tracy was giggling into her champagne flute and it was the happiest Gary had seen her in a long time.

Gary put out his hand. 'Let's do it,' he said with gusto.

Dylan shook it firmly. 'You've got a deal.'

45

It was time for the television crew to say goodbye to Treweham. Len had made arrangements to return, as he planned to film the Straw Man Festival. He half thought Marcus would be around too, judging by the way he was with Finula. It was the only time he'd witnessed Marcus fully relaxed and he was pleased for him.

Libby was eager to get back home. She, too, was looking forward to Christmas with her family, but was under no illusion how hard she would have to work, once the festivities were over. Marcus was a notorious slave driver, expecting all the team to show as much dedication as he did. Whilst she enjoyed working with Marcus, she sometimes found him too intense and longed for him to lighten up a little. Libby also noted the difference in Marcus when he was chatting easily with Dermot, and especially Finula. The chemistry between them was evident for all to see and she wished Marcus every happiness; he deserved it.

Viola had been unusually withdrawn for a few days now. She was anxious to leave Treweham, but for very different reasons. Not particularly relishing the prospect of a Christmas with her parents, she had booked to go away – far from anybody she knew. For the second time in her life, she felt an overwhelming urge to flee and start again. But, realistically, could she do that? After all the attempts she'd made to reinvent herself, Vera had returned, with a vengeance, bringing with her the suspended sentence and that all-consuming threat of imprisonment. The very thought made Viola numb. A cold, blind panic spread through her when considering the consequences of her actions. Yet it wasn't enough to make her stop. If there had been some way of snaring Tobias Cavendish-Blake, Viola would have gone for it, without a doubt. It was paradoxical that the very subject of her obsession had also been her downfall. Hating Tobias, yet still finding him dangerously attractive, was an odd mix of emotions, yet so typical of the complex character Viola was. Any observer looking objectively would instantly recognise she clearly needed some kind of help; that her twisted mind needed straightening out. Perhaps more alarming would be discovering what had initially triggered Viola's violence. Why did she go to the lengths she did without any empathy? What drove her to be so fixated? In fact, if she was honest, Viola sometimes frightened herself, and she was petrified of the repercussions from deleting Tobias' interview. It was about to kick off, big time, and she wanted to be out of the way when it did. So, it was time to regroup. Time to take stock.

She had chosen to hide away on a tiny island off the coast of Scotland. It would be just her, the roaring sea and the old crofter's cottage. Apparently, the only neighbours would be the monks from the monastery on the island. The irony wasn't lost on Viola. Perhaps she could learn something from their simple existence and contemplate a more honest outlook on life.

Jamie was reluctant to leave The Templar, for leaving Treweham meant leaving Sebastian. He had developed real feelings for him, not the schoolboy crush he'd initially had, but genuine affection for a person he was getting to know more and more. He hoped Sebastian felt the same. Jamie had been supportive of Sebastian, which had meant a lot to him. But was that it? Was Jamie only going to be a good friend, offering moral support at a time when he most needed it? Or, could he possibly mean more? Jamie understood Sebastian had been hurt in the past, but wasn't everyone at some stage in their lives? And now he had been diagnosed with MS; surely he, Jamie, being the only person to know this meant something. There were so many questions he wanted answers to, but didn't want to seem pushy or needy and frighten Sebastian off. Then again, he deserved some clarity on the relationship.

With a heavy heart, Jamie packed his case and made his way downstairs. Libby and Len were checking out and Viola had gone first thing that morning. After saying his goodbyes, he wheeled his hefty case through the doors and into the car park. He opened his car boot and was nearly knocked into it by a force from behind.

'What the...?' A black Labrador jumped up at him.

'Zac! Here, boy!' Sebastian called, laughing at Jamie, who had been practically pushed into the back of his car. Turning round, Jamie saw Sebastian making his way towards him. His heart hammered, seeing him in his Barbour jacket, jeans and Wellington boots, very much the country squire. 'Sorry about that.' He took hold of Zac's collar and put his lead on. Smiling up at him he asked, 'So, you're off then?'

'Yep. Time to go.' Jamie's throat dried up. He couldn't say another word for fear of showing emotion. Sebastian stared into those smoky-grey eyes that he had grown so accustomed to. The thought of never gazing into them again gripped him with panic.

'Any plans for Christmas?'

'Er... not really. Probably go to my mum and dad's.' There was a pregnant pause.

'Stay.' Sebastian was still staring. 'At Treweham Hall, as my guest.'

Jamie was floored. It took a moment for the invitation to sink in. Then a warm, blissful wave of happiness washed over him.

'Yes please, I... I'd like that very much.'

46

Immediately after the races, deciding to strike while the iron was hot, Dylan had contacted Graham Roper. Trying to sound nonchalant, he calmly told him he had a possible buyer for his horse. The relief in Roper's voice was encouraging and Dylan was hopeful he would be able to wrap the deal up quickly, without any complications or suspicion. If Roper had any inkling of Phoenix's potential as a jump racer, the whole thing would collapse. The horse would be whisked away and sold elsewhere for a fortune. Dylan again thought about the consequences this would have on Flora and willed himself to stay composed and neutral.

'Good, that's a bloody relief. Who wants it?'

'Some bloke in the village. Lottery winner, apparently. He fancies owning a horse.'

'More fool him,' sniggered Roper. 'What's he prepared to pay?'

This was where Dylan had to be careful. Realistically, the ballpark figure for a horse without any racing promise would be a few thousand. But wanting to entice Roper, who was a businessman, meant pitching it competitively, yet without causing any suspicion.

'Five grand,' Dylan replied firmly, and waited for a response.

'Try and get a couple more out of him.' Anticipating Roper's greed, Dylan had been prepared.

'I'd say two's a little ambitious. Try one more thousand?'

'Hmm,' grunted Roper, 'OK. Six grand and that's it.'

'I'll talk to him and get back to you.'

'Within the hour, Delany. I'm not wasting any more time.' Dylan gripped the phone and bit his tongue. Then he heard the receiver slam down.

After waiting twenty minutes patiently going through some admin, Dylan once more rang Graham Roper.

'Yes, he'll pay six thousand,' he told him curtly.

'Right, if you get the paperwork in order, I'll come and sign. Tell him I want the money by the end of the week.'

Dylan was on the brink of telling him to sort out the admin himself, but managed to resist. This time next week Phoenix would be theirs and he'd never have to lay eyes on that bastard Roper again. Taking a deep breath to control his temper, Dylan replied with a cool voice that the necessary arrangements would be made.

He left the yard office and took another deep breath. The cold air stung his lungs. Blowing on his hands to warm them, he made his way to Phoenix's stable. As he'd predicted, Flora was there brushing him down, talking gently to him. He stood and watched for a moment, imagining her glee at being told Phoenix would soon be here to stay. But no, he'd save that surprise for her birthday tomorrow. He'd also been to the jewellers to pick up her other present from him. He laughed to himself, not knowing which she'd be happiest about.

'Hello, you,' she said, turning and smiling.

'Hi.' He nuzzled into her neck, loving the fresh floral scent of her. He turned her face towards him. They shared a long, sensuous kiss, arousing Dylan and making Phoenix snort with envy. 'Don't be late,' he coaxed, finally releasing her lips. 'I'll have dinner ready in an hour.'

'OK,' nodded Flora, then patted an impatient Phoenix who was demanding her attention.

The next morning Flora was woken with breakfast in bed. Dylan had brought up a tray laden with two full English breakfasts, coffee and a small pile of birthday post. There was also a little silver box with a black ribbon tied round it.

'Happy birthday, Flora.' He kissed her lips, then carefully manoeuvred the tray onto the bed.

'Oh, this is lovely, Dylan! Thank you.' She began opening her mail, swallowing down the emotion when she came to her parents' card. She missed them and was so looking forward to their return from travelling. Then she took the small silver parcel. Unwrapping it with care, she revealed a white velvet box. Opening it up, she gasped with delight. A beautiful silver horseshoe charm studded with diamonds twinkled up at her. It was attached to a thin, silver chain. 'Dylan, it's gorgeous,' she exclaimed.

'You like it, then?' he smiled.

'I love it!'

'Here, let me put it on.'

He leant forward and fastened the necklace round her slender neck.

'Right, eat up,' he said. 'Then we're off to the yard.'

They had arranged to ride together, something they hadn't found the time to do for too long. Dylan had also booked a table at The Templar for lunch, wanting to spend as much quality time with Flora as possible. He hoped that Josh, their stable hand, had followed his instructions.

Together they entered Phoenix's stable and Flora noticed something threaded in his mane. It was a white envelope. Frowning, she took it out from the horse's locks and opened it. Inside was a letter she instantly recognised was in Dylan's handwriting.

Dearest Flora,

Your wonderful Dylan has seen to it that I never have to leave these stables. I am yours for ever.

P.S. Although I know you spend every waking hour tending to me, I think he deserves far more loving attention.

Phoenix

Her face crumpled with joy, tears glistened in her eyes.

'Oh, Dylan... is he actually ours?' she choked.

'Well, half, technically. Me and Gary have formed a joint partnership.'

'Really?' she laughed.

'Really,' he nodded, loving her reaction. 'We've called him "The Last Laugh". Hopefully Roper will rue the day he wrote Phoenix off.'

Flora suddenly looked sombre. 'Could he claim him back?'

'No. Everything's in order. He's no idea I'm involved.'

'Oh, Dylan...' She hugged him hard.

For once Phoenix didn't mind. It was as if the horse instinctively knew he'd found his way home.

47

Treweham Hall stood proud and majestic in the snowy white landscape. Smoke puffed softly from the many chimney pots atop the roof. Inside, the open fires crackled, the mulled wine flowed and the festive music played gently in the background. It was Christmas Eve and, like every year at this time, Treweham Hall hosted a drinks party for family, friends and all the estate workers. This year would see two new guests. Jamie, as Sebastian's house guest, would be there, and also Marcus, who reluctantly had accepted his invitation, due to a very persuasive Finula.

'Oh, do come, Marcus. It'll be fun!' she'd urged him when opening the pale green invitation with gold, italic writing. It was decorated with a holly and berry border and headed with the Cavendish-Blake coat of arms. Even the invitations smacked of pomp and ceremony, thought Marcus with derision.

'Finula, I'm sure Tobias – or indeed any of the Cavendish-Blakes – don't really want to see my face. My name's been included through politeness to you.'

'No it hasn't!' Finula vehemently denied. 'Megan wants you there.'

That, he had to concede, was probably true. He did have a liking for Megan; she was a warm, friendly person. What she saw in her husband he'd never understand.

'Must I?' he looked at Finula pleadingly.

'Yes, you must,' she replied firmly, then wrapped her arms around his body in an attempt to appease him. It worked. Marcus loved being hugged by Finula. She exuded sincerity and comfort, something he had realised he needed. Marcus was missing his mother dreadfully, of course, especially at this time of year. His mind shot back to last Christmas, when he'd been nursing her thin, frail body. He badly needed to talk about it, to confide in someone, but something always stopped him. He just could not let it go. Being an only child meant he'd not had that sibling support. And since being an orphan he'd not had any other parental support either. His thoughts turned, as always, towards the unfairness of his two half-brothers having a very different upbringing. Their childhoods had been blessed with the love of both parents, with all the privileges that brought. He reminisced about how his mother had worked hard to support them both without any help at all.

The injustices raged inside Marcus. At least plotting his revenge had given him some solace, something to focus on, but now that was beginning to give him extra grief, too, because that meant jeopardising his relationship with Finula. He knew this, and the risk he was taking had started to chip away at him. Finula would catch him often in his deep, dark moments, his expression unreadable. Every time he'd brush away her concern, knowing full well she hadn't been convinced of his wellbeing. At night she'd hold him close, soothing whatever it was he wouldn't disclose. Deep down Finula thought it was just a matter of time. She knew there was a special bond between them – it was tangible – and she also knew to trust her instincts. Marcus had come to mean so much to her and this dark, brooding side to him only increased his attraction, being the curious person she was. Subconsciously, the fact that her dad had also taken to Marcus had strengthened Finula's feelings for him.

In turn, Marcus had fallen deeply for Finula. She epitomised everything he craved: love, warmth and comfort. Dermot, too, had taken on a role as a father figure, with his steady presence and guidance. It amazed Marcus how, within such a short period of time, they had grown to mean so much to him, almost like a surrogate family. He couldn't help but wonder if all this had been preordained in some way: that he was always meant to come to Treweham.

'OK, I'll come then,' agreed Marcus with a sigh, knowing when he was defeated. 'But let's go to my place on Boxing Day and spend some time alone?'

Finula thought about it for a moment, then agreed.

'Yes. Dad'll be busy, so he won't have time to miss me.'

Marcus was reminded of Finula's loyalty once more and that feeling of foreboding returned.

The Dowager Lady Cavendish-Blake was in full force, ordering the staff around, overseeing arrangements and fussing like a mother hen. As always, Celia was on hand, smothering her excitement.

'Calm down, Beatrice. It'll all go to plan, it does every year,' she told her sharply.

'Yes, due to my management,' Beatrice batted back. Then she turned to Sebastian, who was strolling down the stairway. 'Darling, the guests will be arriving soon. Aren't you going to dress?'

'I am dressed, Mother.' He looked down to his faded jeans and long, white T-shirt.

'Hardly for the occasion, Sebastian,' cut in Celia with a raised eyebrow.

Sebastian rolled his eyes and made his way back up the stairs.

'Do you think that TV friend of his is a bad influence?' whispered Beatrice.

This time Celia rolled her eyes. 'No, Beatrice, I don't.'

'I do wish he'd find the right girl and settle down,' Beatrice shook her head.

'Then you'll be wishing a long time, dear,' muttered Celia under her breath.

Tobias and Megan were in their rooms, getting ready to join the rest of the family. Tobias looked devilishly handsome in his dinner suit. He sat in the drawing room waiting for Megan, sipping a brandy. This time next year he'd be a father. He looked at the Christmas tree Megan had decorated that day, sparkling in the corner with presents scattered underneath it. Next Christmas would include presents for their child, his heir. What a difference a year makes, he acknowledged. He hadn't even known Megan that long. They had met in early spring and their whirlwind romance had spun them both off their feet; and now this spring would see their first child born.

'Ready to go?' Megan entered the room, looking elegant in a black evening gown. It discreetly hid her ever-growing bump. She was wearing the diamonds Tobias had given her on their wedding day.

'You look beautiful.' He kissed her lips gently. 'We won't stay too long; I don't want you getting tired.'

Megan laughed. 'Tobias, stop fussing. I'm absolutely fine. I'm looking forward to seeing Finula. I've not seen her for ages.'

'Too busy with that TV producer,' he replied tartly. 'I take it he's coming tonight?'

'Yes, of course, as Finula's partner.'

'Hmm.'

'I don't know why you disapprove of him,' said Megan, half smiling. 'In some ways he reminds me of you.'

Tobias' head shot up sharply. 'Don't be ridiculous.'

'I'm not,' she teased, finding his reaction amusing. 'He comes across as being quite a proud person, confident, knows what he wants. You're both tall, dark and handsome, too,' she added with a grin.

Tobias' eyes narrowed. 'Is that so?' he answered, knowing she was playing with him. He softly pulled her closer and stroked her swollen belly. Did he feel a kick? It was an amazing sensation. His hands travelled upwards to her solid breasts and caressed the fullness of them, then slid up her long, graceful neck to rest under her chin. He tilted her face to his and kissed her slowly, his tongue running along her lips and slipping inside her mouth. She tasted so good. He could feel the beginnings of an erection and wished more than anything they could just get in between the sheets of their four-poster bed.

'Tobias! Are you there, darling?' Beatrice's voice boomed down the corridor. Megan giggled as Tobias backed off with a disgruntled moan.

'Coming, Beatrice!' she called back.

Jamie was on cloud nine. Staying at Treweham Hall had been a mind-blowing experience. He had never felt intimidated and Sebastian had gone to great lengths to ensure he was comfortable. He was sleeping in the next bedroom to him. That alone had kept Jamie up at night, just knowing that behind the adjoining wall slept Sebastian. The Cavendish-Blakes were a real mixture of characters, from the somewhat ditsy mother, crusty old aunt, gorgeous brother and affable sister-in-law. They'd all welcomed him, although the knowing looks Aunt Celia kept giving him had proved a touch off-putting. No wonder Sebastian was terrified of her. He was relieved to learn that Marcus would be there that evening. At least it would be another familiar face.

The evening proved to be a success. All the guests were greeted with glasses of champagne in the hall, where the colossal Christmas tree glimmered and holly decorated the sweeping staircase. Beatrice was on fine form, ever the social butterfly, whilst Celia stood back and watched from afar with a frown, accepting a drink every now and then from the passing silver trays.

On seeing Finula and Marcus enter through the hall, Megan rushed over to speak to them.

'Glad you could make it.' She hugged Finula, then looked towards Marcus with a beaming smile. 'And you too, Marcus.'

Marcus smiled politely. 'Thanks for the invite.' His eyes scanned the place, taking in the marble floor, stone pillars, high coved ceiling, stained-glass windows, chandelier, grand staircase, the tapestries and, of course, the huge, ostentatious Christmas tree. Such opulence, it turned his stomach.

Sipping his champagne, he homed in on Tobias, chatting comfortably with his guests, looking every inch the Lord of the Manor in his pristine dinner suit. For a split second Tobias caught his eye. The two men exchanged cool looks – no smiles. Marcus suspected that Tobias wanted him there about as much as he wanted to be there. Then Marcus' eyes turned to Sebastian, his other half-brother. This time he smiled when Sebastian waved and together with Jamie they made their way over to him.

'Glad to see a familiar face,' said Jamie, looking a tad relieved.

Marcus laughed. 'I could say the same.' Then, turning to Sebastian, he shook his hand. 'Good to see you again, Sebastian,' and he actually meant it. From what he had experienced he concluded that Sebastian was the opposite of Tobias, not just in looks, but in personality too. Sebastian seemed warmer, more approachable, compared to Tobias' cold, standoffish demeanour. Marcus would like Sebastian for a brother, not so Tobias. He glanced at Tobias again, looking suave and sophisticated, milling in the crowd. Not that Marcus didn't hold his own in his dark dinner jacket. In fact, he'd go so far as to say the resemblance between the two of them – dressed so similarly, with the same black hair and green eyes – might have been pretty obvious, if people knew what he did. He'd thought about trying to get back into his father's study. Marcus longed to get hold of his diaries and explore more about him.

'Good evening, Marcus.' Tobias cut into his thoughts, startling him a little.

'Good evening, Tobias,' he replied in the same tone.

'So, you're still in Treweham?' Tobias looked almost accusingly at him.

Without missing a beat Marcus replied, 'Yes. Proving hard to shake off, aren't I?' He smiled tightly.

That earned him a hard stare, before Tobias turned his attention to Finula and Megan.

I'll teach you to dismiss me, raged Marcus with a burning hatred.

48

Christmas morning arrived with a flurry of snowflakes, gently dusting the rooftops and hedgerows of Treweham village. The dining table at Treweham Hall boasted the finest silver, cut glass and porcelain, all laid out with precision. It was a particular favourite task overseen by Henry, the butler, who saw it as an opportunity to showcase the utmost care and attention to detail he was renowned for. There were ten places set, as Megan's granddad, mum, dad and brother were coming for Christmas dinner. Henry gave the table one last inspection, before refilling the decanters on the sideboard.

Tobias lay in bed gazing at his wife deep in slumber. He wanted her to have as much sleep as possible, knowing the full day ahead they faced. He deliberately postponed the Christmas morning Mass celebrated in the Hall's chapel, allowing Megan a long lie-in. The service was an intimate affair for family and any members of staff from the Hall and estate who were able to join them. He lay back and enjoyed the peace and quiet. The Hall was still silently waiting to spring into life once its occupants rose.

At The Templar, however, Christmas was already under way, raring to go. Marcus had quietly snuck into Finula's bedroom early in the morning to wish her a merry Christmas. He had woken her with a kiss and, bleary eyed, she smiled lazily.

'Merry Christmas, Finula,' he whispered, holding out his present to her.

'Oh, thanks, Marcus.' She sat up in bed and hastily unwrapped the square-shaped parcel. It was a drawing, capturing a charming, quaint village, surrounded by emerald-green hills.

'It's Kilsalla, the village in Roscommon where I was born. My mother drew it.' He pointed to the right-hand corner.

'Oh, yes, "A. Devlin".' Finula squinted to read the signature. 'Marcus, it's lovely…' She didn't know what else to say, feeling quite overwhelmed. The picture obviously meant a lot to him.

'It's a part of me and now I'd like you to have it.' He looked deeply into her eyes, making her gulp with emotion.

'Thank you, Marcus.' Then, she reached under the bed to get her present for him. 'Hope you like it,' she grinned. He smiled as he instantly guessed what was inside the gold wrapping.

'Can't go wrong with a bottle of Jameson's whiskey,' he chuckled.

Then she reached down again and gave him another present. She looked carefully at his face as he tore off the gold paper. It was a silver-framed photograph of them sitting together laughing and clinking wine glasses, taken by Dermot in The Templar. It captured the moment perfectly, each looking with adoration at each other. This wasn't lost on Marcus.

'Finula...' He could feel a lump form in his throat. 'Thank you.' He bent his head and kissed her.

'Come inside,' she coaxed, lifting back the duvet cover, 'and I'll show you what else you've got for Christmas.' Her eyes danced with devilment.

'Hmm, sounds good,' he replied, slipping off his clothes. Finula ran her hands hungrily over his toned body, losing all her inhibitions. In turn Marcus covered her cream breasts with his mouth, licking the pert, pink nipples. His hand travelled up her silky thigh and rested on the soft triangle of hair. Slowly he stroked, gently gliding against her warm, moist opening, making Finula arch herself into him. He kissed her long and deeply, then ran his lips down her body until reaching the same sensitive area. Finula gasped as his tongue slid into her, firmly and with rhythm.

'Marcus,' she whimpered. Marcus continued with pace, sending her into ecstasy. Then, just when she thought she'd burst, his mouth travelled back up her body and he slipped his hard erection into her with a guttural groan. Finula clutched his buttocks, wanting more of him. Marcus was moving slowly, relishing her impatience for his body. Then, overcome with lust, he pushed firmer and faster. Finula dug into him harder. They were greedy for each other's bodies, desperately needing a release. When it came they both exploded together. Panting heavily, Marcus pulled Finula onto his broad, dark chest.

'Have I told you how amazing you are, Finula?' he asked breathlessly.

'Yes, but tell me again,' she giggled, kissing his cheek.

'You. Are. Amazing.'

Dinner at the Hall was a busy affair, but enjoyed by all. Megan was pleased to see her family and, together with Jamie, everyone blended well together. Sebastian, as usual, supplied the entertainment, making even Aunt Celia chuckle into her sherry glass. She had received a rather tasteful Christmas card from a gentleman friend of hers called Wilfred, whom she'd met on a cruise a few months ago. The kind words inscribed in the thick, cream card had made her glow. Perhaps there was life in the old girl yet.

Jamie was still in awe of the place and its surroundings. Mostly he was more and more in awe of Sebastian, and still couldn't quite believe he was there as his guest.

Finally, when all the splendid food had been eaten, all the wine drunk, all the gifts exchanged and all the parlour games played, the day drew to a close and the guests bade their farewells.

Back at The Templar, Marcus and Finula sat huddled on the sofa, enjoying an Irish whiskey. It was late now and Dermot had gone to bed, leaving the two of them alone after they had all enjoyed a lovely day together.

'Where were you last Christmas?' asked Finula.

Marcus tensed. Although he knew the question was asked innocently, the memory still cut deep. He gulped down his whiskey before answering.

'In Ireland, looking after my mam.'

'Oh, sorry Marcus, I didn't realise—'

'I know,' he cut in.

'Do you want to talk about it?' she tentatively asked, but the closed look on his face said it all. She was hitting yet another brick wall. A flash of impatience shot through her. When would he open up? 'It might help,' she persisted.

Marcus closed his eyes. Could she not take a hint? He'd given her everything – well, as much as he could – far more than anyone else had had.

'What do you want from me, Finula?' he asked wearily. He'd had a lot to drink throughout the day and it had started to creep up on him.

'Transparency,' she replied with force.

He looked at her with narrow eyes, 'Well, that's a very dangerous commodity, Finula.' His voice had an edge to it that sparked Finula even more.

'That depends on what you're hiding.' She stared him in the face.

'What exactly do you want to know?'

'More about you,' she urged, 'your childhood, parents—'

'Drop it, Finula,' he warned.

A few moments passed, then she changed tack.

'And why don't you like Tobias?' He looked surprised at her question, clearly not expecting it. 'It's blatantly obvious you can't stand him, why?' This was a question he most definitely had no problem answering.

'Because the man's a complete arse. A pampered, arrogant, aristocratic arse.'

Finula's eyes widened in shock. 'What? That's my friend you're talking about.' Then the penny seemed to drop. 'I get it now. You used me.'

Marcus' head turned sharply. 'Finula—'

'You bastard, you used me to get inside Treweham Hall and interview Tobias, didn't you? None of this is real. You just needed me to do your dirty work. You'd never have got near the place without me asking him.'

This was true, and they both knew it. They stared at each other in silence. Finula waited for him to say something, anything, and while Marcus hated seeing the look of hurt in her eyes, he couldn't speak. He had no defence.

Finula stood up. Fighting back the tears she made for the door. Finally, she turned to look at him. 'I think it's time you left, don't you?'

49

Sebastian tapped quietly on the bedroom door next to his. There was a moment's pause, before Jamie answered it. Sebastian suppressed a giggle at the stripy pastel pyjamas Jamie was wearing, as they reminded him of something similar he had worn as a child.

'Thought you might like a nightcap?' He held out a bottle of rum and Jamie's face lit up.

'Absolutely, come in.' He held the door wide open. It was past midnight and everyone was fast asleep. Loud snores could be heard thundering down the corridor.

'Aunt Celia,' whispered Sebastian with a titter, 'snores and rattles like an old boiler.'

Jamie started to snigger and suddenly found he couldn't stop. With hushed laughter he quickly shut the door.

Sebastian poured them each a generous slug of rum in the glasses on the bedside table. He held his out. 'To you, Jamie. Thanks for everything.'

Jamie averted his gaze, feeling self-conscious. Extravagant displays of affection like this made him uneasy, yet incredibly happy at the same time. Sebastian was so public and open with his gestures, it often made Jamie wonder if he was in fact still acting.

Sebastian moved closer, sensing his embarrassment. He tipped his chin up to look at him. 'Seriously, Jamie, thanks for all your support.' He spoke quietly, his expression serious, and Jamie knew he was being sincere.

'You're welcome.' Then he paused before saying, 'Sebastian, don't you think you ought to tell your family?'

'About my MS?'

'Yes.'

Sebastian sighed and nodded. 'Yes, in time. My time, when I'm ready.'

'I understand.' Which he did. Having such a life-changing diagnosis must take a lot of adjusting to. Sebastian obviously needed to get his own head round it before sharing the news. In a way, Jamie felt privileged at being the only person to know. 'And thank you for the invite. It's been a great day,' he smiled, taking a sip of rum.

Sebastian gave a wry smile, 'My family not scared you off, then?'

Jamie looked directly at him. With Dutch courage he asked, 'Scared me off what?'

'A relationship with me.' Sebastian stared back, without flinching.

'No. If anything, it would be your superstardom that would scare me off,' he playfully answered.

'It's all bollocks. And anyway, what part could I play now with this limp? Fucking Richard III for ever?' He laughed, despite his predicament.

Jamie smiled at him with real affection. 'It's not that bad, and you know it.'

'I know,' conceded Sebastian. 'Just playing the sympathy card,' he added with a sly grin.

'You'll get none from me. I don't do pity,' Jamie said with humour, still revelling in what Sebastian had said about a relationship.

'Do you do hugs? Because right now I could do with one.'

'Yes, I do hugs.' Jamie put down his glass and moved towards him. The two embraced. Breathing in the scent of his long, lean body, Jamie thought his Christmases had truly all come at once.

50

Finula woke with a thumping headache and a heavy, sickening sensation in her stomach. Gradually fitting back the pieces of last night, she shut her eyes tight again, as if trying to block out the memory. Her mouth was dry, her skull throbbed and she badly needed to vomit. Only just making it to the bathroom, she emptied the entire contents of her stomach down the toilet. Panting, she sat on the side of the bath.

Marcus. She had to speak to Marcus. But once washed, dressed and having knocked on his bedroom door, she found he wasn't there. His room was completely empty, without any trace of him ever having been there. Finula started to tremble. He'd gone. Marcus had left. Well, she'd told him to, hadn't she? Tears stung her pale cheeks. Would he ever come back?

Marcus had driven non-stop to get home to Shropshire. Despite having had a few hours' sleep and copious cups of coffee, he knew he must still be well over the limit. Frustration and anger burned through him, but most of all his heart broke picturing the hurt in Finula's eyes. If only he could just come clean and tell her everything. Like *why* he was so clandestine about his childhood and parents. This time last year even *he* didn't know fully about them. It was all so cruelly unfair.

He banged his fist against the steering wheel when he recalled Finula's words, saying how he'd used her. He had, but only to a degree. She had actually offered to ask Tobias about the interview and access to Treweham Hall. Tobias could still have refused. It was the fee that had swung it, purely the money. Tobias had even said as much in the interview. As soon as Marcus got back he was going to start editing it. With grim determination, he urged his car on to eat up the miles and finally he made it home. Marcus took out all his equipment, leaving his suitcase. He would unpack later; for now he just needed the laptops.

Within the hour he was sitting at his desk, searching through the rushes. The interviews were all labelled, as promised. He tutted with impatience at not seeing Tobias Cavendish-Blake's name. Where was it? Looking more closely and, forcing himself to slow down, he searched again. It wasn't here. Grabbing his phone, he rang Libby.

'Libby, it's Marcus. I thought you said you'd sent me all the footage of the interviews?'

'I have,' replied a somewhat disgruntled Libby. It was Boxing Day, for goodness' sake. Didn't the man ever take a break?

'Well, Tobias Cavendish-Blake's isn't here,' he stated flatly.

'It should be. I definitely sent it.'

'Then send it again, please, Libby,' he finished, and put the phone down with force.

Fifteen minutes later his phone rang. It was Libby.

'Marcus, I don't have it.' The urgency in her voice was evident.

'What?'

'It's not here. It's gone.'

'It's gone?'

'It was there and now... it's gone,' Libby replied faintly.

'Right, I'm ringing Len, see if he's still got it.'

But half an hour later, it was the same scenario. The interview had vanished from Len's camera, too.

Marcus sat motionless, staring out of his lounge window. Slowly anger started to rise in him. He clenched his fists. Where was that *fecking interview*? What had happened? How had the interview vanished? Who would have deliberately erased it? None of his team, he was sure. Libby and Len were professionals, and why would they want to? Same for Viola: she more than anyone saw that interview as a pivotal stepping-stone in her career. Jamie? Doubtful, and again, what would be his motive? None of it made any sense. He was utterly perplexed.

His eyes turned to his mam's photograph on the windowsill. Then his pounding heart gradually began to slow down. His rage was replaced with a sense of calm. His breathing became deeper, steadying him further. It was as if a huge weight had been lifted off his shoulders. Then another thought suddenly occurred to him. Could this be some kind of divine intervention? His eyes remained on the photograph of his mother. If there was no interview to discredit Tobias… he wouldn't lose Finula. Granted, he wouldn't have his revenge, but suddenly that wasn't a priority any more – Finula was. Putting things in perspective gave him time to take stock and re-evaluate. It was all so clear when looking at it objectively, without being caught up in the maelstrom of emotion. That clairvoyant had been right. Revenge was not sweet. It could have cost him dearly. Had it already? Did Finula no longer want him?

51

'So, Gary, meet Phoenix.' Dylan opened the stable door and showed Gary in.

'Hell, he's a beauty, isn't he?' Gary stared in awe at the mahogany-brown-coated horse, quite overcome at the size of the animal. It was the first time he'd been up so close to one.

'He is now, thanks to Flora's loving care.' Dylan grimaced at the memory of Phoenix's whip wounds and rolling, anxious eyes.

Gary patted the side of him. 'Hello, mate.' Phoenix nudged his face into Gary's shoulder, making him laugh.

'He likes you,' smiled Dylan. 'He wouldn't do that to me.'

'Why?' Gary asked surprised, given how good he knew Dylan was with horses.

'Jealousy. He thinks Flora's all his,' laughed Dylan. 'Hardly surprising, judging by the amount of time she spends on him.'

Gary chuckled. He did feel some affinity towards the horse and understood how attached people must become.

'So, what's the plan? When do we start racing him?' Gary rubbed his hands, keen to see Phoenix compete. He rather fancied himself in the winner's enclosure, soaking up the limelight.

'Not for a while yet, Gary.' Dylan looked serious; this was business, after all. 'We need to spend more time training him.' Then he added by way of explanation, 'Phoenix has had quite a rough time of it. We don't want to push him too hard too soon.'

'Oh, right. Yes, of course.' Gary patted him again. 'In your own time, mate,' he murmured.

Flora was in the office with Tracy. The two of them had become close recently and Tracy, for once, had started to feel that she had made a real friend since moving from Lancashire.

'So, what did you do for Christmas?' asked Flora, blowing on her coffee, having handed Tracy a cup.

'We went back home to Preston, stayed at my mum and dad's.'

'Do you still think of Preston as your home?'

'Sometimes. It takes some getting used to, moving completely away from your home town.'

Flora considered it. 'Yes, I suppose it must. But you do like it here, don't you?'

Tracy laughed. 'Yes, how could you not like it here?' There was a moment's pause and she looked down.

Flora observed her. Something was amiss. 'Home is where the heart is,' she said gently.

Tracy looked up and smiled. 'I know, it's just taking a lot of adjusting. Our lives were so different twelve months ago.'

'Would you ever go back up North?'

Tracy shook her head. 'No.' She didn't elaborate on why: it was too upsetting. It still saddened Tracy how their friends had treated them, but she sincerely hoped they could make new ones.

As if reading her thoughts, Flora put an arm round her shoulders.

'Come round here, anytime. Well, you've a vested interest now, haven't you?' she joked.

Tracy smiled. 'Me, owner of a racehorse. Who would have thought it?'

52

Dermot looked sideways at his daughter and sighed. She looked a complete state, with her tired, white complexion and dark bags under her bloodshot eyes. It had been five days since Marcus had left and Finula had grown progressively more and more miserable as each one passed. Obviously the two had not been in touch. He didn't want to pry, but he was starting to feel genuinely concerned about his daughter's health. She was losing weight, having hardly touched food. When he'd found Finula sobbing uncontrollably on Boxing Day, she'd briefly told him what had happened and Dermot had stared at her incredulously.

'You argued over Tobias?'

'Yes, Dad. He used me,' she answered indignantly.

'Finula, Tobias is a grown man. He wouldn't have done anything he didn't want to. Presumably he was paid for the interview?'

'Well... yes...'

'And I take it Marcus has got back safely to Shropshire? Seeing as how you sent him home well over the limit,' he asked in a steely voice.

Finula's head shot up. 'Oh God, I... I don't know.' Her bottom lip quivered.

Dermot shook his head in exasperation. 'Unbelievable,' he muttered, and walked away.

Finula was on the verge of yet another breakdown, when her mobile interrupted her. It was Megan.

'Hi, Finula, had a good Christmas?'

'No,' came the dull reply.

There was a pause. 'Need to talk?'

'Yes.'

'I'm on my way.'

'No. I'll come to you.' She needed to get away from The Templar and the judgemental looks her dad kept throwing at her.

It didn't take long for Finula to hotfoot it to Treweham Hall. She was glad of the change of scenery. Not for the first time, she was seriously considering a life away from The Templar.

Megan was sitting alone by the open fire in the drawing room when Henry showed Finula in.

'Finula, whatever's the matter?' Megan's eyes shone with concern. Finula sat next to her on the settee.

'Megan, it's all gone badly wrong.'

'Why? What's happened?'

Finula filled Megan in, not sparing any detail, even though it involved Marcus' dislike of Tobias. Megan sat and listened.

'Why do you think he's so secretive about his upbringing?' Megan asked, narrowing her eyes. 'And why has he taken a dislike to Tobias?'

Finula shrugged. The two sat still, contemplating. Then Megan faced Finula. 'Do you think there's a link between the two?'

Finula frowned. 'How do you mean?'

'I once commented to Tobias that he reminded me of Marcus.' She paused, remembering the look of contempt on her husband's face. Finula's mind started to tick into overdrive. The green eyes, speckled with amber... she too remembered pointing out the likeness of Tobias to Marcus in the portrait. He didn't like it, refusing to see the resemblance, though it was so clearly there.

'I once asked Marcus about his dad and he clammed up, saying he was dead and he had never met him.' The two stared at each other. Then something else crept into Finula's head, from the day they had filmed inside Treweham Hall. She vividly remembered Marcus standing outside Richard Cavendish-Blake's study when she'd met him at the top of the stairs. Had he really just taken pictures of the chapel? She voiced her thoughts to Megan.

'Follow me,' Megan answered, getting up from the sofa.

'Where are we going?'

'To Richard's study,' she said over her shoulder.

Finula's heart began to pound. Had they stumbled across something?

Entering the room, packed to the ceiling with ledgers, they both scanned the many shelves. One of the spines stood out slightly.

'Look, there!' Megan pointed to the book edging out of line from the others.

Finula quickly reached up and took it from the shelf, her heart now racing in anticipation. She squinted at the side of it: there was a slight gap in the pages, indicating where it had last been opened. Carefully, she reopened it to the same page. Both Megan and Finula's heads eagerly bent over it. Finula ran her finger down the list of names on the left-hand side, then stopped.

'Anne Devlin,' she whispered. 'That must be Marcus' mum.'

'Marcus' mum worked here, at Treweham Hall?' Megan asked in astonishment.

'Yes, look, in the kitchen.' Finula followed her finger across the page. They looked at each other in amazement. 'Are you thinking what I'm thinking?' asked Finula.

Megan slowly nodded. 'I think so.' Then she looked towards the glass cabinets she knew contained her late father-in-law's diaries. Finula followed her gaze. 'They're Richard's diaries, locked away. Tobias will have the key,' Megan told her.

'We need get to them and read them, don't you think?' Finula urged.

Megan nodded. 'I'll speak to him.'

53

Tobias threw his head back and laughed. 'Really? You expect me to believe that Marcus Devlin could be my half-brother?' Megan and Finula looked deadpan into his mocking face. He stopped laughing and took in their serious expressions. 'You are, aren't you?'

A short silence followed. The atmosphere could have been cut with a knife.

'We need to look at your father's diaries, Tobias,' Megan said quietly.

'They're personal and private, Megan.'

'Please, Tobias, don't you see how important this could be?' pleaded Finula.

'They could be holding crucial information,' Megan added gently.

Tobias eyed his wife. She really did believe that he and Marcus shared the same father. It was impossible, of course, but to appease her he nodded.

'OK, but let me read them first.' He opened his desk drawer and took out a small box. Inside was the key to the glass cabinets containing the diaries. 'Leave this with me for now.'

Megan and Finula sighed with relief. At least Tobias was prepared to look.

Despite his refusal to acknowledge what was being suggested, Tobias' mind couldn't help but play tricks on him. His thoughts were cast back to certain occasions, such as when he caught Marcus staring at his father's portrait that time in his study. He always seemed to stare at him, too; was he looking for any likenesses? Any family resemblance? Tobias cursed himself for being so foolish and made his way to his father's study.

Once inside, he closed the door firmly. He didn't want any interruptions. He carefully opened the glass cabinets and scanned along the shelves. The most sensible place to start would be the year before Marcus had been born. On looking Marcus up on the internet, he soon discovered his date of birth. He was two years older than himself, so he started his search in the mid-eighties. Tobias painstakingly ploughed his way through the pages and then the name flashed before him like a thunderbolt. Anne Devlin. She was mentioned in a casual way to start with. Then, as the days, weeks and months went by, her name appeared more and more frequently, and more intimately. It was obvious to any reader that they were in a relationship. A physical, loving relationship. Tobias' eyes widened in disbelief at the commotion this had clearly caused. His grandparents had blatantly disapproved, to the point of forbidding their son to carry on with a member of staff. A part of Tobias felt sympathy for his father, especially when reading how heartbroken he was at Anne's sudden disappearance.

Anne's gone, without any word or trace. Why could she not be strong, like me? My parents are to blame, I'm sure, but I will find her, if it kills me, I'll find her.

Bloody hell... Tobias' jaw dropped. Had Anne Devlin been pregnant when she'd fled Treweham Hall? The dates certainly stacked up. Nine months after the date in his father's diary entry, would be the approximate time of Marcus' birthday. A film of sweat covered Tobias' body, telling him he had uncovered something sinister. Judging by what his father had written, Tobias doubted his knowledge of Anne's pregnancy. Had she panicked and run, knowing what the repercussions would be? And why only now had Marcus decided to show his face?

There were so many unanswered questions, but only Marcus himself could answer them. Obviously, Anne Devlin had sought refuge in Ireland, while Richard Cavendish-Blake had gone on to meet and marry Beatrice. The whole sorry tale left Tobias in a state of shock.

Then the pragmatic, logical side of his brain kicked in. All this was just speculation. If Marcus Devlin had any intention of announcing his parentage, then he'd need evidence. The necessary tests would have to be carried out. Tobias couldn't deny him that. After all, he grimly conceded, Marcus may actually *be* his brother, and not just that, even though illegitimate, he would be the firstborn. That in itself could potentially invite repercussions. My God, what can of worms had he just opened?

54

Having thrown himself into his work from dusk till dawn, Marcus was exhausted. He preferred to feel numb with exhaustion rather than feel the pain of heartbreak. Being completely drained meant that when eventually his head did hit the pillow, he was out like a light. He was also drinking heavily, having finished the bottle of Irish whiskey Finula had bought him for Christmas. Each time he'd poured its amber fluid into a glass he was reminded of Christmas morning and how special it had been. He ached for Finula, but equally resented her casting him away as she had. He'd picked his phone up on countless occasions, intending to ring her, but had bottled it each time. Instead he had occupied himself doing what he did best: working flat out.

He spent hours viewing all the scenes, placing them in order and checking for continuity. This process allowed for revisions and new ideas to be tried and tested, which he wanted to run past Libby. When he did sleep, his dreams were filled with Finula, always ending with the wounded look in her eyes; it devastated him.

Deciding enough was enough and it was time to get some fresh air, Marcus wrapped up and set off to walk into the market town. It was New Year's Eve that night and Deacon's Castle was busy preparing for the evening's celebrations. New Year always depressed Marcus and this year wasn't going to be any different. His first stop was the bookshop café he had taken Finula to, where he was greeted by a cheery Margo.

'Hello, Marcus, all on your own?' she smiled.

'Apparently,' answered Marcus flatly.

'Where's that pretty redhead?' she chuckled.

'At home in Treweham.'

Margo didn't push him. She'd soon learnt when to talk to him and when not to. Today was obviously not a chatty day. Marcus stared gloomily out of the window, watching all the excitement build. Shops, bars and restaurants were brightly decorated, ready to host and bring in the New Year. Marcus wanted to hide away. After half an hour, he paid for his coffee and left. He didn't have the energy or the inclination to go elsewhere, so he slowly made his way home.

As he closed the door and took his coat off, he heard the phone ringing. He stopped still for a second, then bolted into the lounge to pick it up. When he recognised The Templar's phone number on caller display his heart leapt.

'Finula?'

'It's Dermot.' There was a short pause. 'Listen, Marcus, I know this is none of my business, but I'm worried about Finula.'

'What's happened?' The alarm in Marcus' voice was evident.

'You bloody leaving, that's what's happened,' Dermot replied in exasperation.

'I was asked to leave, Dermot,' replied Marcus dully.

Dermot sighed down the phone. 'I know, and to say she's been miserable since is an understatement.'

Marcus took some comfort in this. At least he wasn't the only one suffering.

'If you'd only see the state of her, Jeysus – and I'll wager you're not much better, eh?'

This he couldn't argue with. 'No.'

'Look, Marcus, I'm asking you to come back and at least talk to each other.'

'Does she know you've rung me?'

'Hell, no. She'd kill me for interfering.'

Marcus couldn't help but smile, imagining his feisty Finula giving her dad a good ticking-off. 'OK, I'm on my way, but say nothing, Dermot.'

'Absolutely, Mum's the word.'

Marcus swallowed hard. *Mam.* He looked towards her photograph on the windowsill. Blinking back the tears, he made his way upstairs to pack his case and return to Treweham.

55

Megan sat on the settee, with her legs resting on the footstool. She closed her eyes, then quickly opened them again. She felt a huge kick and then her baby moving inside her. Lifting up her top, she revealed her swollen stomach. She watched in wonder as a small lump poked up from the bare skin.

Tobias walked into the room. 'Look,' she whispered to him. Tobias rushed forward and knelt down to see. His eyes homed in on their baby's movements.

'It's amazing, isn't it?' He stroked his hand over her belly. This was his, all he could think about; how important family really was. Since reading his father's diaries he could think of nothing else. The more he considered what he had uncovered, the more sense it made. With reluctance, he had to admit, at least to himself, the similarity between himself and Marcus. It all seemed so obvious in hindsight, but then wasn't it always easy to be wise after the event? Even so, Marcus' intentions – if indeed he had any kind of plan – would determine what happened next. It was all so unsettling, and yet the underlying issue remained steadfast: blood was thicker than water, and if they truly were brothers, it must be acknowledged.

He'd had to tell Megan and Finula of his findings, but not Sebastian just yet. The one person he'd have loved to be able to talk to was his father. Tobias was resolute that he had not known about Anne Devlin's pregnancy. His father had been many things – frivolous, with no business sense, maybe – but he had a kind, generous heart and loved his family unconditionally. Tobias refused to believe he would knowingly have let Anne bring his firstborn child into the world without ever recognising him. It was important to Tobias to defend his father as he wasn't here to do it in person. His mind spun with all the implications.

'You OK?' Megan touched the side of his face. It troubled her to see him so tense, obviously contemplating the recent revelation.

Whilst Finula had assured them of her discretion, Megan couldn't help but wonder how long it would take for it all to come tumbling out into the open. Would there be yet more press intrusion? Tobias had been plagued by the media all his life. For the first time, she felt a sense of foreboding for her unborn child, the future heir.

56

Marcus had driven with a steely nerve. Whilst he was desperate to see Finula, he also had to get matters straight in his own mind. He found it hard to accept how easily she'd told him to leave, and how she hadn't made contact since. Dermot's words gave him some consolation, but deep down he wished the call had come from Finula, not her father. Then a voice whispered inside his head: *you* hadn't made contact either.

His journey hadn't taken too long, there being hardly any traffic. Entering the village, he drove past Treweham Hall. There it stood, strong and resilient, while he felt anything but. He pulled into The Templar car park and made his way to the front entrance. Dermot must have been watching out for him, as he pulled open the door and ushered him in. It was late afternoon and they weren't opening until early evening.

'Will you just look at yourself,' uttered Dermot, bolting the door. He nodded towards the bar. 'And she's no better, pasty-faced, maudlin thing.' He pushed Marcus gently through. 'I'll see you're not disturbed,' and with that he left him alone.

Finula was behind the bar wiping glasses. She really didn't have the energy to work that evening and was dreading seeing in the New Year. Suddenly she looked up and saw him standing there.

'Marcus... you've come back.' Her voice cracked.

Marcus slowly walked to the bar. 'Yes, Finula, I've come back. But if you tell me to leave once more, you'll never see my face again.' It killed him to see the look of pain shoot across her face, but he had to see this through. He gritted his jaw, then leant across the bar. 'So, you need to tell me exactly what it is you want.' His tone was quiet and determined.

'I want you,' she faintly replied. Her chin started to quiver and tears swelled in her eyes. Still he carried on.

'Well, I don't come cheap, Finula. It's all or nothing.' He stared into her face.

'I... I want all of you,' she choked, the tears spilling down her pale cheeks.

This was enough, Marcus lifted up the bar hatch and she raced to him. He held her tightly, breathing in the familiar scent of her.

'Marcus,' she whispered hoarsely, 'I know.'

He kissed the top of her head. 'So do I, we're meant to be together.'

Finula pulled away to face him. She looked searchingly at him, 'I mean... I know who your father was.'

Marcus froze. He stared at her, speechless.

An age seemed to pass as they stood opposite each other. Finula broke the silence first.

'Sit down, I need to talk to you.' She led him to the settle by the fireplace and explained everything: from how she and Megan had gradually pieced together their suspicions, to finding the ledger containing his mother's name, to Tobias clarifying the relationship with his father through his diaries.

Marcus sat dumbfounded. How had they guessed who his father was? Had he been so transparent?

After digesting all the revelations, Marcus asked, 'Finula, *how* did you suspect Richard Cavendish-Blake was my father?'

'Firstly, your resemblance to Tobias. You have exactly the same eyes. Then the way you were so cagey about your childhood and only spoke about you mum. You told me your dad was dead and you'd never met him. That tied in. But most of all your dislike of Tobias. You resent him for having what you should have had.'

Marcus frowned. 'I don't want a title. The last thing I'd want to be is an aristocrat.'

'No, I don't mean that. I meant you wanted a dad. You begrudge Tobias having both his parents and never having to worry about money.'

How perceptive she was. He wondered if she'd worked out his intentions to discredit Tobias, too.

'What must you think of me, Finula?' He looked carefully for any signs of disapproval.

Instead Finula took his hand and spoke softly. 'I think you're a man grieving. Not only have you lost the most important person in your life, but you have had no one to comfort you.' She put her arm round his shoulders. 'Marcus, you need to speak to Tobias and Sebastian. They're your brothers.'

'But do they believe that? All we have is hearsay at the moment.'

'Do *you* believe you're their brother?'

He sighed and rubbed his hand through his hair. 'Yes, I believe every word my mam said.'

57

Marcus and Finula walked hand in hand up the gravel driveway to Treweham Hall. Dermot had insisted they take time out to be together and had laid on extra bar staff to cover the New Year's Eve shift. Once Finula had rung Megan to update her on Marcus' arrival, she had invited them to spend the evening at the Hall.

Marcus hadn't backed off, as he too recognised the importance of their meeting. It was an unfamiliar feeling, walking towards the Hall, not being an outsider, not invading the Cavendish-Blakes' privacy any longer, but visiting potentially as a family member. He was glad of Finula's warm hand to hold. Looking sideways at her composed profile, he mentally thanked Dermot for his phone call. Where would he be without her?

Megan and Tobias opened the door, so determined were they that Marcus wasn't shown to their rooms by Henry.

'Come in. It's so good to see you.' Megan kissed Marcus on the cheek and hugged Finula.

'Welcome, Marcus.' Tobias held out his hand. The two men exchanged firm handshakes. Marcus was a little taken aback, and a lump started to form in his throat. Coughing slightly, he allowed his eyes to sweep round the great hallway as they had just the previous week at the Christmas Eve drinks party, only this time its opulence didn't turn his stomach. The anger had vanished, to be replaced with calmness. They all seemed to be looking at him, waiting for some kind of response. He didn't know what to say. What was appropriate in such circumstances? Instead he said nothing. It was all too much.

'Let's have a drink… this way,' chirped Megan, anxious to fill the awkward moment.

They made their way to the south wing. Megan had arranged for a simple supper in their dining room, just a quiet, intimate meal between the four of them, much to Marcus' relief. As Megan showed Finula the finished decorated nursery, Tobias turned to Marcus.

'Marcus, follow me. Let me show you something.' He led him to his father's study. Marcus noticed the glass cabinets were open.

'These are my father's diaries,' Tobias walked towards them, 'which I've read now, at some length.' Marcus swallowed. 'Your mother appears in them, Marcus, and I've no doubt they were in a relationship. But for what it's worth, I truly do not believe my father knew anything about your mother's pregnancy, or you.' He stared into Marcus' eyes.

There was a slight pause before Marcus replied. 'You mean she left without telling him?' The tone of surprise was evident.

'That's exactly what I think happened. Marcus, I knew my father. He wouldn't have let you grow up without ever acknowledging you. I'm positive he wouldn't.'

Marcus took a sharp intake of breath. He was stunned. This was not something he'd contemplated. Always, he'd assumed his mam had been banished in disgrace, not bolted. The new version of events took some adjusting to. It shed a completely different light on the whole affair.

Tobias continued, 'I want you to read for yourself.' He beckoned towards the cabinets. 'Come here whenever you want and help yourself. Get to know him.'

Those last words broke Marcus finally. He yearned to learn more about his dad. To his shame, a tear ran down his face and he instantly wiped it away.

Tobias spoke calmly: 'If you want to make this official, we'll do the necessary DNA test, make it public—'

'I'm not ready for that,' Marcus interrupted. 'The test, yes – we all need to be certain – but the rest...'

'Would you take on the family name?'

'No. I'm a Devlin,' Marcus answered firmly.

'I understand.' Any doubts or reservations Tobias may have had disappeared. Marcus wasn't a threat, he just wanted to know who his father was. If anything, Tobias felt humbled. 'I'll arrange for a swab test. I also need to tell Sebastian.'

Marcus looked up. 'He doesn't know yet?'

'No, and I'll need to speak to my mother.'

'Yes... of course.' Marcus was eager to get inside those diaries but knew now was not the time. The grandfather clock chimed in the corridor. It was eight o'clock. In four hours it would be midnight, the start of a new year. A new beginning.

58

'Are you ready yet, Tracy?' Gary was getting impatient waiting at the bottom of the stairs.

'Just a minute!' his wife called back.

He looked in the hall mirror at his reflection. Not too shabby, he thought. Gary had let his hair grow, wearing it slightly longer than his usual crew-cut style and it suited him well. He'd also taken heed of Dylan's comments about losing weight. Although he knew Dylan had only meant it light-heartedly, to be taken in jest, it had made Gary think. Perhaps he was getting just a bit too used to living the good life. His thoughts rewound to his former days, when he actually worked hard for a living. Stacking freezers in Iceland, albeit monotonous, was in fact strenuous, physical labour, and had kept him in good shape. Nowadays, the only thing working him into a sweat was the long walks when he was out shooting. That alone obviously wasn't enough and the pounds had started to pile on. Tracy had often teased him about his chubby tummy, but hearing it from Dylan had hit home. As a result, Gary had installed a few pieces of gym equipment: a rowing machine, treadmill and some weights. The results were beginning to show, even if Tracy had giggled hysterically at him in his Lycra bodice. He gave a smirk in the mirror; she soon stopped laughing when he revealed his toned body in the bedroom.

Tracy scurried down the stairs. 'Right, let's go.'

They were off to The Templar to celebrate the New Year. When Flora had invited them to join her and Dylan, Tracy had been pleasantly surprised, secretly dreading the New Year. She couldn't help but compare it to last year, when she and Gary had had a blast of an evening in the club. She pictured them joining hands with their mates, belting out 'Auld Lang Syne'. What would it have been like if they'd stayed in Lancashire? She suspected Gary was right: it would have been a nightmare, with more threatening letters and abuse. Common sense told her it would never have stopped, and succumbing to their demands would only have encouraged more. Another voice told her that real friends wouldn't have acted that way. So, all in all, it had been the right decision to move away. Tracy kept telling herself this as she slipped into her sparkly new dress. She felt more confident than she had in a long time and her confidence rose at Gary's wolf whistle.

'Very nice, Mrs Belcher.' He plonked a kiss on her lips, then ushered her out of the front door, eager to get to the pub.

Inside The Templar it was heaving. Dermot was rushed off his feet and was so glad of the extra bar staff willing to work New Year. Despite it being one of the busiest nights of the year, he didn't begrudge Finula the time off. She deserved some quality time with Marcus.

He began to consider what quality time he ever had for himself, which was hardly any. For the first time, Dermot was beginning to wonder if his days at The Templar were numbered. Was it time to pack up and say goodbye? He was in his mid-sixties, after all, perhaps getting a little too old for this game? He longed to put his feet up and watch television of an evening, instead of working behind the bar, wearing his most welcoming smile for the public. What he most yearned for was peace and quiet. He'd grown tired of listening to people's requests, complaints and opinions. He'd grown tired of rising early, lugging crates, barrels and serving pints. He'd grown tired of having to feign an interest in customers' stories, being cheery and accommodating, when really he just wanted to soak in the bath and sink into bed. Basically, he'd had enough and tonight's constant, hectic stream of customers shouting orders at him reiterated this.

He suspected Finula, too, had had reservations about her future in The Templar. Maybe she spent too much time here, he reflected somewhat guiltily...

His thoughts were interrupted by another customer hurling demands at him. With an inward sigh and a fixed smile he set about his duties.

Jamie and Sebastian were tucked away in an alcove watching the pandemonium.

'Is it always this busy at New Year?' asked Jamie, steadying the table as it was jostled by the crowds.

'Yes, do you want to go?' Sebastian was starting to regret his suggestion of coming to The Templar. He picked up his pint glass before someone knocked it over.

'Where to?' asked Jamie.

Sebastian suddenly had an idea. With a slow smile he answered, 'Follow me.'

The two pushed their way through the crowd and out of the pub. Despite it being winter, the air was still and not too cold. A full moon shone down and blanketed them with its beam.

'This way.' Sebastian walked Jamie down the dimly lit track leading back to Treweham Hall. But instead of walking up to the entrance, he veered to the left of the Hall into the woods, using his mobile's torchlight and the moonlight.

'Where are we going?' hissed Jamie, feeling like a naughty schoolboy, trespassing on private property.

Sebastian laughed. 'To my secret hideaway.' He used his evil Richard III voice for effect, making Jamie giggle. There was something deliciously clandestine about creeping through the undergrowth in the dark. Then they came to a stop. 'Here it is, the Folly.' He shone his light on the tall, stone building with small slits of windows and a castellated top.

'You'd never know it was here, hidden deep in the woods,' Jamie marvelled.

'Exactly. That's why it's the perfect hideaway,' replied Sebastian. 'Come inside.'

He forced open the heavy, wooden door. Inside it smelt damp. Moonlight shone through the leaded glass of a large, arched mullion window at the back. Jamie made out two dark green velvet armchairs, a wood burner, several picture of hunting scenes hanging from the walls and a jute rug covering the floor. Sebastian was crouching over a log basket and began filling the wood burner. He reached for a lighter on top of a cabinet in the corner. Once lit, the burner provided light and warmth. As the Folly warmed up, the smell of damp began to evaporate.

'Come and sit down.' Sebastian pointed to one of the armchairs. 'I'll pour us a drink.' He opened the cabinet to reveal a fully stocked mini bar.

Jamie chuckled. No wonder this was Sebastian's hideaway.

Sebastian handed him a whisky. 'Cheers.'

'Cheers.'

'Fancy a cigar?' Sebastian went back to the cabinet and took out an expensive box of cigars. He lit one with the lighter and took a few puffs. Jamie watched his silhouette; smooth, graceful and staged, a true thespian.

'I won't, thanks,' he answered. He took a sip of whisky and enjoyed the sharp heat hitting his throat. He was beginning to feel relaxed now, away from the hustle and bustle of The Templar, in the tranquil peace of the secret folly. Sebastian sat opposite him by the wood burner.

'This was my father's bolt hole. He used it to escape all of life's pressures.'

'There is a sense of good karma about it,' agreed Jamie.

'I've started to use it for the same purpose.'

There was a moment's silence.

'Please don't think you're alone, Sebastian.'

Sebastian looked up. 'Thank you, Jamie.'

'I mean it.'

There was another pause.

'When do you start work again?' Sebastian knew Jamie was to go to London, working on a set there filming a period drama.

'Mid-January.'

Sebastian nodded.

'What do you plan on doing next?' Jamie asked.

'Hmm, I'm reluctant to commit to anything just yet.'

'I see.'

'Not because of my diagnosis,' Sebastian was quick to explain. 'I just don't feel ready to throw myself into another role yet. It can take it out of you.'

'I bet it does. Anyway, there's no rush, you've made a name for yourself now.' Then he added, 'You could work for yourself, like before.'

'You mean the travelling theatre?'

'Well, a theatre, yes, but why travel? You could hold productions here, in the Treweham Hall grounds.'

Sebastian sucked in on his cigar and contemplated the suggestion. Why hadn't he thought of that? His ancestral home provided the ideal venue for open-air plays. He imagined captivated audiences lying on the lawns with picnic hampers, or cuddled up with blankets and lanterns in the dusk. The more thought he gave it, the more his imagination ran with the notion. He pictured other events: drama workshops, acting retreats, maybe even speciality dinners with a few of his well-known actor friends giving talks.

'Do you know, Jamie, you could just have stumbled upon a completely brilliant idea.'

'Glad to be of service,' Jamie smiled, saluting with his glass.

Sebastian leant forward and clinked it with his.

'Here's to a new year. May it be filled with peace, love and laughter.'

'It will be, I'll make sure of that,' assured Jamie.

59

After celebrating the New Year at The Templar, Dylan and Flora enjoyed a few quiet days to recuperate. Whilst still seeing to the horses and attending the all-weather meetings, they finished strictly on time every afternoon whenever possible and let the staff cover the evening stables. The yard was almost running at full capacity now and Dylan had decided to extend his team and employ more stable staff, to the delight of Flora. This also meant she would be able to spend more time with Phoenix, but she had the foresight not to voice this to Dylan.

Whilst Dylan was busy with paperwork at home one late afternoon, the phone rang.

'Hello, Dylan. It's Jade Fisher here.' Dylan frowned for a moment before realising who it was. Ah, yes, the journalist from *Hi-Ya* magazine who had contacted him a few months ago.

'Hello, Jade.'

'Dylan, you promised me an interview.'

Dylan gave a soft laugh. 'No, Jade, as I recall, I said I'd think about it.'

'And have you? We're willing to pay a very generous fee,' she coaxed.

Why not? Thought Dylan. The money would come in handy, and Flora had looked favourably upon the proposal of an interview, believing it would be good for business. He also remembered his reply: that it would have to involve her.

'Yes, I'll do it, on the condition that you include my partner, Flora.'

'Business partner or girlfriend?'

'Both.'

Jade's ears pricked up. This was a first. Dylan Delany, the playboy former Champion Jockey, settling down? He'd been pictured with various glamorous beauties on his arm, but that's where it ended. Never had there been any hint of him in a serious relationship. To want this Flora appearing next to him in the interview was a scoop.

'Certainly, it would be a pleasure, Dylan,' Jade smoothed, practically rubbing her hands together. This was going better than planned.

'And be kind, no tricky questions,' he warned.

Jade gave a light chuckle. 'As if. You have my word,' she assured him.

Dylan gave an unconvinced, 'Hmm,' having experienced the gutter press before.

'I'll have the details sent to you. We'd like you to feature in next month's issue, so I'd like to interview you as soon as possible.'

'OK.'

'Could we say next week? Monday?'

'That should be all right.' Then an idea came to him. 'You can interview us at the stable yard.' He was keen to promote the business and maximise coverage.

'Yes, good idea. We'll get some fantastic shots,' gushed Jade, her enthusiasm evident.

'Good. I'll await the details.'

'Yes, I'll get them over to you today.'

'And I want the fee, too. Today,' he replied firmly. He wasn't standing on ceremony; he'd learnt how to deal with these slippery journalists.

'Of course.' Jade smiled to herself. The fee was a drop in the ocean compared to the sales he'd bring in.

Flora was initially edgy about being interviewed, despite having agreed to it before. 'But why do I have to be involved?'

They were in the kitchen washing up after dinner. Flora was standing at the sink, gazing thoughtfully out of the window, and Dylan was behind her. He wrapped his arms round her body and ran kisses up her neck.

'Because we're a partnership and I want you to be there beside me,' he answered in her ear, before turning her to face him.

'But…'

'No buts, Flora.' His lips covered hers. Flora could feel herself beginning to melt. Yes, she would be interviewed – why not let the world know they were a couple?

Monday saw the early arrival of Jade Fisher, accompanied by a photographer. All the stable yard staff had been prepared and the grooms were rather excited by the visit, especially the young women, who had taken extra care of their appearances.

'I hardly recognise them,' muttered Dylan to Flora as he took in their coiffures, painted faces and perfect manicures. Hardly the image he wanted to create, preferring his staff to look like hardworking, practical grooms, not something from a catwalk.

'Oh, leave them alone,' laughed Flora, who also had been at pains to look her best. Whilst not going to quite the same lengths, she had freshly washed and blow-dried her hair and carefully applied a little make-up. Dylan didn't need to try. His natural dark, gypsy looks and twinkling blue eyes always made him picture perfect.

'Right, Dylan, if we can just take a few shots of you tending to a horse, that would be great,' enthused Jade.

Dylan did as he was told. Flora had made sure Phoenix was at hand as a star attraction. Phoenix, however, had other ideas and didn't quite like the way he was being handled by Dylan and not Flora. The horse head-butted Dylan out of the way when he tried to take his reins. Dylan smiled wryly to himself; the old tinker was playing silly buggers.

'I think it would be better if Flora was on this shot, too,' he told Jade.

'OK. Flora, if you could just position yourself next to Dylan – oohh!'

But Phoenix apparently didn't like that either, as he opened his bowels and dumped a huge pile of dung at Jade's feet. Dylan's lips twitched at the horror on Jade Fisher's face.

'Perhaps just have Flora in this shot?' He knew when he was beaten. There was no way Phoenix was going to behave the way they wanted him to. Jade stepped gingerly away from the steaming pile of crap.

'Hmm, maybe we could take a few shots with you at the stable doors, with the horses safely inside?'

'Good idea,' smiled Dylan.

Flora tried not to laugh as she led a disgraced Phoenix away. 'You naughty boy,' she quietly chuckled. The horse neighed in response.

Dylan was a natural in front of the camera, his good looks and charm oozing through the lens. Once Flora had returned they were photographed together in the office. Dylan made sure his arm was protectively around her, in an attempt to instil some confidence in her. It worked, as Flora assertively answered Jade Fisher's questions. Any sign of hesitation was met with Dylan's calm support. The interview was mainly focused on him, however, much to Flora's relief. Dylan was self-assured, artless and keen to promote his yard, praising all his staff, but especially his assistant trainer.

'That Delany's Racing Yard is a success is hugely down to this one's commitment,' he said, squeezing Flora affectionately.

'And yours, too,' she chipped in.

Dylan's head swooped down to kiss her and the camera went into overdrive. Jade slowly smiled to herself. This was going to be one hell of a feature.

60

It had been quite a start to the New Year for the Cavendish-Blakes. True to his word, Tobias had arranged for both himself and Marcus to undertake the swab tests as soon as possible. He had contacted the family doctor, ensuring full discretion. The DNA results had confirmed, as predicted, that Marcus and Tobias undoubtedly shared the same father. This then left Tobias with the duty of telling both Sebastian and his mother.

Gathering them together in his study for privacy, he gave strict instructions to Henry that he didn't want to be disturbed. As best as he could, and as gently as possible, Tobias outlined the whole state of affairs. He was matter-of-fact, but also spoke of the turmoil his father must have suffered. He showed both of them the diaries as if to prove this. He also had the DNA results to hand, in case they needed to see evidence for themselves. Both Sebastian and Beatrice sat, stunned into total silence.

'I know it's a lot to take in,' Tobias spoke gently, 'but give yourselves time to adjust.'

'Bloody hell, another brother.' Sebastian shook his head, hardly believing his ears.

'Half-brother,' cut in Beatrice with force. Both sons turned to face her, understanding the resentment she obviously felt.

'This doesn't change anything, Mother,' Tobias reassured.

'How can you be sure?' she asked, arms crossed.

'Because by his own admission, he's a Devlin. He doesn't want the family name or anything else, just to know more about his father.'

Beatrice's face crumpled with emotion and Sebastian put his arm round her. 'He's no threat to any of us, Mother.'

'But why didn't your father tell me?' she said in a strangled voice.

'Because he didn't know, of that I'm convinced. Anne Devlin bolted, without any trace. I suspect your in-laws had something to do with that.' Beatrice's head shot up in alarm.

'You mean they paid her off, to leave?'

Tobias shrugged. 'I wouldn't be at all surprised, judging by their reaction to the relationship.'

'My God...' Beatrice stared into space.

'I'd say we're the only ones unscathed in all of this,' Sebastian remarked wisely. 'It's Marcus that's been affected the most.'

'I agree.' Tobias turned to his mother. 'I've invited Marcus to read Father's diaries. He deserves to learn all he can about him.'

Beatrice continued to stare into space, making no response. Tobias scrutinised her face. What was she really thinking? For once Tobias saw her in a slightly more critical light. Maybe because he was comparing her comfortable, cosseted life to the harsh reality Anne Devlin had been faced with. Had she any inkling at all about her husband's first love? Had he ever confided in her, especially as they had met soon after Anne Devlin's disappearance?

'Does Marcus want to go public about this?' Sebastian asked.

Beatrice gave a gasp.

'Not for the time being,' replied Tobias, then added, looking at his mother, 'but it's his prerogative if he ever chooses to.'

'Of course,' agreed Sebastian.

61

The DNA results had left Marcus with a sense of peace that he hadn't expected. Although confirming what he already knew deep down, having solid proof validated his place with the Cavendish-Blakes. It also gave him access to his father's diaries, which he fully intended to read and discover all about the man for himself. But just now was not the time. He had a documentary to co-edit and produce, which was going to take much of his time.

Which brought him to the next task: leaving Treweham – and possibly Finula. He had to return to Shropshire and get back to work. He was due to meet with Libby in the London studio next week. Normally, this would fire adrenalin within him, but this time it was dampened by the prospect of having to be parted from Finula yet again. He could tell she was feeling the same, although neither had spoken about it as both knew it was inevitable.

It was early morning and they had just finished eating breakfast when Marcus broached the subject.

'Finula, we need to talk.'

She looked directly at him. 'Yes, we do.'

'I have to go back home. I really need to start working—'

'I know,' Finula interrupted. 'Let me come with you.'

Marcus sighed. 'Darlin', I'll be busy, preoccupied, I won't have time to give you like I did on your last visit.'

'I don't mean to visit. I mean for good.'

Marcus frowned. 'To live together?' His hopes soared, never expecting to hear this. Would she really leave Treweham, her dad and this pub? It was all she'd ever known.

'Yes. I can't be here without you... I'd be miserable.' Finula was baring her all, but didn't she always? That's what he loved about her, and *how* he did love her. He took both her hands over the breakfast table.

'You'd come and live with me, in Shropshire, and leave your dad?'

Finula nodded. 'Yes. It'll be hard, but watching you go alone would be harder.'

He squeezed her hands and leant over the table to kiss her. 'Thank you,' he whispered.

That evening both Finula and Marcus sat Dermot down to tell him the news. Dermot, fully expecting this, had prepared himself. It had also given him the opportunity to reflect on his own future. He, too, had made a life-changing decision. After sitting quietly and listening to his daughter tell him she was finally flying the nest, he nodded sagely and put her mind at rest.

'It's time, Finula.' He patted her hand and looked at Marcus. 'I wish you both every happiness.'

'Thank you, Dermot,' Marcus replied, feeling reprieved, 'and you must come and visit us in Shropshire whenever you want.'

'I will do just that, son, especially as I'll have plenty of time on my hands.'

Finula looked puzzled.

'I'm selling up,' Dermot explained.

'You're selling The Templar?' she asked, surprised.

'Yes,' he laughed. 'I'm not getting any younger and, well… I've had enough. Simple as.'

'Good for you, Dermot,' Marcus smiled.

'But… but what will you do, Dad?'

'Retire, Finula, bloody well retire and put me feet up!'

They all laughed, each glad this difficult conversation had ended so light heartedly. 'Seriously, Fin, I'll sell up and downsize. Get a cottage in the village. I couldn't leave Treweham; this is my home.' He looked warmly at the pair of them. 'And you two have to make your own home now.'

So, the next day when Marcus had to set off for Shropshire, Finula was able to wave him off without that dull, heavy feeling in the pit of her stomach as she'd anticipated. Instead she smiled brightly and kissed him tenderly.

'Have a safe trip.'

'Will do. I'll ring when I get home.'

'Funny to think it'll be my home too soon.'

They had arranged for Finula to drive to Shropshire after Marcus had finished working in London. That way she wouldn't be on her own and it would give her a chance to pack and say goodbye to everyone in Treweham. It would also give Dermot a few days to arrange extra staff to cover for her. He also intended to contact the estate agents and get the sale of The Templar started immediately.

Dermot had quietly taken Marcus to one side earlier on.

'I take it you'll be making an honest woman out of my daughter?'

'You have my word, Dermot,' Marcus replied in a serious tone.

'Good, because I'd like your wedding to be this place's last do for me.'

Marcus smiled, fully understanding where Dermot was coming from. 'Don't worry, it'll happen, if she'll have me.'

'Oh, she'll have you all right. She wouldn't be leaving me otherwise.' The two men shook hands.

Once Marcus had safely left, Finula made her way to Treweham Hall. She wanted Megan to be the first friend to know she was leaving. Walking in the bright sunshine along the lane leading to the magnificent Hall, it dawned on her how much her life was about to change. This village, with its quaint charm, honey-stoned cottages, babbling brook, ancient church, humped-back bridges and village green was about to be replaced with black and white Tudor cottages and sleepy, rolling green hills. It both excited and frightened her. Above all else, though, one thought kept her stable: she would be with Marcus.

Henry opened the door with a polite, stiff nod.

'This way, please.' He led Finula to Megan's drawing room in the south wing. It still made her grin the way Henry stood on ceremony.

'Finula!'

'How are you? Tired?'

Megan was fully blooming with only eight weeks to go before her due date.

'Absolutely. Come and sit down. I'll put the kettle on.'

Henry hovered awkwardly and coughed. 'May I arrange tea, madam?' He'd been given strict instructions by Tobias to look after Megan, which meant in Henry's book to wait on her hand and foot.

'Oh, would you? Thanks, Henry.'

'Certainly, madam.' He bowed slightly and left. The two of them exchanged knowing smirks.

'So, what brings you here, any news?'

'Well, apart from making sure my best friend's not having to move an inch,' she grinned, 'I do have news. I'm moving to Shropshire to live with Marcus.'

'You're going? To Shropshire?'

'Yes,' Finula laughed, 'are you surprised?'

'No. It's just strange hearing you say it. Makes it real, I suppose.' Whilst being happy for her friend, Megan couldn't help but be saddened. She'd miss her dreadfully.

'And Dad's selling The Templar,' Finula added. 'He wants to retire and downsize to a cottage.'

'Really?'

'Yep. So it's all change.'

'It certainly is. When will you be going?'

'In two weeks.' They faced each other, neither spoke for a few moments.

Megan gulped. 'So soon.'

There was an empty silence.

'I'll keep coming back to see you and the baby, and you must come and visit,' Finula's voice cracked. Her eyes filled and she quickly blinked.

'Oh, Fin, come here.' They hugged each other.

'It's a new exciting chapter – embrace it,' Megan spluttered between tears.

62

Libby sat in the studio patiently waiting for Marcus to join her. She glanced at the various screens and equipment before her, itching to get started. For the umpteenth time she searched her laptop for the missing interview. She was utterly bewildered. What on earth had happened? It was unheard of. Never in her thirty-year career had something so drastically wrong occurred. It both baffled and disturbed her. Was she losing her touch? No. Libby reminded herself that both Len and Marcus hadn't been able to locate the interview with Tobias Cavendish-Blake on their laptops either. It was a mystery. She grimaced, imagining the wrath of Marcus. However, when he did arrive Libby was pleasantly taken aback.

'Hi, Libby. Good Christmas?' he smiled, taking a seat next to her in front of the screens. Libby stalled for a moment, totally unprepared for his congenial manner.

'Er... yes, and you?'

'Marvellous,' he beamed.

She paused again. Was he being sarcastic? But no, he hummed merrily to himself as he unpacked his laptop. Libby decided to address the elephant in the room.

'Marcus, what are we going to do about Tobias Cavendish-Blake's interview?' She scanned his face for some kind of reaction with baited breath.

Marcus sighed and turned to face her. 'In all honesty, Libby, I don't know.'

'Where did it go?' She was beginning to sound panicked.

'Hey, Libby, don't stress. I'm the producer, as well as the co-editor,' he added drily. 'If anyone's head's on the chopping block, it's mine.'

Libby blinked. Who was this sitting next to her and where was the real Marcus Devlin?

'But... he was paid a hefty fee... questions will be asked.'

Marcus gave a curt laugh. 'Oh, I know that.' He ran his hand through his hair, showing the first sign of any pressure.

'What do you think's happened?'

How should he answer that? Say he suspected it could be some kind of divine intervention, paving the way for his future happiness?

Instead he shrugged. 'I have no idea, Libby.'

'What are we going to do?' she persisted.

'Like I said, I have no idea, Libby.'

Libby blinked once. Had he had some kind of personality transplant? Where was the confident, ambitious, tell-it-like-it-is, highly successful, award-winning TV producer? 'Let's work on what we do have until I think of something.'

'Do you think Tobias would give another interview?'

Marcus shook his head. 'No, and I wouldn't ask him for one. How unprofessional would it appear to admit to losing the footage of his first one?'

Libby nodded in agreement.

'Listen, let me worry about it, OK?'

'If you say so,' she reluctantly answered.

Soon they were deep in concentration, scanning every one of the rushes, making the necessary cuts to carve out a cohesive story, with not only narrative, but substance with an interesting slant. Each selected scene was placed in order and checked for continuity. As they were only working on the rough cut at this stage, revisions and new ideas could always be added at a later stage.

The two worked well together. Marcus was quick to offer suggestions, his creative imagination running wild, which was counterbalanced by Libby's level-headed logic and experience. The combination was a winning formula. Their track record proved this.

They couldn't help but smile to themselves at the Belchers' interview. Gary's enthusiasm and *joie de vivre* was in stark contrast to the stilted, clipped tones of the other interviewees.

'Replay that,' laughed Marcus. Libby giggled and pressed the rewind button. Gary's animated face lit up the screen again. He'd just been asked by Viola how it felt living on the Treweham Hall estate.

'*Smashing. All this space is a far cry from where we came from, innit, Tracy?*'

Marcus and Libby chuckled.

'Turn the volume up, let's capture his northern accent. It's an interesting angle for the Cotswolds.'

They carried on watching.

'*We came into money,*' Gary told the camera with a big beam.

'Pause,' said Marcus. 'That's another good slant, and look at his wife's face. She wasn't comfortable with him announcing that.'

'Should we home in on it?'

'Definitely, let's get a close-up of her reaction.'

Together they worked through the rushes and made excellent progress. After nine hours, and only thirty minutes stopping for lunch, they eventually called it a day. Hiring the studio cost good money, so Marcus was keen to get as much done as possible.

'Let's go for something to eat,' said Marcus, 'or do you want to head back home?'

Again, Libby couldn't help but notice the change in Marcus. He seemed much more relaxed somehow. Perhaps having dinner with him would be a pleasant experience after all.

'No, let's eat. We deserve it after that.'

'Libby, I haven't worked you too hard, have I?' He genuinely looked concerned.

'Yes,' she laughed, 'but I enjoy working with you, honestly. You may be a slave driver, but you produce awesome documentaries.'

Marcus smiled. 'Well in that case, dinner's on me.'

63

The last two weeks Finula had left in Treweham were going so fast. Each day she'd packed more and more stuff, not bearing to part with anything.

'Will you just look at all these boxes?' Dermot exclaimed, poking his head inside his daughter's bedroom.

'I know, I've tried my hardest to have a good sort out and get rid of any rubbish, but I can't. It's all precious.'

'What, even your Brownie manual?' Dermot squinted his eyes at the piles of books.

'It's part of my childhood, Dad!' Finula insisted.

Dermot rolled his eyes and left her to get on with it. He had contacted the estate agents and the Templar was officially on the market, causing great concern amongst the locals. Dermot was a popular landlord and he was going to be a hard act to follow. Whilst he appreciated a huge change in lifestyle was imminent, he knew it was for the best. The timing was right. Dermot also knew his girl was in safe hands. Marcus had rung daily, always chatting to him as well as Finula. As clichéd as it sounded, he honestly felt he'd gained a son, not lost a daughter. His thoughts projected to grandchildren, giving him a warm, comforting glow.

After finally boxing every single item up, ready to be packed into the back of her and Marcus' cars, Finula decided to call Megan. As she'd thought, Megan was anxious to see her.

'I'll come to you,' she told Finula. 'I desperately need a change of scenery.'

'Are you sure you're all right walking to The Templar?'

Megan let out an exasperated sigh. 'Don't you start. Tobias is bad enough. I can't move without him hovering over me and when he's not here Henry watches me like a hawk.'

Finula laughed. 'That's because he cares!'

'I know, I know, but seriously, Fin, I'm desperate to get out.'

So, a very pregnant Megan slowly and carefully made her way to The Templar. She looked at the 'For Sale' sign and smiled to herself. Only just under a year ago she had first got a job here. It seemed much longer, probably because so much had happened since. She glanced down and patted her bump affectionately. Tobias wouldn't be pleased when he returned from his estate meeting to find her out visiting Finula, but even so, she needed to see her best friend before she left for Shropshire. A lump formed in Megan's throat. How would she manage without Finula's happy-go-lucky presence? Then she recalled Tobias' opinion that she'd be too busy with their baby to miss Finula. Still, life was going to be so different, for both of them.

Finula had the decaf cappuccinos ready and waiting when she arrived.

'Come on, we'll sit in the cosy alcove. Don't want you propping yourself up by the bar in your condition,' she laughed.

Megan gave her a warning look. 'Don't. I get enough of that at home.'

Finula cocked her head on one side thoughtfully. 'You think of Treweham Hall as home now?' She remembered how Megan had been in awe of the place when she'd first met Tobias.

'Yes, I do now. It's funny how quickly you can adjust. I've even grown fond of Henry.'

Finula threw her head back and hooted and Megan's eyes filled with tears. This was precisely what she'd miss: Finula's loud, hearty laugh. As if reading her mind, Finula suddenly went quiet.

'All packed?'

'Yep. Ready to go,' Finula swallowed.

'You'll come back, won't you, when the baby's born?'

'Of course!' Finula looked almost offended by the question. 'You'll come and visit me in Shropshire, see my new home?'

'Try and keep me away,' grinned Megan. There was a pause, then she asked, 'What are you going to do over there, job-wise, I mean?'

Finula's face lit up. 'I've been thinking. I want to set up my own business.'

'Doing what?'

'Still cooking, or baking, but in my own time. I've thought about a catering company...' She looked for Megan's response.

'Excellent idea!' This encouraged Finula to continue.

'Perhaps cakes to begin with—'

'Finula's Fancies,' butted in Megan.

'Not Finula's Buns then?' she batted back with a smirk, making them fall around in giggles.

'Oh, Fin, I'm so going to miss this,' Megan managed to say once they'd both calmed down.

'I know. Me, too.' They embraced.

Dermot passed by the doorway and stopped for a second. Watching them brought a tear to his eye, then he shook himself and carried on lugging the beer barrel down into the cellar.

The next day saw Marcus pull into The Templar car park, ready to collect Finula. All hands were on deck as Dermot, Finula, Marcus and a couple of bar staff carried down all the boxes. After only just managing to shut both the car boots, they were ready to go. Finula hugged her dad hard.

'Drive carefully, do ya hear me?'

'I will.' Her chin started to quiver.

'Now, none of that, Fin. I'll be on your doorstep before you know it,' reprimanded Dermot. He gave her one last squeeze, then parted from her with a forced smile; inside he was falling apart. He turned to Marcus. 'You look after her.'

'I intend to, Dermot.' Marcus shook his hand. 'We'll ring once we're back.'

'You do that.' And off they went.

Dermot stood and waved until they disappeared completely, then went directly to the bar and poured himself a stiff drink.

64

Sebastian sat at the desk he had installed in the Folly. Since deciding this was going to be his headquarters from now on, he'd spent many hours in his secret hideaway, nestled amongst the estate woods. After giving Jamie's suggestion of setting up his own outdoor theatre company some real consideration, his mind had run into overdrive. He seriously thought it was a contender, running his own events at Treweham Hall. Sebastian had confided in Tobias, who had seconded it, thereby making him even more determined to make a go of it.

Today he had contacted several actor friends, eager to gauge their reactions to his proposal. Sebastian aimed to produce his first play in the summer, giving him five months if he wanted to stage the show in early June. He wanted his theatre company to perform plays that reflected class and sophistication to the more discerning audience, not cheap and cheerful farces played to tipsy crowds booing or cheering. His immediate thoughts gravitated to Shakespeare.

After all, what could be more appropriate? But which one? *Richard III* was out; he'd had enough of King Dick to last him a lifetime. He also didn't want to be solely associated with that role and was keen to take on another. It obviously couldn't be a leading one, though, as he wouldn't have the time to dedicate to it with overseeing the whole project. He narrowed his eyes as he pondered. Then it came to him. What could be better than *A Midsummer Night's Dream* to play in summer, especially with these woods?

Jamie, once again, had shown nothing but support. Sebastian liked the idea of the two of them perhaps working together. Jamie was ambitious, but not in a hard, ruthless way, more eager to gain experience and offer assistance wherever he could.

He had contacted Sebastian regularly since working on set in London and was due to come back to Treweham Hall that evening. Sebastian found himself excited by the thought of seeing him again, and silently rejoiced that he was able to feel this way. Gone was the dark, depressing mood that had occupied his inner being for so long. He cast his mind back just a few months, when he thought he'd never get over the heartache Nick Fletcher had inflicted. It all seemed unbelievable now, when comparing the self-obsessed, callous Nick, to the compassionate, caring Jamie.

Fortunately, enough of the friends and colleagues he'd contacted were happy to be involved and were available. Now he had to think about everything else: the costumes, props and scenery. He had to arrange the scripts and decide parts, get programmes, posters and flyers together, and decide on the dates for the production. He needed to get a website designed, a Facebook page set up, his social media all lined up, which then posed the question, what to call his theatre company? The list of things to consider and do was endless.

Thankfully, his thoughts were interrupted by a knock at the door. Sebastian frowned. Who could that be? He didn't think anybody knew where he was. As he opened the door, his face lit up with joy.

'Jamie!'

'We finished early, so I thought I'd surprise you,' Jamie grinned, thrilled with Sebastian's reaction.

Soon they were sitting opposite each other in the armchairs by the roaring log burner. Sebastian had poured them each a drink and the two were relaxing and unwinding from a hectic week of work.

Jamie slung back his whisky. 'I still can't believe what you told me about Marcus.'

Sebastian nodded. 'I know, Marcus Devlin, my half-brother. It beggars belief.'

He'd told Jamie the night he had first learnt the news, anxious to confide in him. To say Jamie was stunned was an understatement. 'But I need your discretion, Jamie. It's not common knowledge. Well, not yet, anyway.'

'Absolutely.' Then Jamie added, 'Do you think it ever will be?'

'Common knowledge? Don't know. I suppose that depends on Marcus.'

'But what if it leaks out? These things have a habit of doing so, especially where the Cavendish-Blakes are concerned.'

Sebastian knew Jamie was referring to the tabloids, which had hounded his brother practically all his days and had exposed, exaggerated and, in many cases, lied about his lifestyle.

Sebastian looked solemn. 'It would kill my mother.'

'Perhaps it would be better to announce it yourselves then, as a family, rather than leaving it to the gutter press to put their spin on it.'

Sebastian paused to reflect on Jamie's words. He had a point.

'I've got an idea. Marcus could appear in the documentary.'

Jamie sat up, impressed with the suggestion. 'That,' he pointed to Sebastian, 'is a brilliant idea. The three brothers together, showing a united front. It would be fantastic viewing!'

'Hmm,' Sebastian nodded. 'But let me run it past Tobias first.'

65

Megan looked out of the drawing-room window. Despite it being February, the grounds still looked lush with evergreens neatly manicured. In the distance she could just make out the white railings of the racing track. Tobias was at the training yard that morning, where he'd gone to meet Dylan. She was pleased for both of them that the yard was such a success. Judging by Tobias' more relaxed mood, it was obvious the money it generated was contributing well to the Treweham Hall estate.

Megan was looking forward to the Hall being reopened to the public in spring. For her, it made the place come alive. Tobias and Beatrice, she knew, thought it was intrusive and an inconvenience, perhaps because they had always had the Hall to themselves as a home, whereas she'd never known any different. Megan pictured her little cottage that had once been her gran's. She missed the cosy bolt hole at times, but had grown to like living in Treweham Hall, with its vast history and character, plus its quirky inhabitants. Her cottage, and her granddad's next door, were both rented out as holiday cottages now.

Her thoughts turned to Finula. They'd spoken a few times since her move and Megan couldn't wait to go and visit. She let out a bored sigh… Suddenly a sharp pain shot through her lower back, making her cry out loud. Clutching the back of the armchair, she doubled over in agony as another stab ran through her. She felt damp, and looking down she saw a small pool of pink water at her feet. Her waters had broken! Panic stricken, she looked out of the window. Tobias wasn't here and she was about to go into premature labour! The baby wasn't due until next month.

'Ahh!' Another searing pain hit her hard. She couldn't walk to the phone, nor even reach the pull for the bell to summon Henry. Megan cried out in torture and gripped the chair again.

Meanwhile, Tobias was in the training yard office where Dylan was showing him their feature in *Hi-Ya* magazine. Tobias threw his head back and laughed, when Dylan told him how badly behaved Phoenix had been.

'He literally dumped, right at the journalist's feet.'

'Good for him. Most journalists deserve it,' chuckled Tobias. Then he sobered for a second, remembering Sebastian's proposal for the three brothers to be interviewed together for the documentary until Dylan broke into his thoughts.

'So, not long to go now, eh? Just another month, then you'll become a daddy.'

'We won't know what's hit us.'

★

Back at the Hall, Megan knew what was hitting her, sheer agony. She had managed to ease herself now onto the floor, as wave after wave of pain engulfed her. Fear and panic started to set in. She tried to remain calm and started to pant as instructed in her antenatal class. Then, through blurred vision, she saw two black polished shoes.

'Madam!'

Looking up, she gasped, 'Henry… the baby's coming.'

A stricken Henry rang the bell, then crouched down next to her.

'Don't worry, help is on its way.' He reached for a cushion and placed it under her head. Then he held her hand. Megan squeezed his hard and let out another piercing cry. Moments later another member of staff entered the room and stopped short when she saw Megan on the floor and Henry bent down next to her.

'Quick! Ring for an ambulance!' he ordered.

'Tobias!' Megan screamed. 'I need Tobias!'

Tobias was sipping on a coffee, reminiscing about the scrapes him, Dylan and Seamus had got into back in the day, when his mobile rang.

'Just a minute, Dylan.' He reached inside his Barbour jacket.

'Sir, you must come quick,' urged Henry. 'Madam's in labour!'

Tobias' eyes widened. Not bothering to reply, he jumped up.

'What is it?' Dylan asked, startled.

'It's Megan. She's having the baby,' he called over his shoulder as he ran at full pelt to his car.

Tobias' chest thumped hard, especially when seeing the ambulance pull up behind his car on the driveway. The great door was flung open by a distressed Beatrice.

'Quickly, she's in your drawing room.'

The ambulance staff and Tobias tore down the corridor and up the stairs to the south wing. Entering the room, Tobias dashed over to Megan and knelt down. Henry stood up out of the way and left the room.

'Tobias, it's coming,' panted Megan, pouring with sweat. She clutched his hand. Tobias smoothed away the hair on her forehead.

'You're in safe hands, Megan,' he soothed, while the paramedic popped a white sheet under her body and rolled up her dress. After quickly removing her knickers, one of the medics examined her.

'Not long to go, Megan,' she said gently. 'You're fully dilated.'

Tobias gulped. Hell, his baby was about to be born in his own drawing room. This wasn't exactly what he'd envisaged. He jumped as Megan screeched and dug her nails into his palm.

'You're doing great, Megan,' he encouraged, petrified inside.

'I want to push!' Megan shouted.

The paramedics glanced at each other. One of them took another look.

'I can see the head,' she confirmed. 'OK, Megan, let's have a big push on your next contraction.'

'Ah!'

'That's it, good girl, and again.'

'Ahh!'

Tobias closed his eyes and prayed hard.

'It's coming. Keep going, Megan.'

One mammoth thrust brought the tiny bundle out.

'Well done, Megan, it's a boy!' the medic exclaimed, taking the squawking baby. They swiftly cut the umbilical cord and wrapped him in a blanket from the emergency bag.

'Let me see,' gasped Megan, straining her neck. Carefully the baby was placed in his mother's arms. Tobias stroked the top of his head, all wet with dark hair. 'He looks like you,' she whispered to him, and Tobias kissed her cheek.

'Well done, my love,' he croaked, his eyes welling up with emotion.

The medic carried on attending to Megan whilst Tobias took hold of his son.

'Is he all right?' He spoke urgently under his breath to the other paramedic. 'He's a month early.'

The nurse smiled. 'We'll need to get mother and baby to the hospital for a good check-up, but he sounds fine to me.'

Tobias looked down at his crying son, so tiny, so fragile, he wanted to wrap him in cotton wool. Megan had been an absolute star. Outside the drawing-room door he could hear anxious low voices. He walked towards the sound, holding the baby. Beatrice and Henry were waiting desperately on tenterhooks.

'Meet your grandson, Mother.'

'Oh, darling!' Beatrice rushed to his side. 'He's the image of you, Tobias.'

Henry waited patiently to be invited.

'Look, Henry.' Tobias beckoned him over. Henry gazed at the heir to Treweham Hall and smiled tenderly. 'Thank you, Henry,' Tobias said, 'for being there to alert me.'

'Not at all, sir. It was my pleasure.'

The ambulance took Megan and baby to the hospital, while Tobias followed in his car. After spending all day there, and having been examined by the doctors and midwife, the new mother and her son were able to come home in the early evening. Although born a month early, the baby still weighed well and hadn't shown any signs to cause alarm, to the huge relief of both his parents.

Later that night, Megan was tucked up in the four-poster bed cradling her newborn, and Tobias was sitting next to her with his arm round them.

'What shall we call him?' he asked her, unable to take his eyes of his son.

'Edward, after my granddad.'

'Edward Richard, after my father, too?'

'Yes. Edward Richard Henry.'

'Henry?' laughed Tobias.

'Yes, if it wasn't for Henry, God knows what could have happened.' Megan shivered with the horrific memory of being immobile on the floor in agony, unable to call for help.

'Edward Richard Henry it is, then.'

That night all the staff and family celebrated by wetting the baby's head. Champagne flowed, music played and Tobias said a few words of gratitude to Henry, who blushed pink with pride. Upstairs in the south wing, Megan spoke to her elated parents, then rang Finula with the good news. After a light supper of chicken soup, she fell into a deep slumber, while little Edward slept in his Moses basket beside her, oblivious to the commotion his early arrival had caused.

66

The next few days were a whirlwind of visitors. Megan's parents came to see their new grandson, her brother to see his new nephew and Kate, Megan's friend from the Midlands, also paid an impromptu visit. Finula and Marcus were due to come the following week.

Sebastian knocked on the bedroom door.

'Come in,' called Megan. She was sat in an armchair by the large bay window overlooking the grounds and had just finished breastfeeding Edward.

'Just thought I'd check on young Eddie,' he grinned.

'Don't let Tobias hear you call him that,' laughed Megan. She ran her finger down the side of her baby's face and kissed his forehead. Sebastian looked on affectionately, thinking it must be a wonderful feeling.

'How are you?'

'Great, just a little tired, that's all.'

'You were amazing, according to Tobias.'

Megan rolled her eyes and smiled. 'I know, so he keeps saying.'

'He's in a good place. I've never seen him so happy.'

'*I've* never been so happy,' she replied, then added, 'You seem much happier too, Sebastian.' Her head was tilted to one side, as if assessing him.

'Yes. I am.' He walked over and gazed down at the now sleeping baby. Megan noticed him limp slightly.

'Do you want to hold him?'

'No, I won't disturb him, he looks so peaceful.' He stroked his tiny fist and instinctively it uncurled and wrapped round his finger. 'Oh, isn't he adorable?' Sebastian's heart melted.

A week later, as promised, Finula and Marcus came back to Treweham. Megan and Tobias arranged to meet them in The Templar and wheeled Edward in his Silver Cross pram, which Beatrice had proudly presented to them. As they entered the bar, Dermot's voice boomed, 'Congratulations to you both. The drinks are on the house!'

'Thank you, Dermot,' said Tobias, shaking hands with him, then turned to Marcus. 'Marcus,' he nodded.

'Hello, Tobias, and congratulations.' Marcus held out his hand.

'Oh, let me see him!' Finula poked her head into the pram. Edward was wide awake, his eyes looking straight into hers and she saw they were exactly the same as his father's, and uncle's. 'He's beautiful.' Her hand went out to touch him and Megan noticed a ring on her finger.

'What's this?' she asked, taking hold of her hand.

Finula gave a wide smile. 'An engagement ring.'

'And... you didn't think to tell me!' spluttered Megan.

Finula laughed. 'It only happened last night.' Then lowered her voice. 'It was Marcus' mum's ring.'

'I see. Here, let me have a proper look.' A huge emerald dazzled brilliantly against a collection of diamonds surrounding it. 'It's gorgeous, Finula.'

'I know,' she giggled.

'So, when's the wedding?' Megan turned to Marcus, who had been quietly watching them with a warm smile.

'As soon as,' interrupted Dermot overhearing. 'I intend to put on a good show for them here, before I sell the place,' which made everyone laugh.

67

Whilst Finula and Marcus were in Treweham, the question of the interview was put to Marcus. Both Tobias and Sebastian had quietly approached him and outlined their proposal and although Marcus had been quite taken aback initially, he soon saw it as an opportunity to rectify the issue of the missing footage.

They were in Tobias' study, Tobias and Sebastian having collared Marcus as Finula made her way to the south wing to see Megan.

'Are you prepared to go public, Marcus? It will mean a hell of a lot of press interest and intrusion.' Tobias stared gravely at Marcus.

What choice did he really have? Marcus considered. He had to come up with something for the BBC. Besides which, the revelation would be sure to make the documentary a smash hit.

'Yes,' replied Marcus, 'I'll do it.'

'Just one condition,' said Tobias, crossing his arms, 'Viola Kemp has no involvement.'

Marcus nodded, understanding his dislike of her after the way she had previously interviewed him.

'I'll make some calls, get—'

'Let Jamie do it,' cut in Sebastian. The two looked at him. 'He's more than capable, and it would be a chance to give him a real break.'

'That's not a bad idea. We'll compose the questions, though,' replied Tobias, 'and make sure he sticks to them,' he added in a dry voice.

'Jamie's hardly likely to make it difficult,' Sebastian answered in his defence.

'OK. I'll brief Jamie and get hold of Len,' said Marcus decisively.

Two days later and the interview was good to go. The lights and camera had been set up in Tobias' study. His desk had been moved out of the way and the Chesterfield was placed under the portrait of Richard Cavendish-Blake.

Butterflies fluttered in Jamie's stomach as he reread the questions on his clipboard. It was an amazing opportunity he'd been given and he intended to make the most of it. He knew Sebastian trusted him to do a good job and he so badly wanted to make him proud. Marcus had organised just the minimum of assistance with make-up, lighting and sound. Jamie scanned the room: all the equipment was in place and Len was ready. All they had to do was a sound check once Tobias, Sebastian and Marcus had been fitted with microphones. He took a deep breath when the three of them calmly sat down before him. Sebastian gave a discreet, sly wink, making him relax a little, and then Jamie took the huge, furry microphone, coughed slightly and spoke into it.

'Testing one, two three. Testing one, two, three.'

'OK, let's roll,' replied Len. There was a pause, then Jamie began.

'Thank you, gentlemen, for agreeing to be interviewed. Marcus, it must be especially challenging to you?'

'In a way, yes. Then again, I'm glad it's all out in the open now.'

'How did you feel when learning of your true parentage?'

'I was always led to believe that my father had been killed in an accident. To be told the truth by my dying mam was astonishing.'

'Tobias and Sebastian, how does it feel to have Marcus suddenly in your lives?'

'He's our brother and the family accepts this,' Tobias answered resolutely. 'I'm sure if our father had known of Marcus' existence, then we would have been brought up with him.'

'Diaries, written by Father prove he knew nothing about Marcus, which is a tragedy,' confirmed Sebastian.

'But they do document a relationship with my mam,' explained Marcus.

'And the DNA tests confirm we all share the same father,' said Tobias.

And so the interview continued; three brothers united in one family. They spoke agreeably together, giving clear, concise answers, gelling seamlessly, with the picture of their father hanging above, looking down on them.

Inside the library next door, Megan, Beatrice and Finula sat quietly together, hoping to hear the interview through the open doors. Luckily Edward was peacefully sleeping in his pram. Tobias had allowed Len to film him for just a few minutes, much to the delight of Marcus – and Megan – who thought it would add a nice touch, showing the new heir of Treweham Hall in the documentary.

Beatrice moved to hover over Edward... What would her husband have made of all this? A new grandson as well as another son he didn't know about? She'd accustomed herself to the situation now and had found a way to accept it. Sighing, she gazed in adoration at her beautiful grandson and gently rocked his pram.

Megan and Finula strained to hear the voices in the study, but couldn't catch it all. They would have to wait until next autumn, when the documentary was due to be aired. Megan looked at Finula's ring again.

'I've just realised,' she murmured, 'we'll be sisters-in-law.'

'I know!' Finula exclaimed, then quickly covered her mouth. 'Who would have thought it?' she whispered.

68

It was the day of Edward's christening. February had passed in a blur at Treweham Hall, with all the hullabaloo of his unexpected, early arrival, and the days had shifted into early spring, bringing the cheery sunshine. Daffodils waved in the grounds, crocuses peeped out from the earth like colourful jewels, and the early blossom of the trees was bursting into life. The smell of freshly cut grass and a warm, mild breeze filled the air, whilst the birds sang their merry songs.

As expected, Beatrice was in full swing organising the event, whilst Aunt Celia stood on the sidelines, showing her usual signs of irritation. Megan was just plain relieved that Beatrice was acting true to form and taking over as it gave her more time to catch up on her sleep, after what had seemed like endless nights of tending to Edward. Only now, two and a half months after he'd entered their lives, had her son allowed her a fairly decent nap. Tobias had helped, but instinctively it was Megan who lay in bed listening and watching his tiny chest rising and falling.

The two couldn't imagine life without him. Grandma Beatrice worshipped him. Uncle Sebastian adored him. Even Henry was enamoured, in his own way. Megan gently poked his wriggling little arms and starfish hands through the sleeves of the very elaborate white christening gown. It was a family heirloom, which each generation of the Cavendish-Blakes had worn for decades. Megan imagined Beatrice doing the same with Tobias and she smiled to herself.

'All ready?' Tobias entered the nursery, looking handsome in a navy-blue suit. He lovingly stroked his son's head, then kissed Megan.

'Almost. It's quite a tricky thing to get on.' She pointed to all the folds of silk and lace draped over the changing unit.

'I know,' laughed Tobias. 'It's hard to think of me and Sebastian in that.' Outside, from down the corridor they could hear the commotion Beatrice was causing in preparing for the event and they exchanged knowing smiles.

Sebastian couldn't fail to hear it too. Chuckling to himself, he straightened his tie in the mirror and ran his hands through his blond hair. There, that'd do, he told himself and then he reached for his phone to ring Jamie, who ought to have arrived by now.

'Hi there, everything OK?'

'Yeah, just running a bit late. I'll be about fifteen minutes. The posters look amazing, by the way.' Jamie had collected them from the printers that morning. They depicted the cast of his upcoming production of *A Midsummer Night's Dream* all resplendent in their costumes, surrounded by the lush, green woods of the Treweham Hall estate, in bright, vibrant colours.

'Excellent!' gushed Sebastian.

His new theatre company, The Folly Players, was really taking off now, due to his relentless determination and effort, although he was often fighting fatigue. He was regularly counselled by Jamie to ease off and take time out; that the main benefit of running your own company meant doing things at *your* own pace.

He had attended his first appointment at the MS clinic, which had proved encouraging. There had been no change in Sebastian's symptoms and it looked like his condition had stabilised for the time being, rather than worsening.

Marcus and Finula had just arrived at The Templar. As usual, Dermot stood waiting at the entrance with a huge beaming smile on his face. Finula hugged him hard, then stood back in astonishment.

'You've sold it!' She looked up at the 'Sold' sign standing outside the pub.

'Certainly have. Only just, though. Thought I'd let you see for yourself,' he laughed. Already he had his eye on a cottage in the village, which had only been on the market a week.

Marcus joined them. He was looking forward to his stay in Treweham. Having made good progress with the documentary, he was treating himself to a bit of a break. He was keen to put his time to good use and fully intended to read his father's diaries whilst he was here.

'Who's bought it?' he asked.

'A young couple. I think it's a huge investment for them, but they seem pretty keen.'

'Oh, good. I'm so glad it's not been swallowed up by a big brewery wanting to rip out the heart and soul of the place.' Finula gazed at the beautiful stone pub, which had been her childhood home. Now it looked like it would be someone else's.

Dylan and Flora were rushing to get ready. Dodging each other as they pelted about their bedroom, Flora suddenly gasped.

'I forgot to get a christening card!'

'But you did get a present?' Dylan asked, buttoning his shirt.

'Yes, but—'

'Oh, it'll do. Come on, or we'll be late.'

Together they scrambled into the car and drove past the training yard on the way to Treweham Hall. Flora saw Phoenix in the paddock and blew him a kiss through the window and Dylan shook his head in amusement.

Gary and Tracy Belcher had remembered to get both a card and a present. Tracy was wrapping the silver spoon engraved with the baby's name on it in pale blue paper.

'Very apt,' chuckled Gary.

'Why?' asked Tracy.

'If ever there was a baby being born with a silver spoon in its mouth, it's Edward Richard Henry Cavendish-Blake,' he answered with mirth.

'They won't think we're having a dig, do you?' Tracy asked concerned.

'Nah, will they 'eck.'

Together they walked through the estate leading onto the gravel driveway of Treweham Hall. Gary was pleased he managed the brisk walk easily, without puffing for breath. Due to his fitness regime, he had once more transformed his body into the toned, muscled one he had had previously. It hadn't gone unnoticed by Tracy, or Dylan for that matter, who had given him a few horse-riding lessons as promised.

All the guests were greeted at the Hall by the proud parents and guided up the stairs into the chapel. Rays of sunlight shone through the stained-glass windows and the air was filled with the scent of roses and tulips that decorated the sills in pretty arrangements. Friends and family shuffled sideways into the small, wooden pews, then turned to face the stone font. Finula and Marcus stood next to Tobias and Megan, as godparents to baby Edward.

'Edward Richard Henry, I baptise you in the Name of the Father, and of the Son, and of the Holy Ghost,' the priest recited, whilst sprinkling the crying baby's head with holy water.

Marcus looked into the font and saw his mam's face reflected in the water. Not the sallow, sick face of a dying woman, but one with a healthy glowing complexion, rosy cheeks and a wide smile, just as he remembered her as a little boy being chased through the wildflower meadows of Roscommon. There she was, grinning at him. He gave a shaky smile back. In his heart he knew she'd guided him to Treweham. He was meant to find his brothers. He was meant to find Finula. He was no longer alone.

Acknowledgements

Researching for this book led me into the exciting world of theatre and visiting Stratford-Upon-Avon with all its cultural, thespian charm. It also sadly brought a sharper focus of the debilitating disease of multiple Sclerosis, and I'd like to thank Professor S Chhetri, Consultant Neurologist, and all his team for their valuable time and advice given.

As always a huge shout out to my publishers, Aria and its amazing team, especially to Sarah Ritherdon, my wonderful editor, Caroline Ridding, publisher, Yvonne Holland, copy editor and Michelle Jones, proof reader.

My publishing journey so far has had lots of support and I sincerely thank all the reviewers for their kind words and most of all, you the reader. It really makes all the writing angst worthwhile!

Love,
Sasha x

SASHA MORGAN lives in a rural, coastal village in Lancashire with her husband and Labrador dog. She has always written stories from a very young age and finds her fictional world so much more exciting than the real one.

Hello from Aria

We hope you enjoyed this book! Let us know, we'd love to hear from you.

We are Aria, a dynamic digital-first fiction imprint from award-winning independent publishers Head of Zeus. At heart, we're avid readers committed to publishing exactly the kind of books we love to read – from romance and sagas to crime, thrillers and historical adventures. Visit us online and discover a community of like-minded fiction fans!

We're also on the look out for tomorrow's superstar authors. So, if you're a budding writer looking for a publisher, we'd love to hear from you. You can submit your book online at ariafiction.com/we-want-read-your-book

You can find us at:
Email: aria@headofzeus.com
Website: www.ariafiction.com
Submissions: www.ariafiction.com/we-want-read-your-book
Facebook: @ariafiction
Twitter: @Aria_Fiction
Instagram: @ariafiction

Printed in Great Britain
by Amazon